THE
BALANCING ACT

THE
BALANCING ACT

Matthew Cullen

First paperback edition 2022

Illustrated cover by Moinak

ISBNs
Paperback: 978-1-80227-940-5
eBook: 978-1-80227-941-2

Dedicated to my parents, and gin & tonic.
Not necessarily in that order.

PART ONE

None of this happened.

(Or so they'd like you to think…)

CHAPTER ONE

It had been such a *remarkably* massive bulge, and that was the problem. He just couldn't have missed it. It wasn't a hump, it wasn't a protrusion, it was a great, big, bulbous swelling and he hadn't known where to look. The incident had happened over an hour ago, but he still couldn't get the image out of his head.

And so it was that Mike Nation found himself seated at his desk that morning, attempting in vain to wash the earlier incident from his mind and glumly pondering life. His mood was totally out of character. Normally, he was extremely self-confident; after all, he was the complete success story! He was a businessman and entrepreneur. A wheeler-dealer with a gift for earning money. And most of all, he was a genius; Lord knows he was sure of that. Yet despite his unshakeable belief in his own abilities, the self-made millionaire executive found himself feeling not quite the mastermind his confidence would generally suggest.

He had a scrap of paper in front of him and was absent-mindedly doodling across the page. Nation always doodled when he was stressed, and this was no exception. He was finding it difficult to concentrate; his mind was wandering all over the place.

Doodling and wandering, doodling and wandering...

Mike's thoughts drifted to the Birmingham suburb of Moseley, which was the location of his office and had been the home of his business empire for the last four decades. God, how it had changed over the years and, in his opinion, entirely for the worse. It was so different to the Moseley he recalled from when he had first opened his doors to the business world in the 1980s. For a start, that morning's unpleasant incident just wouldn't have happened back then. In those days, the good old days, it wouldn't have been acceptable for elderly gentlemen to do their Marks and Spencer's food shopping in nothing but their cycling lycra. All those rubbery, swollen lumps poking out from their ageing, saggy bodies – it simply wasn't right.

Nation had innocently popped into the Moseley *M&S* earlier that morning to grab a sandwich for breakfast and had quite literally bumped into one such sweaty, bulging specimen. Talk about unexpected item in the bagging area. Unexpected item in the ballbagging area, more like. Horrified, Nation had fled the store and retreated to the safety of his office empty-handed, so he was bloody starving and that wasn't helping his mood.

And the residents! They had all changed too. Poncy champagne socialists, the lot of them. And, without exception, wannabe chefs as well. Everyone was a bloody cook in Moseley these days. He reckoned that within the suburb's boundaries there would be more recipe books per square metre than anywhere else in Europe. Possibly the world.

He recalled the Great Moseley Harissa Shortage of 2019 and how, as stocks ran dry, fights had broken out in the supermarket aisles. A harissa black market had developed, and those little jars of spiced paste had been traded for ever-increasing amounts of organic wine and vegan chocolate as those desperate Moseley foodies attempted to secure even the smallest of supplies. The crazy bastards.

Mike harked back to when Moseley was a different place, a better place, with a more refined feel. There'd even been a Pizza Express back then! Great days. Long since gone, of course. It was a Lebanese food store now. On a couple of occasions, Nation had glanced at the strange array of foodstuffs in the window of the shop as he had walked past, but he hadn't ventured inside. He'd never seen the point.

Nation leaned back into his chair, closed his eyes and transported himself back to the High Street of yesteryear. That trendy bar opposite his offices: twenty years ago, that was a bank. And the Peruvian restaurant down the road: what was that? Actually, he was pretty sure that was a bank as well. Thinking about it, you couldn't bloody move for banks back then. Good times. Now it's all tapas this or tagine that. Microbreweries and independent coffee houses. Give him a Starbucks any day of the week.

People would tell him that his views were misjudged. They would say that the bohemian, cultural 'Moseley Village' was where Birmingham was at its finest. It was where the city's diversity was celebrated most fully, with row after row of independent shops, stalls, restaurants and bars. Where an eclectic mix of locals could be found standing shoulder to shoulder over a pint of local ale, discussing everything from politics to pole dancing. Where hippies and luvvies, artists and scientists, professors, bloggers, shaggers and boozers, and even bloody rugby fans would meet up as equals for a night out. But Nation wasn't interested in all that crap. He had lost all affection for Moseley. Despite it being where he had made his first million, and indeed each subsequent million, the place just depressed him.

Not that this had anything to do with why Nation was doodling and wandering that morning. Moseley's changes and spandex-clad appendages, while both vexing in the extreme, were not the causes of his anxiety. The throbbing stress in his forehead had an altogether different cause. Mike had come to realise that he had a very specific problem, in that a very specific person, with very specific responsibilities, had very specifically screwed him over. Ever since he had uncovered the issue, this fundamental breach in trust, he had been mulling over his options. And he had finally decided what to do.

Nation was chairman, chief executive and owner of the Nation Group of Companies, a conglomeration of three different businesses that he had formed over the past four decades. Nation Construction, Nation Investments and Nation Wholesale Foods were known in the organisation by their initials NC, NI and NWF, and the abbreviations had the rather unfortunate coincidence of being acronyms for Mike's recruitment policy: No Cocks; No Idiots; No Weird Fucks. Mike's HR Department had stressed the importance of perhaps not writing that policy down anywhere.

Nation had formed his first company, Nation Wholesale Foods, back in the early 1980s. Mike's father had been a fishmonger who had set up a small shop in the Kings Heath area of Birmingham, a couple of miles from Moseley. Mike had joined the family business at sixteen, and when his father retired through ill health, he bought his dad out and moved from retail to wholesale, focussing on selling meats and fish to the bars and restaurants of the city.

The business satisfied Mike for a while, but it wasn't earning him the sort of return he considered worthy of his obvious genius. Fortunately for Nation, it was around that time that the council commenced an extensive 'urban regeneration' programme or, as Nation put it, fixing all the cock-ups. Mike quickly launched Nation Construction and started bidding for council tenders across all sorts of projects. He made close business contacts in the building trade and rapidly expanded his operation into both the demolition of old, defunct structures and their replacement with new-build developments. This addition to Nation's business portfolio proved beneficial for two reasons. First, it was quite legitimately a profitable enterprise in its own right. But crucially, it also lent itself to some additional, rather less legitimate revenue streams. Nation discovered that tender awards could be heavily influenced in his favour by using a carefully applied combination of bribery and blackmail, particularly if targeted at the political leaders of the city. Mike became very good at both.

Success followed, and once again Nation's thirst for money was satiated for a period, but now he had the taste for ill-gotten gains, he wanted more. Much more. So, to scratch that itch, Mike launched Nation Investments at the turn of the millennium, a business that started vaguely legitimately but over time became an utterly corrupt property investing division of his group. He used the business in part to earn quick cash by flip-flopping properties, but in the end, it was essentially just a front. Far more importantly, it became Nation's vehicle for laundering substantial sums of money on behalf of the less salubrious business contacts he had made over the years.

In order to wash such large quantities of cash, Nation soon realised that the level of creative accounting required necessitated an equally creative accountant. After an extensive search, he finally found his man. A quiet, extremely clever and morally flexible professional, the gentleman Nation hired was most certainly neither a cock nor an idiot, thereby meeting two of Mike's three golden criteria. However, the accountant was undoubtedly somewhat of a weirdo and so, strictly speaking, failed the final crucial test. For any other role in his empire, Nation would have taken a pass and continued his recruitment hunt, but he desperately needed the man's rather bespoke skills, and so, finally, a contract was drawn up.

The accountant was never formally on the Nation Group employee roster, but he nevertheless worked exclusively for Mike and had done so ever since Nation Investments had gone completely dodgy about ten years before. Throughout the subsequent years, Mike had considered his relationship with the accountant rock solid; consequently, he had rewarded his man handsomely. Nation never once dreamed that this bent bookkeeper, his chief washer of money, had been fleecing him since the start.

Doodling and wandering, doodling and wandering…

Nation stared at the small set of files lying haphazardly across the desk in front of him. He had spent the last week reviewing the whole lot. All of the documents related to the work his specialist accountant had been undertaking on his behalf, and at first, Nation had found the information difficult to follow. But he had eventually got the gist of the paperwork, and the pattern had finally become clear. He had the proof he needed, he had confirmed the accountant had been robbing him blind and he had decided on what would come next. Which all meant he needed to get his head back in the game. After all, he had a very busy day planned.

He leapt to his feet. 'Snap out of it! Let's get this show on the road!' he instructed himself as he stretched his short, tubby body from top to bottom in an effort to get the blood pumping. He grabbed the day planner with his little plump hands and skimmed through the morning's activities.

First, he had a meeting with Rosie Bell, the Michelin-starred chef with whom Nation had various vague but influential business arrangements. She had specifically requested the get-together, and Mike knew she was going to whinge to him about some produce that Nation Wholesale Foods either had or hadn't sourced for her that week. But that wouldn't be a problem; she just needed to get something off her rather attractive and ample chest.

Second, he needed to get down to the construction site at Moseley Railway Station to check on progress. Eighteen months ago, Nation Construction had been successful in securing the contract to build three new train stations in south Birmingham. Nation had to make damned sure those works were completed before the big branch line opening in a week's time, so it was imperative that he got on site to check in with his foreman.

But third, and most importantly, it was critical that Nation had a very serious discussion with his trouble-shooter and fixer, Brian Wood, the man he turned to when he needed access to rather *specialist* assistance. Nation reached for the intercom to speak to the ever-reliable Beryl, his secretary of over forty years. Now in her seventies, she would be dragged out of the office dead rather than ever consider retiring.

'Beryl, pop in here a moment would you, bab?'

'Certainly, Michael,' came the chirpy reply.

Nation was fond of Beryl. She followed instructions without question, and she followed them to the absolute letter. Nation regarded her diligence as a sign of loyalty, although it had caused him some difficulties in the past. He recalled one email that he had recorded on his dictaphone, which he'd left for Beryl with the instruction to send 'precisely as dictated'. Sure enough, the next day, out came the mail:

'To all staff. It is imperative that no department exceeds expense budgets this month. Any breach will be seen as gross misconduct and that decision will be final, right that's it I'm pissing off for lunch.'

The mail had created somewhat of a stir, but when push came to shove, he would rather have a reliable Beryl in situ than pretty much anyone else.

The ageing secretary knocked once and shuffled in. 'What can I do for you, Michael?' She flicked her pad to an empty page and waited for her instructions.

'Ah, Beryl, good. Get hold of Rosie, will you? Tell her 11 a.m. at my office is fine. And call Derek Penrice at the Moseley Station construction site. Tell him I'm coming down later. And Beryl? Sort us a bacon sandwich will you, bab? I'm famished. On second thoughts, make it a bacon and egg sandwich. Actually, a bacon, egg and sausage sandwich. Red and brown sauce. Better make that two sandwiches. Ta, bab.' That should fill the hole, he thought.

Beryl scurried back to the reception area to make the calls and order the food. Meanwhile, Nation grabbed his mobile phone and skipped to his contacts list. He swiped down until he reached Brian Wood and sent his text.

Need your services. My office, ASAP.

CHAPTER TWO

Paul Dixon was in the large and airy lounge of his Edgbaston home, working through his daily exercises. A rubber mat was rolled out onto the floor, and he stood at one end of it, heaving his scrawny upper body from one side to the other. His shiny, skin-tight, salmon tracksuit caught the mid-morning sun streaming through the window, and with arms outstretched, balancing precariously on one leg, he had the vague appearance of a rather absurd giant flamingo.

Dixon had an unfortunate affliction in that his skin always looked rather pallid and grey. He gave the impression that he was constantly a little bit clammy to the touch, as if he were forever getting over the flu. Not that anyone would volunteer to touch the strange and awkward-looking man. His curiously unattractive appearance was accentuated by the copious amounts of sweat he was producing while he laboured through his routine.

Dixon was painfully thin and bony, with peculiarly angular features including a very narrow and pointy nose, but behind that nose, he had a big and powerful brain. And that brain was particularly powerful when it came to numbers and statistics or, more accurately, the manipulation of numbers and statistics. Dixon was thinking about one number in particular whilst he worked through his exercises, and that was eight hundred thousand precisely.

After thirty minutes of work-out, his smart watch announced his time was up. He puffed out a breath of air and cautiously lowered his raised leg, wobbling as he did so. He lost his balance at the crucial moment and fell flat on his face, hitting the exercise mat with a slap. Limply he rolled over, got back up and reached for a towel, all the while cursing under his breath and pondering whether all this keep fit bollocks was worth it. He had previously tried jogging for exercise but, like all joggers since the beginning of time, he soon realised that he absolutely hated it. So he had switched to indoor exercise drills and had come to tolerate, if not exactly embrace, his new work-out.

He threw the towel down and set off for the kitchen to fix some toast and a black coffee. With breakfast in hand, he headed back to the lounge to check on the array of computer screens that sat on his desk in the bay window. The three monitors were dancing with numbers portraying Dixon's latest illegal trades on behalf of the Nation Group of Companies. He took his seat and got back to work, his skeletal fingers tapping away at the keyboard with remarkable speed.

Paul found money laundering, as a profession, fairly straightforward. It was essentially moving figures from one place to another. All one had to do was move dodgy money into a business transaction, then shift that money elsewhere through another transaction, while collecting clean money at the end of the deal. Once washed, the clean money could be passed back to the original owner, minus a suitable fee, of course. And this was precisely what he had been doing for Mike Nation for the best part of ten years.

The way Dixon washed Mike's dodgy money was fairly routine and typically involved the Nation Investments arm of Mike's operations. The investments that Nation held in other firms frequently came about through rescuing failing businesses and bailing them out. Once they were saved, Nation could exert significant influence over the owners, often blackmailing them with fear of further failure into cleaning money on his behalf. For example, Nation had an interest in a hotel in Solihull that had been struggling financially. As part of the rescue deal, Mike had persuaded the hotel owner to artificially inflate the number of room bookings they secured from one day to the next. With those fake, non-existent guests now on the books, their bills were paid with dirty money. Once it had been cleaned through the hotel's accounts, Nation would take a dividend of clean money out of the business and pass it back to the person who needed the money washed.

Nation had dozens of such interests in firms across the city, and so the investment arm of his company was Dixon's most useful route for washing money. But on occasion, Dixon had found ways to layer the money through Nation's Wholesale Foods business as well. If Nation had bailed out companies that purchased fresh meat and fish as part of their business, such as pubs and restaurants, then over-inflated food bills would be drawn up and settled to Nation Wholesale Foods by those desperate business owners. The resulting payments would pass through the books all shiny and clean.

All in all, Nation's businesses lent themselves very well to laundering, and Paul had cleaned the best part of twenty million pounds of dirty money in the decade he had been working for him. It sounded a lot, but at around two million a year, and with Nation's powerful influence infesting so many local firms, they were only pushing fifty or a hundred grand through any given firm in any financial year. It was just about workable.

Mike's typical fee for services rendered was twenty percent, so all that laundering had netted Mike Nation four million pounds of pure profit over the course of Dixon's employment.

To Dixon's impressive brain, the actual process of legitimising the tainted cash was rather simple; even an idiot could do it. Well, maybe not an idiot. Mike Nation was an idiot, and he quite clearly *couldn't* do it. Which was precisely why he had paid Dixon to wash all his money over the years. And while Dixon had accepted the salary Mike had offered him without any real negotiation, he had considered his remuneration package to be largely underwhelming, all told. It was for that very reason that, from the very first moment he had started working for Mike, Dixon had been skimming money off the top of each and every transaction. In the beginning, the numbers involved were not large; it was just a little extra commission that Dixon considered fully deserved for his financial expertise. However, he quickly realised that Nation was not following the money trails that he had devised at all, and there was, therefore, the potential to earn some significant bonuses.

Nation's cut for laundering his dodgy mates' money had always been twenty percent of the transaction. Long ago, Paul had decided he was going to take twenty percent of that twenty percent and keep it for himself. Logically, since Mike had earned four million pounds over the years, Paul had surreptitiously taken eight hundred thousand pounds of that money and kept it for himself. Which was precisely why the number eight hundred thousand continued to pop into Dixon's mind.

All had been going to plan, and Nation hadn't picked up a single clue as to Dixon's scam. The strategy could, theoretically, have continued indefinitely, with the only determining factor being the timing of Dixon's decision to stop working for Nation, take the money and run. However, circumstances had very recently changed, and quite radically at that. All of a sudden, Nation needed to get liquid. He needed access to the full four million pounds for some huge, career-defining final deal he was putting together, and he needed the money quickly. Nation had been asking questions of Dixon that he had never posed before. He'd started instructing Dixon to consolidate all his dodgy accounts, and the pace at which he had wanted to bring his money together had taken Dixon by surprise. Paul wasn't able to cover his tracks adequately, and he was sure Nation was getting closer to realising what any half-intelligent businessman should have realised from the start: that Paul had conned him out of eight hundred grand.

Dixon took a bite of his toast and rubbed his aching eyes. He was nervous about Nation finding out the truth, and he was anxious about the days to come. He realised he had an urge to pee. His prostate had been playing up for months and it seemed to get worse the more anxious he got. These days, he was in the downstairs loo more often than he was in the lounge.

He got up from his desk and walked across to the hallway, then on to the toilet. He hovered over the bowl for what seemed like an eternity, but nothing happened. Finally, he managed to squeeze out a few drops but they missed their target entirely and dripped onto his smart, salmon-coloured trainers. He sighed in disappointment.

Back in the lounge, he wandered over to the far side of the room towards the chimney breast and reached up towards the big mirror above the mantelpiece. He slid the frame of the mirror to one side, revealing a tiny electronic button. It was flush with the wall and painted the same colour, so unless you knew what you were looking for, it was imperceptible to the naked eye. He pressed the button and heard a hushed click echo into the room. Bending down, he extended an arm deep into the fireplace and pushed a panel on the left-hand side. The panel snapped inward, then popped outwards, revealing a small secret compartment deep within the hearth. With the door shut, the compartment was invisible. Even a rigorous search of the fireplace would fail to reveal its location, just as Dixon had designed.

Reaching as far as he could inside the compartment, Dixon felt the soft leather of a large duffle bag. He smiled. It was still there. Of course it was still there! Why wouldn't it be? No one knew it was there in the first place! The security arrangements were excellent; without knowing the location of the secret locking button and without knowing where to push the panel, the chamber would forever remain hidden.

Dixon tugged at the bag, dragging it from the fireplace and onto the floor of the lounge. He unzipped the top and pulled it open. Inside, neatly wrapped into bundles, were thousands and thousands of pounds, all in fifty-pound notes. Those bundles were carefully stacked one upon another in bandings of two-and-a-half thousand pounds per banding. Over three hundred bundles all told. Grand total, eight hundred thousand pounds sterling. He smiled.

Dixon, being a very smart money launderer, knew that every single electronic transaction left a digital trail, and every digital trail could be followed and analysed if you were smart enough. Dixon also knew that, as stupid as Mike Nation appeared to be, he would eventually come to realise some of his money was missing and he would want it back. For a decent finder's fee, Nation could easily locate another computer finance expert who would have the skills to follow the money trail, track down the stolen cash and thereby locate Dixon himself. Hard cash, on the other hand, leaves no electronic trail. You just have to hide it.

It was for this reason that, about a year ago, Paul had come to three conclusions. First, he needed to start withdrawing his self-rewarded bonuses from their accounts, converting it all into cold, hard currency; second, he needed somewhere to store the money until it was time to depart for pastures new; and third, he realised that regardless of whether his money was in a bank or a bag, he couldn't stop Nation from looking for him. Nation was going to be apoplectic when he found out, and he would want his revenge. This meant that, unless

Dixon wanted to spend a lifetime on the run, he would need to do something about Mike Nation.

The first of those tasks was an easy one. Dixon had been splitting his unauthorised cut of the transactions he'd been making into various bank accounts for years, so he could comfortably make regular, monthly withdrawals from each of those accounts without sending up any red flags. For the past twelve months, this was precisely what he had been doing.

The second task turned out to be no more difficult than the first. It just so happened that his neighbour was having some redecoration work done at about the same time Dixon was formulating his plans, so he approached the neighbour's tradesman on the street one afternoon. The labourer was a tall, good-looking Polish lad who, by all accounts, lived nearby and who often carried out a little building and decoration work on the side to supplement his main income. He seemed discreet enough, so Dixon had hired him, and the guy had spent a week in Dixon's lounge, carefully digging out and then perfecting the hiding place in the chimney breast. Dixon paid a fee that he thought was certain to buy the man's silence, but regardless, Paul had an excellent security system at his house, and the hiding place was merely a further layer of protection.

The final conclusion that Dixon had come to, however, had proven more problematic to resolve. Whichever way he analysed his options, however he covered his tracks and whatever he did in the way of protection, he had realised that Mike would never stop searching for him. Nation was a vengeful man at the best of times, and ripping him off to the tune of eight hundred grand was the height of betrayal. The guy would search the corners of the earth for him, so Dixon had come to the inescapable deduction that he had to get rid of Mike Nation. Permanently.

The conclusion caused him no guilt. After all, no one would miss the dreadful little man, other than maybe his ghastly wife, Barbara. The problem was finding a realistic and foolproof method of getting rid of him. Dixon toyed with the idea of doing the deed himself but, as morally malleable as he most certainly was, he wasn't sure he was capable of carrying out an actual murder. And regardless, he knew he didn't have the expertise to bump off Nation and guarantee he would get away with it. Sure, Dixon could cover his tracks *financially* with the best in the business, but when it came to disappearing *people*, he was very much a beginner.

To that end, Dixon had started making some discreet enquiries with a select number of trusted people. People who were either friends of his, of which there were depressingly few, or more likely those whom he could rely on to keep quiet with the gift of a small bung. He hadn't rushed those enquiries because, until recently, there seemed no hurry on this particular issue. After all, a fortnight ago, Mike had no suspicion there was any money missing. However, things had moved on very swiftly, what with Nation's insistence on cashing out on the full four million. Now, there was very much a degree of urgency. Finally, after a succession of false leads, Paul thought he had got a hit. He was to go to a café on York Road in the Kings Heath area of Birmingham and ask for a man called Terry. Terry would tell Dixon what could be done about his little problem. Terry, by all accounts, knew a man.

CHAPTER THREE

B rian Wood heard his mobile phone buzz from its docking station on the other side of the bedroom. Groaning, he slowly opened one eye and peered at the clock next to his bed. 10.30 a.m. Four hours' sleep. Bugger, he thought, as he gave a yawn. He was starting to feel every bit of his forty-eight years, and four hours' sleep was just not enough.

Brian had spent the previous night providing security for a rather rich man of dubious repute who had travelled up to Birmingham from London to check on his various interests in the city. The man tended to make the trip every six months, and each time he would call on Brian for protection. Yesterday had been the most recent of those occasions, so once again, Brian had spent a tedious evening looking on while his client went from bar to club to casino, all the while checking on staff, reviewing the books, drinking heavily and generally annoying everybody he met. Nonetheless, the night had passed without incident, and Brian had left his VIP at the hotel just as the sun was coming up. The man was drunk out of his head but not dead. Another happy customer.

Brian rolled over and opened the other eye. As he did so, he knocked a heavy book from his bed and it toppled onto the floor with a thud. It fell open to a page somewhere in the middle, and a large photo of Old Joe, the nickname for the memorial clock tower that dominated the Birmingham University campus, stared back at him. More lucidly now, Brian reached down, picked the book up and carefully placed it on the bedside table.

Brian loved books, and he was going through a phase of reading up on all of Birmingham's buildings. He was on his fourth loan, and between them, they had covered most of the city. He'd read about old buildings and new buildings. He'd explored renovated buildings and decaying buildings. And he'd spent a great deal of time studying the city's long-since demolished buildings. Birmingham had a particular penchant for knocking things down, which rankled Brian. But all the city's important structures were covered in the books he had found, and, just as with any topic he chose, he devoured the information with relish.

Brian knew precisely where this love of books had come from. As a boy, he had never known his father, who had walked out on him when he was just two years old. He had been brought up entirely by his mother in a small terraced house in the Hall Green area of the city. She was employed part time at the local library, and she had regularly taken Brian to work with her. He loved everything about the place. He loved the smell of the library building, he loved the way the endless rows of different publications resembled a maze, but most of all, he loved the feel of each individual book.

The way the strong, hard backing of the book cover slowly revealed the shiny, delicate pages within. He would spend hours leafing through them, shelf after shelf, examining the pictures and reading those words that he understood. The memories lived with him long into his adulthood.

Naturally, for a boy who had spent his life surrounded by volume after volume of wonderful artistic and literary works, when he grew up, Brian joined the army and learned how to kill people. His mother was unconvinced of the plan, but the family were short of money, and the armed services would provide them with a steady income, so Brian's mind was made up.

He trained hard and developed into a strong and dependable soldier. He was always careful with his rather meagre earnings and was mindful to send money back to his mother each month. He steadily rose through the ranks from private, to lance corporal, to corporal and was well respected by his superiors, who saw him as a safe pair of hands; he never got into any trouble with the authorities, either military or civilian.

But all that changed when, out of the blue, his mother became gravely ill. Brian was given compassionate leave to come home and care for her. She was very poorly and he did his best to make her comfortable, but eventually his mother succumbed. Heartbroken, he realised he was suddenly alone. He became furious with the army for robbing him of all the precious time that he could have spent with his mother, so he never went back. He was soon regarded as absent without leave, eventually being dishonourably discharged for desertion.

He became a ghost, with no paper trail to speak of, but he needed a source of income to survive. He had only his army skills to call on, so he fell into the role of a fixer of sorts. An enforcer, a gun for hire and an occasional contract killer. Over the years, he had become rather good at it.

Brian dragged his body from his bed, limped over to his phone and pressed his thumb to the scanner. It was a text message from another of his clients.

'Mike bloody Nation,' he muttered to himself before opening the text.

Need your services. My office, ASAP.

Brian yawned again and scratched his leg, then his buttocks. Not the news he wanted to hear. He was craving a quiet day, but there were always bills to pay and Nation was a good customer. Nation and Brian went back years; he was one of Brian's very first clients after he had left the army, and he had called on Brian regularly ever since. There had been quite the number of less-than-pleasant tasks Brian had performed on Nation's behalf, and Mike had rewarded him handsomely for his services. It all meant that Brian begrudgingly resigned himself to making the meeting, so he headed for the shower to freshen up.

Around an hour later, Brian was turning into the small car park at the front of Nation House in Moseley. He pulled into a spare space, climbed out and headed for the main entrance at the side of the building. The ever-faithful Beryl was at her desk in the main reception area. Above her, a preposterously big portrait of Mike Nation hung on the wall, staring down on the rest of the room like some kind of deity.

Brian picked up a faint scent of bacon, and it made his stomach groan with hunger. When did he last eat? Christ, he had no idea, but he was going to have to get some sustenance inside him sooner rather than later.

'Good morning, Mr Wood. He says you're to go right in,' Beryl said with a cheerful smile.

Brian was about to nod his thanks when he picked up on the muffled sound of raised voices emanating from Mike's office to the rear of the building.

'He sounds busy,' he replied, pointing in the direction of the noise.

'He's in with that chef lady, Rosie something? But he said he wouldn't be long, and he said for you to go straight in as soon as you arrived.'

'Fair enough,' he said with a smile. He reached the office door and gave it a nudge. The voices within grew louder; he seemed to be walking into a full-blown row. He poked his head round the corner and was spotted by Nation, who indicated for him to come in. Brian entered, closed the door and lingered at the back of the office. The smell of bacon grew stronger, and his stomach grumbled loudly.

Brian had had many a meeting in Nation's office, and he knew it like the back of his hand. The sad-looking spider plant tree in the corner of the room was still clinging onto life; it would have perished long ago if not for Beryl. The window that looked out onto Moseley High Street still needed a clean, but the sun's rays were nonetheless strong enough to throw light across Nation's big, ugly desk at the back of the room. Three large posters displaying the logos of Nation's businesses hung proudly on the rear wall, accompanied by a hideous portrait of Margaret Thatcher dangling at an angle over Nation's seat.

God, Nation had bad taste, Brian thought. The only unique feature on this particular visit was the angry, red-faced Rosie Bell, standing in the middle of the room, wagging a finger and yelling at a confused-looking Mike Nation.

'*Halibut!*' Rosie yelled, with such force the word seemed to reverberate around the room.

'Do *what* now?' asked Nation, clearly perplexed. He shrugged his shoulders in Brian's direction.

'Bloody halibut, you dope! That's what I'm on about! Your bloody halibut! You knew I needed all of it for this weekend. And not only that, Gary in your wholesale unit knew I needed all of it for this weekend. Everyone knew I needed all of your halibut for this weekend. But what did I find when I got to the market this morning? Go on, Mike! Guess!'

'I don't know, love.'

'Gary had sold it all! He'd sold the goddamned lot!'

'Rosie, calm down, bab…' Nation complained.

'I will not calm down, Mike! Guess who he sold it to!'

'I don't know, Rosie.'

'I said guess!'

'Rosie, I really don't know.'

'Glynn blooming Purnell!' she snapped.

'Really? Glynn blooming Purnell?'

'Yes, Mike, Glynn blooming Purnell.'

'Well, to be fair, Rosie, he *is* Glynn blooming Purnell… Look, piece of advice, bab. What you need to do is get yourself on *Saturday Kitchen*.'

'What?'

'You know, *Saturday Kitchen*, on the telly.'

'What the hell are you on about?'

'The programme, Rosie. On the Beeb. It's Gary, you see; he loves the show. Swears by it. And Glynn's never off the bloody thing. So, you see, if Gary sees *you* on *Saturday Kitchen*, Gary sells you the halibut, not Glynn.'

'It's not as good since James Martin left,' murmured Brian from the back of the room.

'You're not wrong there, Brian,' Mike conceded.

Rosie looked distinctly unimpressed. 'Look, Mike. Given our relationship, and given that Nation Investments does have a bloody investment in my restaurant, I would have liked to think that I would get some sort of preferential treatment from that dick in your wholesale team. It would help us both. It's logical, for Christ's sake.'

'Fair enough, Rosie, fair enough. Look, I'll get Brian here to go down to the market and have a word with Gary. We'll straighten this all out, I promise you.'

Rosie looked at Brian for the first time and scrutinized him for a moment. So this was Mike's fixer, Brian, that she'd heard about. She'd never been impressed by intimidation and violence, but her first impressions were that this guy didn't *look* the violent type. Not that she knew what the violent type actually looked like in the first place. This guy was tall, certainly over six feet, and probably quite strong by the size of his shoulders. Not entirely unattractive, either, she thought, but in a rough-and-ready, knocking-on-a-bit kind of way.

'I don't want anyone beaten up over this, mind...' she said finally, assuming the worst.

Brian was surprised to find he felt somewhat offended by the inference, but he nonetheless smiled back at the red-faced chef. 'Don't worry, I'll be delicate, I promise.'

The pair held each other's gaze momentarily, and it was Brian's turn to study Rosie just a little. A bit of a pocket rocket, he thought. Small but athletic looking, with a kind of magnetic sparkle in her deep green eyes. The way she had been hammering away at Nation had impressed him; not a lot of people would have the balls to speak to him like that. She was obviously not short in confidence and was determined to fight her own corner. Brian admired it.

He realised they were still holding each other's gaze, the lingering glance more sustained than would perhaps be considered normal. Was there a slight sense of a connection? Brian dismissed the thought as ridiculous. There was no reason why a Michelin-starred chef would have the faintest interest in him. But still…

Brian needed to break the silence. 'So, is this what you wanted to see me about Mike? You want me to go and see Gary about some halibut?'

'No, Brian, you hang on. I need a word with you about some other matters.' Nation turned to Rosie. 'Rosie, Brian here will go to the market, and he will sort this all out with Gary, ok? Oh, and he promises no fishy business!'

Nation grinned proudly at the punchline and leaned back in his chair, waiting for some recognition. There was silence from the others in the room, much to his disappointment. Rosie finally interrupted the awkwardness.

'OK then, Mike, fair enough,' she said.

'Good. And Barbara and I will pop in soon for dinner. We loved it last time we were in.'

'Better not order the sodding halibut,' she said. Brian let out a little snort, and he was sure Rosie smiled, just a touch. Nation was annoyed. That wasn't as good as his fish joke, surely?

Rosie turned and hurried out of the office. As she passed Brian, she glanced up. They caught each other's eye once more. Just a moment in time, and then she was gone, slamming the door behind her. Brian was already looking forward to seeing her again.

Mike stood and stretched. He checked his watch. Just after midday.

'Right then, Bri, sun's over the yard arm; let's go for a drink. We need to have a chat concerning matters that are significantly more important than a load of bleeding halibut.' He gathered up all the accounting files from his desk and stuffed them under his arm. He ushered Brian towards the door and followed behind him. In the reception area, he turned to Beryl and dumped the papers on her desk.

'Send all this lot to Mr Dixon will you Beryl, love? Courier it over. The usual address. No rush on it though, bab, so use the cheap firm, ok? Delivery for tomorrow will be fine.'

Beryl nodded and waved a cheerful goodbye as Brian and Mike made their way outside. Once they were gone, she stood up and walked uncomfortably over to the filing cabinets at the other end of the room. She opened the top drawer and reached in for a courier bag, before hobbling back to her desk and lowering herself gingerly back into her seat. Next, she gathered up the pile of work Mike had planted on her desk.

She noticed a big smear of bacon grease on the top of one of the files, so she grabbed a tissue and wiped it clean as best she could, shaking her head while she did so. Nation's food did tend to get everywhere.

Carefully, Beryl flicked through the documents once more, counting one, two, three folders full of paperwork and a single sheet of A4 paper with what looked like doodles on it. Doodles and some random words, it seemed. Well, Mike had instructed her to send *all* this lot over… so that's what she would do.

She picked up the courier bag and carefully inserted the three folders and the solitary piece of paper. She sealed it firmly and added the address to the delivery label. Finally, she picked up the phone and put in a call to the local courier firm.

CHAPTER FOUR

Brian and Mike strolled purposefully down Moseley High Street in the noon sun, past the Peruvian restaurant and the Lebanese grocery store that irritated Nation so much. It was a warm summer's day with clear blue skies and very little breeze, so Brian took off his jacket and flung it over his shoulder as they ambled up the road.

They headed towards a bar called The Phoney Negroni, which had been Nation's local haunt of choice since he had opened his head office in the locality all those years ago. It wasn't called The Phoney Negroni back then, of course, and Brian doubted whether Nation had a clue what a negroni was, let alone had actually tried one. Back then, it was known as The Jug of Ale, and despite seeing the place being reincarnated several times over, he had stayed loyal to the venue. He'd kept coming back partly out of habit but partly because Nation Investments had a small financial interest in the current business, and Nation liked to check on the books from time to time.

As they walked and talked, Brian was once again reminded of Nation's stocky, compact stature; he towered over the fat little man. His companion had a rather distinctive visual appearance as well. For a start, his clothing seemed to be from a different era. As ever, Mike was sporting grey trousers, a white shirt, and a dark blue double-breasted blazer with a Nation Group of Companies crest adorning the pocket. The normally spotless white shirt was today smeared with what Brian assumed must be tomato ketchup. Once again, his stomach groaned with hunger.

The clothing all sat over Nation's curiously orange-toned skin tone, and the colour was particularly pronounced across his perfectly circular face. His head resembled a pumpkin, Brian thought. The whole look reminded Brian simultaneously of a short, round, 1980s football manager, and a short, round, 1980s coach driver, although Brian doubted that Nation would be capable of either.

Brian would never ask about the curiously bright skin, but he had once brought up the subject of Mike's double-breasted blazer, only to be told that double is exactly 100% more than single and that all businessmen knew that was a good thing. The comment didn't make any sense to Brian at the time, and it still didn't. He hadn't brought up the topic since.

As they continued their summer stroll, Brian wondered what nasty piece of business he was about to be contracted to do this time. Over the years that they had been working together, Brian had come to realise that Nation had a rather warped sense of morals. It had become quite obvious that Nation would shaft everyone and anyone, up to and including his own ninety-year-old granny, to make a fast buck. He had no scruples and didn't care who he trod on as he made his way to his next million. But none of this particularly bothered Brian. He reasoned that if people were daft enough to get themselves into bed with Mike, they had to take the consequences. And if it wasn't Nation doing the shafting, someone else would just step into his place.

They reached The Phoney Negroni, a large, detached building on the edge of Moseley Village, and walked inside. Large prints of cocktails hung on the walls, accompanied by various landscape pictures of Italy, the spiritual home of the famous drink. The lighting was dim and moody despite the relatively early hour, and there were a surprisingly large number of customers already in the bar.

'There's a bit of a healthy drinking culture in Moseley, Bri,' remarked Nation.

They wandered over to Mike's usual table in the bay window and took a seat. They didn't need to wait long for a waitress to join them.

'Two pints of lager, please Sandra, there's a love,' said Nation.

'And a bowl of chips as well, thanks, bab,' added Brian, relieved he could finally get some food inside him.

'You'll get fat,' Nation remarked without any sense of irony, despite having polished off two bacon, sausage and egg sandwiches only an hour ago. Then he had second thoughts and called Sandra back. 'Better make that two bowls, love. Oh, and a bag of crisps while we're waiting, ta.'

'Plain?'

'Yes, bab.'

The drinks and crisps arrived quickly, and they charged their glasses before taking a big gulp each.

'Funny, isn't it, Bri?' Nation said while munching on a crisp. '*Ready Salted*. I mean, why's it not just called S*alt*?'

'Eh?' said Brian, wondering what Nation was going on about this time.

'Well, you don't get *ready cheese and onioned* crisps, do you? Or *ready salt and vinegared*? No, it's just plain *salt and vinegar*. But if you have the salt, minus the vinegar, suddenly it has to be *readied*. Why's that?'

'I really haven't thought about it, Mike, to be honest.'

'Well, that's the difference between you and me, Brian. If you want to make money in this world, you've got to analyse the details.'

'You're probably right. Anyway, what did you want to talk to me about?' asked Brian.

Mike settled back into his seat, rubbed his brow and was silent for a moment as if he were trying to build up some sort of suspense. Brian waited patiently and took another gulp of his beer. Finally, Nation began.

'Let me tell you a little story, Brian, to set the scene. You see, me and Barbara, we were on holiday in Florida about a month or so ago. We love the place, Bri; go every year. Sunshine and steaks coming out of your arsehole. Anyway, we were in a bar in Kissimmee one night, when we met a nice couple from Texas. The husband introduced himself as "The Colonel", but his full name was Colonel John P. Kicklighter.'

'You're kidding.'

'Nope, I shit you not, Bri. Colonel John P. Kicklighter. Got a face the size of Dallas. Anyway, the four of us, we got talking. And the Yanks, they were all friendly and that, like the way Americans can be sometimes. We were having a nice time shooting the breeze and making small talk. You know what I mean, favourite wine, favourite restaurant, favourite machine gun, that kind of thing. The machine gun was The Colonel's question. Turns out he quite fancies an M2 Browning thingy, whatever the hell that is. He likes his guns, does The Colonel. Mind you, he is an actual Colonel, so I guess that makes sense. But I digress. What I'm getting at is it's all pleasant and we're all having a fun time together, you get the picture.'

'I do.'

'So, we were chatting away, and it turns out they were staying in the same hotel as me and Barbara. So, we all agreed to meet up for dinner the next evening.'

The chips arrived, together with a couple of forks and a little dish that was spilling over with condiment sachets. The men nodded their thankyous to Sandra, who asked whether they wanted two more lagers. They said they did, so she hurried back to the bar to fetch the refills. Meanwhile, Nation continued his story.

'We met up the following night as planned, and we had a big old dinner followed by drinks back at the hotel. We got onto the topic of Hollywood movies. Turns out The Colonel is a big cowboy movie fan; he loves all that kind of thing. His favourite one is that old flick *Slow Train to St Louis*, you know, the one starring that Brummie actor, Sir Johnny Weaver. I said that I lived in the very same town as the fruity old fella, and he got very excited! He asked if I'd ever bumped into him in a 7-Eleven one time. He was blown away when I said we didn't do 7-Elevens...'

'What *are* you going on about, Mike?'

'Getting there, Bri. Anyway, eventually the conversation turned to work stuff, what we did for a living and so on. Turns out The Colonel is a bit of an entrepreneur, much like myself.

After he left the army, he went into business for himself. He quickly found that he had an eye for a good deal and he took full advantage. Made his first million dollars within two years of leaving the armed forces. Not bad at all. I tell you, Bri, we were getting on like a house on fire.'

'Sounds lovely,' said Brian, trying to hide his boredom.

'It *was* lovely, Brian. It was like we were brothers. It was as if we had known each other for years. Eventually, Barbara and missus Colonel John P. Kicklighter headed off to bed, so it was just the gents, up late, talking shop over a beer or two. And it was at that point that The Colonel told me about his latest business venture. It was a once-in-a-lifetime opportunity, and it was going to change his life forever. And in a flash, he invited me to join him in the deal.'

'So, The Colonel ripped you off?' Brian interjected, trying to speed things up.

'Christ, no! Not at all. I'm not stupid, Bri. I wasn't going to sign up to any old deal after ten pints of lager. He told me all about the project, but then I did my homework. Over the course of the next few days, we talked through the numbers and worked through his plans. There was no doubting it, The Colonel was right. This thing was a goldmine.'

The second round of beers arrived, so they hurriedly downed their first pints and handed the glasses to Sandra. Nation burped loudly and patted his stomach before grabbing some chips with his podgy orange fingers and cramming them into his mouth. Brian struggled not to pull a face.

Chewing loudly, Nation nonetheless started up his story again, and small bits of fried potato escaped his mouth and tumbled onto the table as he did so.

'Brian, do you know how many old people there are in America?'

'Go on, how many?'

'Well, I don't know exactly, but probably fucking loads. And that's the point. There's badly permed silver hair everywhere you look, and there's only going to be more. Colonel John P. Kicklighter knew this, and he knew they all had to live somewhere. And this was the plan. He was buying a retirement village. *Golden Valley Retirement Community*, in Phoenix, Arizona, to be precise. You see, the construction company that was building the place had gone bust during COVID. But the village is pretty much complete. Just a few odds and sods to finish off. We can pick it up for a song, get the work completed on the cheap and then lease out all those lovely little condominiums to the blue rinse brigade. The returns are going to be ridiculous. The grey dollar, Bri, it's the future. All we need are the funds for the upfront purchase out of administration.'

Brian had finished his chips and was feeling much better. 'Following you so far, Mike,' he said.

'The upshot is that if we're going to go in fifty-fifty, I will need to pony up the dollar equivalent of four million quid.'

'Jesus Christ!' exclaimed Brian.

'Yes, I know. But trust me, Bri, it's a bloody bargain. This investment, it's going to be Barbara and my retirement fund. It's the final deal I'll ever need to make. It will keep us in luxury for the rest of our lives!

'Anyway, I was obviously excited, so as soon as I got back to Birmingham, I started pooling all my resources. You see, I have certain savings put away in specific bank accounts, and they are all administered by my private finance guy. I was pretty sure I could just about get the four million together, but I needed to consolidate all those accounts and quickly. Consequently, I asked my accountant for all the financial details, the statements and the headline numbers of these accounts, and this is where the problems began.'

'So, the *accountant* ripped you off, not The Colonel,' remarked Brian.

'It would seem so, Bri; it would seem so. At first, my finance chappy was very reluctant to hand over the information I was asking for. Finally, he gave me the data but in as complicated a format as was humanly possible. This pissed me off, so I started doing the work myself. I followed the transactions he had conducted for me, trailing the paths from start to finish. I ran the numbers, backtracked the accounts, compared the totals. Turns out that, all told, I *should* have had, near as damn it, precisely the four million quid I needed.'

'And how much did you actually have?'

'About three point two million. It seems the scrawny little Judas has stolen eight hundred grand of my damned money.'

'I see.'

'It's a betrayal, Brian, that's what it is, a damned betrayal. I mean, I've worked my backside off all my life. Three successful businesses I've set up! Three successful businesses, each employing dozens of people. I provide for people, Brian. I create jobs and I create lives. And you know what? "I chose to do these things not because they were easy, but because they were hard." Thatcher.'

'Erm, I think that was JFK, Mike.'

'Thatcher, Bri. But anyway, now, when it's time to reap the rewards of all my years of labour, some nasty, deceitful tosspot has pulled the rug out from under me. I trusted him, Brian. I rewarded him handsomely and yet he stabbed me in the back. I tell you what, mate, some people are like squirrels. You can be as nice as you like to them, but they'll still munch on your nuts…'

Nation paused for a moment and took a glug of his lager while Brian, slightly confused by the last metaphor, just sat quietly, waiting for his client to continue. Eventually Nation re-focussed and started up where he'd left off.

'Suffice to say, I want my money back. But the trouble is there is a degree of urgency in this. It's not as if I can decide to handle my accountant problem at a later date and just earn a different eight hundred large over the next few months as a replacement. You see, The Colonel is flying into Birmingham from Texas in three bloody days to seal the deal. And I must have the money by then. The full four million.'

'That does, indeed, seem to be a bit of a problem,' Brian conceded.

'Precisely. And this Colonel fella, he's a nice bloke and everything, but he is not a guy to be messed around. If he flies all the way here from the States and finds out I'm short, the shit will hit the fan. He'll get really pissed, in a way that only the ex-military seem to get pissed. You know what I mean, Brian?'

'I know what you mean, Mike,' Brian said, not having a clue what he meant, despite being ex-military himself.

'Look, I've got a lot on my plate at the moment, Brian, what with train station contracts and the halibut and everything.

So, here's what I need you to do. Within the next seventy-two hours, I need you to find out what that bloody accountant has done with my eight hundred grand. I need you to find the money and get it back for me. Once you've done that, I want you to disappear the dirty scumbag.'

'Understood, Mike, understood. What's this chap's name, then?'

'Paul bloody Dixon. Lives over in Edgbaston.' Mike dug into his blazer pocket and pulled out his mobile. He flicked to the gallery app and found a photo.

'This is a picture of Dixon from about six months ago. He came round for dinner at my place one evening. Barbara did a shepherd's pie. It was nice. The shepherd's pie, I mean, not the evening. That was absolutely terrible. He's a boring old bugger is Dixon, and a right old weirdo with it, too. Plus, he was forever running off to the toilet. Very odd. I can only guess the glands around his old chap are packing in. Serves the man right, too. But I digress again.'

'Hang on, I thought employing weirdos was against company policy?'

'Yeh, my mistake there, Bri. It's true, I don't make many, but it appears Dixon was one of them. Anyway, I'll send you a copy of the photo, and I'll forward you his mobile phone number, address, all the usual guff as well. Look, Brian, I need you to get this resolved for me, and I need it done quick. As I say, The Colonel is flying over in just three days.'

'Understood. Does this Dixon bloke suspect you are onto him?'

'Well, I'm playing dumb at the moment.'

'Shouldn't be too tricky, then.'

'Shut up, Bri. As I say, I'm playing along for the time being. In fact, I've just had Beryl send all the paperwork back to him to make it look like it's business as usual. But to be honest, he'd be some sort of an idiot if he didn't suspect I had kind of an idea, given all the data I've been asking for over the last two weeks. I imagine he has a pretty good inkling, to be honest.'

Sandra came over to clear the table. Mike asked her to stick the drinks and the chips on his tab, and she nodded politely. The men both stood and stretched, preparing to leave.

'Look, I need this deal, Brian. It's the nest egg. I can't let this one slip. You understand the importance of your role in all this, I take it?'

'Loud and clear, Mike, loud and clear.'

'Good.'

The pair left The Phoney Negroni just as the lunchtime rush started.

'They do like a drink in Moseley, that's for sure,' commented Brian as they sauntered back down the High Street to Nation House. Once there, they paused for a moment in the quiet of the office car park.

'One other thing, Brian. Your little protégée, Sammy. Is she free this afternoon?'

'Not sure, to be honest, Mike. I've not caught up with her for a day or so. But I'm bound to need her for this job, so I presume it's ok to loop her in on all of this?'

'That's fine, not a problem. I guessed as much. But listen, get her to meet me at Moseley Station later today as well, will you? I have another little task for her.'

'Will do, Mike. I'll call her from the car now.'

'Thanks, Brian. And keep me informed of developments. Every step of the way, Bri. Every bloody step.'

Brian nodded and the two men shook hands. Mike wandered back into Nation House, pondering what to order for lunch, while Brian unlocked his car and climbed in. After a couple of moments, his mobile phone pinged. As promised, Nation had sent an email with all the information he had on the accountant Paul Dixon. Brian would have a proper read of all that later. But first, he needed to contact his twenty-year-old partner, Sammy. He scrolled to her name in his contacts list and hit the dial button.

CHAPTER FIVE

York Road is a popular little side street, just off the main drag that runs through the south Birmingham suburb of Kings Heath. Dixon's house wasn't far from the location, maybe five miles in total. But the accountant had been driving for almost three-quarters of an hour and he still couldn't find a way of turning onto York Road legally. The council's new one-way systems, bollards and traffic calming measures were all well-intentioned, for sure, but in Kings Heath, they seemed to defy all logic. To Dixon, it felt as if he were trapped in an Escher painting, much like the famous never-ending staircase, although this time he was destined to drive round and round forever in his car, without ever reaching his destination.

Finally, having done four laps of the same route and failing, on each occasion, to find a way onto York Road, Dixon gave up. Exasperated, he abandoned his car in a nearby Asda car park and chose to hike the final half mile in double-quick time. He was late, and he was getting anxious.

He had been told that his contact, Terry, the man who 'knew people', would be at the café on the side street that very afternoon and that Dixon was expected. He found the premises about ten shops down from the impossible and impassable junction with the high street, and once outside, he took a moment to catch his breath.

His heart was beating hard as he contemplated entering the tired old café. From the outside, it looked like a hygiene death trap. Dirty, stained, yellow paint was flaking off the walls that bordered the grubby and steamed-up centre window, while a crumbling wooden sign reading Allison's All-Day Breakfasts hung precariously over the entrance door.

Dixon felt the sweat pour from his brow and the dampness ooze underneath his arms. This was beyond clammy; his body was humid. He was his own microclimate, and it was tropical. He wondered whether the whole plan was a bad idea after all and considered ditching the meeting and getting out of there. He realised he didn't know anything about this Terry fellow, other than that the guy had contacts who could get things done, so he didn't know what he was walking into. But at the same time, he also knew he needed specialised help with his Mike Nation problem and that he had come too far to pull out now. There was no turning back, so Dixon composed himself as best he could and tentatively pulled the door open.

The smell of grease hit him like a truck. Already feeling nauseous, Dixon struggled to maintain his composure. He was sure he was going to be sick. He closed his eyes and took a couple of slow breaths through his mouth to avoid taking in the dreadful aroma. After a moment or two, he felt somewhat calmer. He opened his eyes and was confronted by an ageing, red-faced woman with curly grey hair and wonky teeth, wearing an apron which may well have been white once upon a time but probably not since the 1970s. The nausea returned.

'Sit anywhere you like, bab,' said the woman cheerily. Dixon took the table nearest to him. He needed to sit down urgently, and he doubted he would have made it to any other table without passing out. He was breathing heavily. Was he having a panic attack? How does one know? He made a mental note to look it up when he made it back home. God, he hoped he would make it back home.

The woman brought him a menu and placed it in front of him.

'Just a black coffee, thanks,' he said meekly. She rolled her eyes, nodded, and made her way back to the counter at the other end of the café. Dixon watched the lady pop the kettle on and grab a dirty jar of supermarket own-brand instant powder from the shelf. He shuddered at the thought of it. He really was going to be sick. And now his prostate was playing up as well; he realised he desperately needed to pee. Bloody hell, what a nightmare. What was he doing to himself?

The woman brought him the mug of coffee and plonked it down heavily in front of him, spilling some of the brown liquid as she did so. She mopped the splashes up with her badly stained apron.

'I, erm, I...' Dixon garbled.

'Yes, bab, spit it out!' said the woman, hovering over him.

'I was... told to ask for Terry?'

'Bloody hell, not another one,' she complained before turning to another table on the other side of the café. It was only then that Dixon realised he wasn't the sole customer in the place. There were two other men sharing a table across the room.

'Terry...' she called.

No reaction.

'*Terry!*' the woman yelled, scaring Dixon half to death. One of the men looked up from his newspaper.

'Another one for you, Tel. Look, you've got to stop using my caff as your own personal office, bab. You don't drink enough tea for that. Not even close.'

'Heard it all before, Alli!' said the man, giving the owner a little wink. Allison glared back at him, then wandered back to the counter and her own mug of tea.

'You'd better come over then, chap. Here, take a seat.' Terry pointed at a chair nearby.

Dixon's legs felt like granite. He wasn't sure whether he could make it to the other side of the room; he might as well be climbing the north face of Everest.

'What are you waiting for, son? I don't bite, do I, Pete?'

Terry turned to the other man at the table. Pete had put his newspaper down and was staring at Dixon intently. 'No, Tel, you don't bite. Much…'

Dixon closed his eyes again and heaved himself to his feet. Concentrating as hard as he could, he slowly made his way over to Terry's table. He dragged a chair into position and collapsed into it with a groan.

'Very good, son. Very good. Now. You are Paul, I take it?' Paul nodded.

'Excellent. And I understand you have a little problem.'

Again, Paul nodded. He had lost the ability to speak.

'Furthermore,' Terry continued, 'I understand that you want someone to remove this little problem for you, pal. Is that about the sum of it? A bit of pest control? A bit of *human* pest control?'

Sweat was streaming down Dixon's face. He wiped it away with his palm. 'Something like that, yes,' he spluttered, finally getting his mouth to work.

'And you don't want your own dirty mitts anywhere near it, eh? Don't want to end up in the clanger now, do you, son?'

'No, no, I don't,' agreed Dixon.

'Course not. And that can happen, can't it, Pete? Oh yes. Sure, it can. You see, I had a pal once. He did a bit of human pest control. But he got caught, though, didn't he? And where did he end up? Doing twenty-to-life in Carlisle Prison, isn't that so, Pete?'

'I guess so, Terry,' said Pete.

'He was a resourceful lad, though, this bloke. Oh yes. Resourceful and convincing. As persuasive as an ox...'

Dixon wondered why Terry would think an ox would be particularly persuasive but dismissed the thought quickly.

Terry continued. 'Anyway, this pal, he convinced the driver of the refuse truck to smuggle him out of the prison by hiding him in the garbage at the back. Isn't that so, Pete?'

'That's what I heard, Terry.'

'Yep. He bribed the driver to take him all the way from Carlisle back to his home here in good old Brum, while all the time he was hiding in that stinking, putrid cesspit in the rear of the wagon. Amazing. I mean, can you imagine the stench, pal?'

'God, no, how awful,' stammered Dixon.

'Awful indeed. Of course, they did stop off in Manchester for a bit, to allow the chap to come up for air and a stretch... Turned out he preferred the garbage...'

'Blahahahaha!!' Terry and Pete burst into laughter, banging the table as they did so. Ketchup bottles and salt and pepper pots went flying, smashing to the floor.

'Oi! Cut that out!' yelled Allison from the counter, her red face turning even more crimson.

'Sorry, Alli. Pete here will clean it up for you, won't you, Pete?' Pete nodded compliantly.

Dixon was speechless once again. He would have done anything not to have been at that table, but all he could do was smile gingerly at the bad joke and tentatively nod his approval.

'Nah! Only kidding you, pal. Manchester's alright, really. You're not *from* Manchester, though, are you, fella?'

'Um, no.'

'Good lad, good lad...'

Calm was eventually restored in the café and Terry returned to the business at hand, much to Dixon's relief. The sooner this meeting was over the better.

'OK, Paul, let's talk turkey as they say. Now then, I've got a guy. He specialises in this sort of thing. Not cheap, mind, but you're paying for quality. I can contact him on your behalf. He won't speak to you on the phone; he'll only speak with me. But if he's interested in hearing you out, I can set up a meeting for the two of you face to face. He always needs to see the whites of a client's eyes before accepting a job; I'm sure you understand.'

'I understand, and thank you.'

'You're very welcome. So, let me tell you what's going to happen. If he's interested, he will give me a time and a place. Somewhere nice and open and in public. It will probably be in town somewhere, and it will probably happen in the next day or so. When I have the exact details, I will text them to you. You and he will meet at the given time and place, and you will explain the full details regarding your pest control problem. When he's heard you out, he will decide whether he is amenable to helping or not, ok?'

'Ok.'

'Now, I need to tell him exactly what you'll be wearing to the meeting so that he recognises you. We can't have him wandering up to the wrong bloke in the street and start chatting about who he's going to whack for you, now can we?'

'No, certainly not.'

'Indeed. Which means I need you to be wearing the exact same clothes you're wearing now when you go for the meeting. You understand? The exact same clothes. So that's black jeans, white t-shirt, black shoes and a light grey jacket.'

'It's more of a blue jacket, I'd say,' said Pete, who had been listening quietly to the conversation while tidying up the mess.

'You what, Pete?' said Terry.

'The jacket. It's blue.'

'Shut up blue! Are you blind, pal?'

'Well, I think it's blue.'

'It's grey, Pete, for God's sake!'

'Well, let's say blue-grey then,' conceded Pete.

'Jesus bloody Christ!' exclaimed Terry in frustration. He turned to Dixon. 'You settle it. What colour is your jacket then, son?'

'Umm… well… you see I had it made bespoke. I got a tailor to match it to a tin of paint I liked.'

'Bleedin' hell, son, I don't need the bloody jacket's life story, do I? Alright then, what colour was the stupid paint?'

There was a pause before Dixon responded.

'Umm… Hippopotamus Sunrise.'

'What?'

'The paint. It's Hippopotamus Sunrise…'

'*Hippopotamus Sunrise!* What the bloody hell is that?' asked Terry incredulously.

'Well, it's this,' said Paul, pointing to his jacket.

'For crying out loud, son. I am not telling my contact, a guy who, may I remind you, kills people for a living, that he's meeting a bloke who's wearing black jeans and a hippopotamus bloody sunrise jacket, now am I? Christ. Bollocks. It's grey. I'm telling him grey. When you meet him, make it look grey.'

Dixon nodded rapidly in acknowledgement. He would definitely make his jacket look grey. In fact, to be safe, he would just go and buy a grey jacket that afternoon.

'Good stuff. Alright then, so I'll be in touch. You'd better give me your mobile number.'

Dixon did as he was told. He mumbled some sort of thanks to Terry and Pete and he left a five-pound note for the terrible coffee he hadn't touched. Allison asked if he wanted the change, but he said she could keep it. He just had to get out of there.

Dixon waved his goodbyes, staggered out of the café, took a couple of steps forward and was promptly sick all over the pavement. He wiped his face with the back of his hand and stumbled over to the nearest lamppost for support. He glanced back at the café door, only to see Terry and Pete falling about with laughter, watching him through the steamed-up window. Allison just shook her head in disdain.

He was starting to think the whole thing wasn't worth the eight hundred thousand after all. He gave himself a moment to compose himself, then took in a couple of gulps of air and lurched forwards in the direction of the car, remembering to check on panic attack symptoms when he got to the safety of his house. Before that, though, he needed to buy a very grey jacket.

CHAPTER SIX

Brian was back at his two-bedroomed flat in the Hall Green area of the city. He had spoken with Sammy from the car park of Nation House and had run through the details of the new job they'd been assigned. Sammy had been highly amused at the thought of a supposed 'business genius' accidentally losing the best part of a million quid but had nonetheless agreed to go and meet Mike at Moseley Station that afternoon. Nation was going to be racking up a lot of billable hours over the coming days, Brian thought. It was always satisfying when business was good.

He took a sip of the coffee that he'd fixed himself and stared at the file he had compiled on the accountant Paul Dixon. He'd spent an hour searching the web for any detail that might prove useful, but there hadn't been a lot of information available online; the guy seemed to keep a very low social media profile. Not surprising really, Brian surmised, given Dixon's speciality.

He flicked through the material that Nation had emailed over, but again, it was all a bit basic. There was his address, his mobile phone number and the number of a current account that Nation used for paying Dixon his salary. There was a photo of Dixon and, confusingly, a photo of Barbara's shepherd's pie as well, which didn't seem to be overly helpful. It did look nice, though. Finally, there was a stack of other information, such as the guy's date of birth, place of birth, and so on, none of which gave Brian a clue as to what Dixon was up to. There was nothing to explain why he had chosen to rob Nation blind, nor where he had put the money.

The eight hundred thousand certainly wasn't in Dixon's current account; Brian had already used a less-than-legal computer programme on his laptop to check that out. So he searched the registry of births and deaths to see whether Dixon could have moved the money to a relative's bank. He quickly learned that he was an only child, had never married and both his parents had passed away. Another dead end.

The computer was still on, so Brian grabbed it and loaded up another dodgy programme of his, a mobile tracking application that he had acquired through a contact he'd made a few years ago. He tapped in Dixon's number, half assuming Dixon would have protected his phone from monitoring devices. But no, the device homed in on Dixon's phone and beamed the coordinates of its location straight to Brian's screen. Dixon was in Kings Heath. Brian flipped the programme to map view and studied the phone's movement for a few minutes. It seemed as though his target was endlessly going round and round in circles in the middle of Kings Heath, and Brian wondered whether the app was faulty. But eventually the phone changed course and came to a stop in a supermarket car park.

Brian checked Dixon's home address once again. A small leafy road in Edgbaston. Very fancy. He estimated he could make the journey from Hall Green to Dixon's house in about fifteen minutes and decided it was time for a road trip. He collected up his laptop, his lock-picking kit and a small bag of electrical gadgets, tucked them all under his arm and set off for the communal parking area just outside his block of flats.

The traffic was surprisingly light, so Brian passed the cricket ground and headed into the main Edgbaston residential area well ahead of time. He pulled into a side street one block away from Dixon's home and parked up next to the kerb. He had no idea what the security would be like at the house, so there was no point risking getting his car registration seen directly outside the premises. Home CCTV cameras were becoming the norm these days, and it was making snoopers' jobs much more difficult.

Brian leaned over to the laptop and once again tapped in Dixon's mobile phone number. He was still in Kings Heath. Good. He climbed out of the car, put the laptop in the boot and slung his little bag of tools and electronics over his shoulder before heading for Dixon's home.

A couple of minutes later, Brian arrived at the accountant's house. He recognised the place instantly from the Google Maps search that he had conducted before he left Hall Green. There was a small but secluded driveway, which Brian was thankful for; he would be camouflaged from the quiet road while he had his little nose around. He loitered on the pavement for a moment to ensure the road was deserted before darting up the driveway and out of the sight of any prying eyes.

From the outside, the home looked rather grand. It was an Edwardian semi-detached spread over three floors and it was maintained, it seemed, to a very high order. Dixon must take pride in the place, Brian thought. The driveway was framed by mature but well-cared-for borders, suggesting the guy was either green-fingered or more likely employed a gardener.

Brian studied the exterior of the building for a moment and determined that there were no visible signs of any digital cameras or recording devices, so he quietly approached the front door of the house. Once there, he dug the lock-picking kit out of his bag in readiness, but when he turned back to the door, he noticed the complete absence of any keyhole. Clearly, the door was not opened with conventional keys. Instead, there was an electronic numbered keypad to the side of the door, securely fixed to the brickwork and most likely tamper-proof. An interesting security measure, thought Brian. After all, keys can be lost. Keys can be stolen. Keys can be copied. A keypad had none of these issues. And a keypad had the added benefit that if, at any time, Dixon thought his security had been breached, he could simply change the code. Hypothetically, if the accountant were using a standard six-figure passcode, there could be a million different combinations. The lock-picking kit he had brought was useless, and Brian knew he didn't have a gadget in his little bag that could help him with this particular lock.

Resigning himself to his misfortune, Brian stooped down and peered into the tiny gap between the door and the frame. He took a small torch from his jacket pocket and directed it towards the divide. He could make out the faint shadows of several deadlock bolts running the length of the door and he quickly realised it would take a tank to knock through that doorway.

Next, he pushed open the letter box. It revealed a clear view of the bright and spacious hallway of the house. What looked like an antique hall table stood to the left-hand side, with the door to the front room off to the right. The floor was wooden and polished and ran the length of the hall. At the far end, Brian could see another two doors, one of which was ajar. Through the open doorway, Brian could see the large kitchen to the back of the property, with a smart kitchen island in the centre. Everything he could see looked very neat, tidy and expensive.

To the side of the kitchen door on the back wall of the hallway was an alarm panel, and a small, red LED light flashed on the front, indicating the system was activated. There was no electronic keypad controlling this device, though. Instead, Brian could make out a thumb print sensor next to the control box. Biometric security. Very interesting, he thought, knowing that once again, there was nothing in his little bag of tricks that could help him get around that.

Brian quietly shut the letterbox flap and stood upright. He wandered down the three steps that led up to the door and returned to the driveway. Then he continued over to the large bay window to the side of the house. Peering inside, he scanned the generous-sized room with the high ceiling and the luxurious furnishings. There was a grand fireplace to one side of the room, and in the bay window was a desk which looked oak and was probably also antique. On the desk were three computer screens, all in a line. The computer was either off or asleep as the screens were all blank. An exercise mat was rolled up and placed on the four-seater sofa at the other end of the room, and three matching occasional chairs were dotted across the space. All in all, the room seemed fairly plush but pretty unremarkable.

From one side of the bay window, Brian inspected the interior of the other side of the bay. He could make out vibration sensors attached to each frame, which would no doubt be linked into the alarm and would be very difficult to overcome. The windows themselves looked like they had been manufactured from toughened glass, and Brian assessed that he would probably disturb the entire neighbourhood if he tried to break into the house by smashing through the glazing.

There didn't seem to be any easy route around to the rear of the premises, but Brian assumed the security on the back door and rear windows would mirror that at the front. All things considered, the house was extremely well protected, and that made Brian suspicious. What was Dixon protecting? Was it the money? It's true that people were more security conscious in general these days, but the accountant was living in a three-storey Fort Knox. Puzzling. Brian knew he needed to get inside somehow to have a proper snoop around.

Opposite the front door, helping protect the driveway from the glare of the pavement beyond, there was an old ash tree. Brian wandered over and dropped his bag of electronics on the grass. He reached in, rummaged around and finally found what he was looking for. A battery-powered motion sensor miniature camera, about the size of a computer mouse. Brian grabbed at a couple of branches and hauled himself up around three feet from the ground. He looked at the front door, and then back at the main trunk of the tree, then back to the door and back to the tree again. He did this double-take two or three times until he was sure he had found the right place. When he was satisfied, he fixed the camera to the trunk and dropped back down to the driveway. He walked back across the gravel and turned to the camera. It was pretty well hidden by the branches of the ash tree. You could see it if you knew what you were looking for, but, to the casual glance, it wasn't easy to detect.

Brian dug into his trouser pocket and fished out his mobile phone. He flicked to the camera app on the device and, once opened, activated the camera and paired it with his phone. Immediately, an image of himself appeared on the phone screen, being recorded by the camera opposite. Brian adjusted the camera lens using the controls on the app. He zoomed in to the keypad next to the front door and refocussed the image. Having done that, Brian approached the keypad and acted as if he were tapping in an imaginary code to make sure his body wasn't blocking the angle of the camera. The keypad was still in full view. Excellent. Job done.

He stepped off the porch steps, went back to his bag of goodies, zipped it up and slung it over his shoulder. Quietly, he paced down the driveway to the entrance way, and having checked the coast was clear, he strode onto the pavement and returned to the car.

As he climbed back into the driver's seat, Brian's phone pinged. It was a text from Terry, an old contact of his. Terry often pushed work his way for a small fee, and it seemed he had a prospective new client for him. He was asking when Brian would be free to meet him to give him the once-over. Brian pondered for a moment. He was a bit bloody busy to take on another client, especially a brand new one, what with Mike

Nation's urgent issue on the go. It always took a little while to work out whether new clients were likely to be reliable. That said, it was never wise to turn down good business. Brian knew from experience that it was quite possible to go weeks without a piece of work, given the specialist nature of his trade. Fair enough, he'd meet Terry's contact. He texted him back.

Fix a meeting for tomorrow. In town. Top of Hill Street, 11am.
    Send me the guy's details.

CHAPTER SEVEN

Three years previously, the Nation Group of Companies, via its Nation Investments subsidiary, had made three different but very generous charitable donations. First, a healthy contribution was made to the metropolitan mayor's successful re-election campaign. The position of metro mayor held significant responsibilities across a number of areas, including housing and, in particular, public transport. Phillip Bland was delighted to secure his second term of office.

Second, a large cheque was sent to the city council's famous Goodwill Foundation, an extremely worthwhile trust that was chaired by the council leader, Colin Smith, who was well known as a bit of a trainspotter and sat on the council's transport committee.

And third, a generous grant was made to the largest local community transport charity in the region. Mike Nation was very proud of the public-spirited donations he was able to make through his various businesses; they were sure to have a positive effect on the city and be of real benefit to its residents.

Eighteen months previously, entirely coincidentally, Nation Construction had managed to secure the contract to build three brand new train stations for a branch line that was to open up in the south of the city. The line was to run from the city centre, through the suburbs of Moseley and Kings Heath, and finally on to Stirchley. Each one of those districts would get a brand new station to serve its residents, and Nation Construction would build them all.

The railway line itself was already in place, so Nation Construction's contract was to reinstate all the station infrastructure, ready for passenger use. Mike Nation had been very pleased with the new contract; it was excellent for business and just reward for a thorough and professional response to the local government tender his team had put together.

Ground had been broken at each of the stations just over a year ago, and work was complete at the Stirchley and Kings Heath locations. Nation had personally made final inspections of both sites a couple of weeks earlier and had approved the finished buildings. The Moseley Station was running a little behind the other two but was almost complete, so he headed down to the site to check on progress.

The location of Moseley Station was within an easy walk of Nation House but, having forced down a lunchtime baguette on top of the two bacon sandwiches, bowl of chips, packet of crisps and two pints of lager that he'd consumed so far that day, Mike felt a little bloated. He chose to take the Mercedes for the quarter-of-a-mile journey.

Three minutes later, he turned into the station car park and pulled up next to the portacabin unit that was used as the base for the construction team. He heaved himself out of the car and paused for a moment, staring proudly at the huge sign that was fixed to the office roof.

NATION CONSTRUCTION
We build more than for any other reason!

Nation was an expert in marketing, he was convinced of it. And as a marketing expert, he knew that a catchy slogan was a vital tool in raising a business's profile. He had come up with the tagline for his construction division himself, and he loved it. The fact that it was gibberish seemed lost on him, and no one had dared ask him what it was supposed to mean. So the catchphrase had stuck and had become quite the talking point across the city.

He lingered proudly for a moment more, then finally pulled himself away from the massive poster and wandered up the steps, through the door and into the portacabin. A young worker was seated on the tatty sofa at one end of the office, eating a packed lunch. Nation vaguely recognised him and guessed the lad's name was Tomasz, or something equally foreign, but he didn't chance actually using it.

'Is the foreman around, lad?' he asked.

The labourer nodded while gulping down the mouthful of sandwich he was chewing. Finally, with throat clear, he was able to reply. 'Yes, boss. He's down on platform one. On the left-hand side of the train tracks.'

'Good lad; finish your sarnie.'

Tomasz nodded and Nation turned to the other end of the cabin, where the hard hats and orange jackets were stored. He rummaged through the pile, trying to find a jacket that looked even remotely clean. Finally, he picked one and slid it on. He left the portacabin and strolled towards the main station building on the other side of the car park. At the entrance to the ticket hall, he waved at a couple of workers as if he were some heroic returning general, back from a long battle overseas. His loyal servants courteously returned the gesture.

The train tracks were in a cutting at this point of the line, and the ticket hall and waiting area sat above them, straddling the railway and effectively forming a bridge which gave access to the platforms on either side. Nation took the left-hand stairway as instructed by Tomasz. At the bottom of the stairs, he turned onto the platform with the long concrete surface disappearing into the distance ahead of him. The unmistakable smell of fresh paint hung in the air, and a small pile of station signs, yet to be hung, leant on the fencing panels that separated the platform from the slope of the railway cutting beyond.

He saw his foreman, Derek Penrice, halfway down the platform. The man was at the top of a stepladder, inspecting the guttering of the steel platform roof. Nation ambled over, calling Derek's name as he did so.

'Afternoon, boss. All good with you?' asked Penrice as he climbed back down the ladder.

'Not too bad, thanks Derek, not too bad. This all seems to be coming along nicely.' Nation took in the view, surveying the building work on both sides of the track, as well as the main station hall that hovered above them. 'It's like a giant, real-life train set isn't it, Del?'

'You mean a railway then, boss.'

'Don't be a smart arse, Derek,' chastened Mike. 'I'm building a whole bloody transport system here, Del. Christ, they should call it *The Nation Line*, after me.'

'Whatever you say, boss.'

Nation was glowing with pride. Of all the projects he had been involved in over the years, this was his most favourite. A whole bloody train line! It would only ever be topped by the upcoming Golden Valley Retirement Community venture with The Colonel, in the good old U.S. of A.

'So, are we on time, Derek? The bloody grand opening is in less than a week, as you will be acutely aware. It's all going to be finished, isn't it?'

'No problems, Mike. We were only ever delayed here because of that minor security issue we had a little while back.'

'What was that, then?'

'Oh, you hadn't heard?'

'No.'

'Dogging.'

'Do what?!' said Nation disbelievingly.

'Dogging, boss. Turns out that when we left the site for the evening, some locals decided to use the empty station car park to, well, you know, watch people in cars doing things with other people in cars.'

'Chuffing hell…'

'Precisely. Dirty degenerates. It turns out there's quite the official organisation locally, entirely dedicated to dogging. All very formal and that. They meet up monthly to arrange events and outings, that sort of thing…'

'What, like the Rotary Club?'

'Well, not really, Mike, no. But regardless, we were put back a few days while we improved the perimeter protection. We're all pretty much there now, though, boss. We had the health and safety visit yesterday from the authorities – no problems there. We got the certificate through this morning. So, it's just a bit of snagging work to go.'

'OK, good. Christ… dogging… bloody weirdos. Anyway, Derek, more importantly, the materials you've been using. I presume you've still been ordering from our friend in the Far East?'

'Oh yes, boss, absolutely; all the supplies have come from your Far East contact. That was quite the little discount you negotiated there. The final shipment that we ordered arrived last week, so we have everything we need on site now. No concerns on that count…'

Derek Penrice had been Nation's head foreman for years, having started in the business in the demolition arm of Nation's operation. He had risen rapidly through the ranks to head foreman and had become quite the trusted employee. Mike knew he could rely on Derek to follow orders without any opposition, and that included the sourcing of questionable pieces of equipment from some less-than-legitimate suppliers when instructed to do so.

Derek paused momentarily before adding, 'Although, you had better be aware, boss, that architect lady who designed the stations, Stephanie something? She was down here again the other day complaining. She repeated what she's been saying these last few weeks. You know, that this Far East stock we've been using was inferior. She reckons the type and quality of the steel and the concrete we were sourcing, and I directly quote the bloody woman, "has the potential to compromise structural integrity," end quote.'

'Unbelievable! We're building a little platform with a shed on it, not the bloody Empire State Building. Look, Del, don't worry about Stephanie bloody Sutton. I've been assured by our Far East friend that there are no problems with the quality of the stock.'

'I'm just a bit nervous, though, boss. She has the potential to cause us some problems with the authorities if she goes running to them with her ridiculous theories.'

'Seriously, don't you be concerned with Ms Sutton, old pal. The Nation Group of Companies has quite the meaningful investment in her little architectural firm, which means that as much as she may have a whinge and a whine, that will be as far as old Stephanie will take the thing, I'm certain of that.'

The two men sidled over to a bench at the rear of the platform and took a seat, staring at the trackside opposite.

'There's another thing I need to ask of you, Derek. It's a little delicate in nature, but I know I can rely on you. I want a hole dug up, on this very platform, just here.' Mike pointed to an area in the middle of platform one. 'You see, I have a certain problem that needs resolving. Now then, that problem is soon to be brought to a satisfactory conclusion by other parties. But once resolved, this problem needs to be disappeared. And I want it to be disappeared under this exact spot. Is this something you can arrange for me? As you might imagine, the hole needs to be the approximate dimensions of a lying, deceiving, little snake.'

Derek nodded knowingly. A wry smile appeared across his face. 'No problems, boss. We can arrange that for you, and I can have the hole ready for later today.'

'Good. So, here's what I want you to do. I want you to get the hole dug and then I want you to stick a big metal box next to the hole. But make sure you leave the box open. When you get on site each morning, check on the box. If it's locked shut and it's been put in the hole, bury the whole thing in concrete straight away. If it's still open, then it means the problem remains unresolved, so leave it all alone for a further day. Understand?'

Derek smiled again. 'Yep, got it, Mike. No problem.'

There was the sound of footsteps on metal. People were coming down the station stairs to the platform level, so the two men stopped discussing the burial of dead bodies and turned in the direction of the station building. One of Derek's construction workers was approaching them. He was accompanied by an attractive young lady with short, cropped hair and an obvious air of confidence, and the two strode over to where Nation and Penrice were sitting.

'This lady says she's here to see you, Mr Nation.'

'Yes, thanks, lad. Off you pop. Hello, Sammy. And how have you been, bab?'

Sammy Joseph was a twenty-year-old woman and Brian Wood's number two. She was strong, fit, healthy and skilled, which was all a far cry from her physical and mental state when she had first met Brian more than three years ago. Brian had tripped over her, quite literally, as Sammy lay homeless in the street near Birmingham Cathedral. It was winter, and her dirty sleeping bag was leaking. She lay there, numb to the core, in the cold and the wet, waiting to succumb to the ultimate darkness.

Brian had stumbled into her while heading home and was horrified to see such a young, fragile girl all alone on the streets in that temperature. He had never done anything like this before, but rather than give her money or buy her a cup of soup, he took her home. He fed her, offered her a chance to get warm and volunteered a bed for the night in the spare room of the flat.

The next morning, Brian found a note of thanks in the hallway, but the girl had gone. However, a couple of days later, there was a knock on his door. Sammy had come back. He let her in, fed her once more and made some small talk before she retired to the spare bedroom for some sleep.

Again, come morning, she had gone, leaving a note of thanks in the hallway. And so the routine continued; every few days she would be back, they would chat, she would eat and sleep, and in the early hours she would leave. Brian had no idea where she went.

There was never anything sexual between them. The age difference was far too great, for one thing, but anyway, the feelings Brian had developed for her were far more concern and care than anything else. He felt like a father figure to her, so each time she returned, Brian would breathe a sigh of relief and feel happy for the company.

During the course of her visits, Sammy started flicking through Brian's books on Birmingham and would occasionally ask him questions about them. He would do his best to answer, and if he didn't know the answer he would find out for next time.

Eventually, the topic of conversation would change from Birmingham to Brian, and his past. He would tell Sammy stories of his youth, of his mother, of his deserting wretch of a father, and of his time in the army. Brian considered that this would be the catalyst for Sammy to tell her story, how she had ended up alone on the streets. But she never did. It was almost as if she had become a new person from the moment she had met Brian and her old life related to someone else altogether.

Slowly the conversations were brought up to date, and Sammy asked about Brian's current occupation. Brian didn't lie, but he was very delicate with the truth. However, Sammy caught on very quickly. And, far from being scared or appalled, she seemed to embrace the profession. She wanted to learn the trade. She wanted to know all the skills required to be a fixer. So, over the subsequent months and years, Brian taught her all the essential qualities for the role.

They started on some basic self-defence strategies but rapidly moved on to more specialised skills. They practised high-performance driving; weaponry and shooting; surveillance and counter-surveillance; the use of electronics and other devices; the list was endless. Sammy absorbed it all like a sponge. She improved her skills as the months passed, and while doing so, she pretty much moved into the spare room of the flat. Sammy was already doing odd jobs for Brian to earn a little money, so finally, having been bullied and browbeaten to death, Brian agreed she could be his partner.

'Hello, Mike,' she said cheerily as she strolled across the concrete. 'I've been great, thanks, and how are you this fine day?'

'All the better for seeing a pretty little face like yours!' Nation replied.

'Don't be gross,' she retorted.

'No. Quite. Look, give me two ticks, Sammy, would you?'

Sammy studied Nation for a moment and came to the conclusion that the violently orange high viz jacket Mike was wearing was the exact same colour as his face. She decided not to mention it. 'Sure thing,' she replied and took a couple of steps away, staring at her phone screen to pass the time.

Nation turned to Derek and in hushed tone said, 'OK, I need a little chat with young Sammy here. But you've got all that, yes? The hole, and the box, by this evening. Check on it every morning. If the box is shut, bury the back-stabbing cheat.'

'No worries, boss, leave it with me.'

'Good lad. We'll catch up later.' Nation turned to Sammy. 'Now then, young lady, let's take a little stroll.'

Derek Penrice set off back up the stairway to arrange the box and the hole. Meanwhile, Sammy and Mike turned and began wandering in the other direction. Ahead of them, they could see the long section of platform stretching out towards the tunnel at the far end of the station, beyond which the tracks headed north towards Birmingham city centre.

'So then, Sammy, a couple of things I need to discuss with you. First of all, would I be right in assuming that you are up to speed with the discussions I had with Brian this morning?'

'I think so, yes. He phoned me from the car after the two of you had finished your meeting. He said you had some jobs for us both. Broadly speaking, they involve finding a load of robbed money of yours, and then getting rid of some tosspot accountant, a chap called Dixon. Brian also said I was to meet you here for some extra reason. Which is, you know, what I'm doing.'

'Excellent, excellent. Right. Well, listen, this is important. I've been mulling over the removal of that skinny little bookkeeping weasel a bit more since I spoke with Brian this morning. We obviously need the body to disappear permanently, but at the same time, I'm keen for one final "screw you", and I've worked out what it is. I have a place where Mister bloody Dixon needs to be buried. It's perfect, and it's what I want. So, you need to tell Brian this, ok?'

Nation explained to Sammy his box and hole plan and how he wanted Dixon buried six feet under Nation's own train station. 'It will be my final act of revenge on the thieving little scumbag,' he explained.

'How's that then?'

'You see, every time I stand here, Sammy, waiting for a train into town, I'll be dropping my trousers and showing him my big round backside.'

Sammy looked completely confused. Mainly because she was. 'You what, Mike? You're saying you're going to come down here and get your buttocks out on the platform while you're waiting for a train? In the middle of the rush hour? You absolute breadbasket! That's disgusting.'

'Don't be ridiculous. I won't actually take my trollies off. I'm on about metaphorical bum-flashes. Each time I'm down on this platform, waiting for the nine-thirty-whatever to Birmingham, I shall stand here with a smile as broad as you like, and I shall be metaphorically buns out, waving my butt cheeks at Dixon's dead, stupid face.'

There was silence. Finally, Sammy spoke. 'I'm sorry Mike, I don't know what the hell you're on about.'

'Metaphorical bum waving, Sammy! Come on, girl, keep up!'

'Well, ok then, metaphorical bum waving. Whatever you say, Mike. Lovely plan…'

'Precisely. Lovely indeed. No one else will have a clue, of course. But I'll know. I'll know exactly where the miserable old git is buried. And I will be stood on top of him, metaphorically baring my big old pert behind right at his ugly head. I tell you, if I'm alive to see ninety, I'll wheel myself down here just to flash my arse at the man. Metaphorically, you understand.'

'Alright, alright, Mike! Enough with the bum talk! Message received, loud and clear. Although I still don't understand what the hell you're on about.'

They had reached the very end of the station. The jet-black tunnel was bearing down on them only metres away. They turned round and started sauntering back the way they came, back toward the main passenger buildings.

'So, there we are. That's what I want. Make sure Brian has got the instruction, ok, Sammy?'

'Sure thing, Mike. You said there were a couple of things you wanted discussing?'

'Yes, indeed. Ok, so, the main reason I wanted to see you – and to stress, this is equally important to me, Sammy – I have a very special guest flying over from the United States on Friday. He's landing at Birmingham Airport at midday, our time. I've booked a rather nice and bloody expensive room for him at the Grand Hotel in town, for a night or two. What I need you to do is to come over to the offices an hour or so beforehand, pick up the Mercedes, run out to the airport, collect the guy, and take him to the hotel. Full chauffeur and security experience, ok? Perhaps get the Merc valeted beforehand. But make sure he has everything he wants. Make sure he's comfortable, and make sure nothing happens to upset him, ok?'

'No problem, Mike. Who's the Yank?'

'Colonel John P. Kicklighter.'

'You're kidding!'

'Why does everybody say that? That's his bleeding name, Sammy. And just to be absolutely clear here, while it's true to say he's normally a very friendly Texan cowboy, this guy does not mess around. Make sure you address him as Colonel, got it? And none of your weird small talk on the drive over to the hotel. Oh, and maybe don't try and have sex with him.'

'Eewgh… Not necessary, Mike. Jesus.'

'I'm being serious here, Sammy.'

'Gotcha. So, it's "Hello, Captain Cockfighter," and "Welcome to Birmingham, Mister Cockfighter. Fancy a quick bonk in the layby, sir?" Roger that, boss.'

'Piss off, Sammy. Don't screw this up; it's important. Understand?'

'Yes, ok, Mike, all understood. I'll pick up the Merc mid-morning, get it cleaned inside and out and be the perfect hostess.'

'Good.'

They had finished a full lap of the platform and were back at the base of the stairwell. Together they climbed the stairs and headed out of the ticket hall, back into the Moseley sunshine.

'See you Friday then, Mike.'

'See you Friday. And tell Brian about the hole.'

'I will.'

Sammy unchained her bike and wheeled it out towards the main road while Mike went back to the portacabin to take off the stinking orange jacket.

CHAPTER EIGHT

The Town Hall of Birmingham dominates the skyline above Victoria Square in the centre of the city. Built in the 1830s, it was designed to resemble a Corinthian temple, or so Brian had read in one of his books. He wasn't sure he knew what a Corinthian temple was, but he knew he liked Birmingham Town Hall. Whenever he was in town, he would find himself wandering in its direction. Many of the city's thoroughfares meet at the Town Hall, so it was easy to stumble across. Colmore Row runs to the Town Hall, as does New Street, and so does Hill Street, Brian's choice of location for the meeting he was about to have with Terry's potential new client.

Hill Street is a busy road in its own right, running as it does from the Town Hall at the top of the hill down into the Chinese Quarter at the other end. Its location near shops, bus stops and stations means it tends to be bustling and open and an ideal place for meeting people for the first time. Especially when the topic of conversation was delicate, to say the least.

Terry had followed up his text from the previous day with a phone call that morning, in which he had described the potential new client in detail. Terry had mentioned something about a hippopotamus which Brian hadn't really followed, but he now knew what he was looking for. Skinny man by the name of Paul, in his forties, wearing a grey jacket, black trousers, black shoes, and a white t-shirt. The meeting was fixed for 11 a.m. at the top of Hill Street, and so, as ever with these things, Brian had got there half an hour early to make sure there was nothing suspicious about the get-together.

After fifteen minutes of surveillance, Brian decided that everything was as it should be, so he bought a coffee from a nearby shop and settled down on a step in Victoria Square, overlooking the brow of Hill Street. His mind wandered to the other Paul in his plans, Paul Dixon the accountant. He had to get into that guy's house somehow and search it from top to bottom. He needed access to his computers, and he needed access to the passwords, but he was at a loss as to how he could accomplish it all. The more he thought about the level of security at Dixon's house, the more convinced he was the money was going to be inside.

He was acutely aware it was now only two days until Colonel John P. Kicklighter landed in the UK, and Mike Nation had already been hassling him for an update. Brian concluded that after this meeting, he would quickly deal with the halibut issue at the wholesale markets since he was in town anyway. With that done, he planned to track down Dixon and break into his car. Brian figured that if he could get a thumb print from the interior of his vehicle, maybe from a discarded pop can or something similar, he could perhaps trick the alarm panel into thinking it was the real thing. That and the camera that was hopefully capturing the front door keypad might be enough. He would bounce it all off Sammy later, but it sounded like a good plan. With any luck, he would have the money by late afternoon.

Brian cast his eyes across the busy city centre and finally spotted a painfully thin man skulking up New Street, heading towards the top of Hill Street. Brian watched him carefully. There was something familiar about him, but he couldn't put his finger on it.

As the man reached the top of Hill Street, he stopped and checked his watch nervously. He was wearing a shiny grey jacket, a white t-shirt, black trousers and black shoes. There seemed to be a small piece of paper dangling in the wind behind the man, as though the price tag was still on the jacket. A bit odd, Brian thought, but he concluded this had to be the prospective client.

There was still something troubling Brian, though. That feeling of familiarity, he just couldn't place it, but it was strong. It was certainly more than merely matching Terry's description with the real thing. He studied the man's face more intently, concentrating, straining his eyes, thinking.

Then it hit him like a brick. Holy shit. Holy. Fucking. Shit. It's *Paul Dixon*. It's the bloody mark! Terry's potential new client was his target! This was unbelievable. The man Brian was hired to kill had arranged to meet Brian, presumably to ask him to kill someone!

Brian was dumbstruck. Well, there's a first, he thought. I mean sure, this was Birmingham, not Moscow. There probably weren't a huge number of contract killers in the area to choose from. They didn't exactly have their own section in the *Checkatrade* booklet. But Christ, what were the odds?

What to do, what to do? Brian's mind was working overtime. He was telling himself to remain calm, to think the situation through logically, to walk himself through the different scenarios. Should he continue with the meeting or pull out? Could he even work the situation to his advantage?

He pondered for a moment and worked through what could potentially happen next. He quickly realised that this situation could turn out to be a very handy coincidence. If they met, Dixon would presumably hire Brian to kill someone. After all, why else would he be here? And if it was an easy job, Brian could potentially fulfil that contract in double-quick time. He would then go to Dixon's house to get paid. *Dixon would let Brian into his own house!* Brian gets paid by Dixon, and then Brian kills him. He finds Mike's money and fulfils Nation's contract. Brian gets paid again. That could just work. Tricky, but probably worth exploring.

Brian resolved to take the meeting just as if he were meeting a normal new client. As if it were someone he wasn't planning to assassinate in the next forty-eight hours. He would do his usual thing, intimidate the guy a bit just for show, make some small talk to relax the guy, then hear him out. If there was a chance of getting both contracts done, then great. But even if the meeting only served to help him get access to Dixon's house, it was worth it.

Brian got to his feet, straightened his jumper, threw the empty coffee cup into a nearby bin and walked purposefully over to where Dixon was standing.

Dixon, meanwhile, was hovering awkwardly at the corner of Hill Street and New Street. He was sweating so much it looked as though he had just taken a shower and thrown his clothes on without drying. And of course, he needed to pee. He'd started to realise that when he had put his cunning plan together; he'd dramatically underestimated the stress levels caused by meeting up with hitmen and their greasy spoon café middle men. He couldn't wait for it all to be over.

He spotted a tall, combative-looking man advancing boldly towards him. He gulped nervously and realised his mouth was the only dry part of his entire body. He tried to remain as calm as possible, desperately attempting to keep control of both his nausea and his bladder. Finally, the hitman reached him and, after what seemed a lifetime of silence, he started up a conversation.

'I believe you were looking to have a little discussion with me,' said Brian.

'Erm, I think so,' stammered Dixon.

'It's a yes or no question, my friend.'

'Well, in that case, yes. Yes, I do.'

'Good. So, what shall I call you mister? What's your name?'

'Err, well, I'm not sure; do I give you my real name?'

'Yes, Paul, your real name.'

'It's P... oh.'

'Terry told me your name, Paul. I'm just messing with you.'

'Yes, of course, sorry. And you are?'

'You can call me Brian, Paul. Good to meet you. Now then, let's take a little walk.'

Brian steered Dixon down Hill Street, towards the Chinese Quarter. They walked quietly, side by side, for a minute or so, through the crowds of people busy going about their day. Brian still found it difficult to believe his mark was next to him, trying to hire him to kill *another* mark. It just was not computing. But he needed to stay professional. And it was time to get Paul Dixon relaxed. He would make a bit of small talk, but what to talk about? His mind went back to his books on Birmingham buildings. He decided to chat about them for a bit.

'Brutalism!' Brian exclaimed abruptly.

Dixon almost had a heart attack. 'Excuse me?' he replied wide-eyed, looking scared to death. Having a hitman bark the word brutalism in your general direction was bloody frightening. Various images of torture rapidly ran through his mind, and he wondered whether he was about to be brutalised himself. Christ, this whole murder business was going to be the death of him.

'Brutalism, Paul. Look over there.' Brian pointed over towards the railway lines. 'See that? That's the New Street Station signal box. It's brutalism. It's an architectural style, Paul.'

'Oh. Ok,' he replied and puffed out a sigh of relief. Sweat was gushing off him.

'I'll tell you what it is, Paul. It's beautiful. It's angry, all straight lines and sharp angles, but beautiful nonetheless.' Brian had read this in his book, so he knew it to be true.

'I hadn't considered it, to be honest. I mean, it's just a signal box, isn't it?'

'It's not even that now, Paul. At least, it won't be. Train movements, they're all electronically controlled these days, miles from here, by a man in an office somewhere. But the building itself? Bloody beautiful. Birmingham was famous for its brutalist buildings once, Paul. We had dozens of them, spread about everywhere across the city. And what did we do with them?'

'I don't know.'

'We knocked the sodding things down, Paul. That's what we did. We knocked the sodding things down.'

There was a pause. Paul nodded carefully, pretending to know what was going on, although he had to admit to himself he had absolutely no idea. Why were they talking about a signal box, for God's sake?

'Take the old library, for example,' Brian continued.

'What?'

'The old library.'

'Oh, yes. Right, now I've seen pictures of that. Victorian, I think? Very ornate. Very nice.'

'No, Paul. That's the *old* old library. Victorian, true, and very grand. It was just up the hill from here. Granted, bloody beautiful. And it's true, we knocked that sodding thing down too. But I'm on about the *new* old library. The one *after* the old old library. A bloke called Madin designed it. A good Brummie lad. And a Brutalist.'

Dixon shuddered at the word again. Brian continued. 'All corners and edges and concrete and stuff. It looked like an upside-down pyramid. Bloody beautiful. Or pig ugly, frankly, depending on your point of view.'

'Umm... Right...'

'Yeh. Controversial, you see. That style of building, it splits opinions.'

'I see.'

'But love it or hate it, you had an opinion on it. You just had to. Very interesting piece of work, that library. And what did we do with that one, Paul?'

'I don't know Brian.'

'We knocked that sodding thing down as well.'

'Erm, right...'

The pair were still strolling down Hill Street, and Brian thought that to the rest of the world, the two men probably looked like two good pals out for a walk, shooting the breeze. In reality, Dixon was so confused he could have cried.

'And now we've got the *new* new library. All golds and blues and circles and what have you. Interesting. And bloody b......'

Brian stopped. The book he was reading hadn't got this up to date. He hadn't been told whether to think the new building was bloody beautiful or pig ugly. He had no reference point.

'Yeh... bloody Broad Street... that's where that is.'

He made a mental note to look up what his opinion was meant to be on the new library. He would need to find a more up-to-date reference book. Later though, when he had a bit more bloody time on his hands.

Meanwhile, Dixon continued to wonder what the hell was going on. Why was he now discussing library buildings with a contract killer when he was supposed to be arranging a hit on his boss? It was bewildering, and he was sweating more and more. He wiped his brow with a handkerchief. He needed to get out of there soon, otherwise he was sure he was going to have another panic attack.

Tragically for Dixon, Brian continued. 'And then you've got New Street Station itself, just over there, Paul. All space age and silver and shiny and what have you. Wall-to-wall gleaming metal. Bloody beautiful. Must be a pain in the arse to polish though, don't you think?'

'Well, I guess so, Brian, yes.'

'Of course, it didn't always look like that. Back in the day, you know, in the 1800s, it was a grand old thing. Big hotel at the front, massive old train shed at the back. And what was it?'

Paul paused and thought carefully. 'Erm... Beautiful?' He dared.

'Damn right, Paul. Bloody beautiful.'

Dixon calmed down a little. He'd spotted the pattern. It seemed buildings were bloody beautiful and then we knocked the sodding things down. He could actually add something to the conversation now. Relieved, he waited for the next question.

'And that lovely 1800s station, Paul, what do you think we did with it?'

'Umm... We knocked the sodding thing down!' asserted Paul.

'Correct, Paul, correct.' Brian offered a smile in Dixon's direction. Paul was suddenly feeling much better.

'And so, we built another one. Nineteen sixties this was. Brand new station. And what was it, Paul?'

'Bloody beautiful!' Paul stated, triumphantly.

'*No!* Absolutely not; it was a total shithole! Christ, man, did you never go there? Dear God, that place! It was one of the nine circles of hell! Even the rats moved to Wolverhampton.'

'Oh, right, sorry…' Paul whispered weakly. Perspiration appeared on his brow once again.

'Oh, indeed. Thankfully, we knocked that sodding thing down too, Paul. And now we've got that shiny old place. There it is, look, sparkling in the sunlight. Bloody beautiful. Sort of. I mean, in fairness, it does just look like it's been smothered in tin foil, but it's futuristic. Resembles a spaceship of sorts, like the UFO out of *Mars Attacks*. You'd be forgiven for thinking that if you ventured inside you'd get probed up the arse while you're in the queue at *Boots*. And then there's the weirdest thing: when you want to leave, you can't. There's something like four hundred and twelve different exits, but none of them are in the same place as they were yesterday. All very strange.'

They stopped walking for a moment and stared at the metal-clad building, gleaming in the summer sun.

'Beautiful,' Brian stated again, but this time with some sort of finality. That was enough small talk, he thought. It was clear Dixon didn't know anything about buildings, so the discussion was fruitless.

With a final flurry, Brian added, 'Of course, the trains are all still cancelled, mind, the arseholes. But some things never change, eh? Anyway, to business… Paul, tell me your story.'

And so Paul started talking.

He described in detail how he had been employed by a narcissistic moron called Mike Nation for the last decade, how he worked for him as his money launderer-in-chief. He described in detail many of the dodgy deals that Nation had put together over the years and gave examples of the people his boss had trodden all over on the way to making his millions.

He accepted that he was no angel himself but he wanted to get out. He was trapped in this murky world and the escape route was to get some money together and run. He had managed to gather enough cash to guarantee his freedom by skimming off some of Nation's own profits. He'd been doing it for years and Nation had never figured it out because, despite his boss's self-confidence, the man was an idiot. But circumstances had changed and Nation was now getting close. It had dawned on Dixon that once his boss found out what he had done, he would never let it go. Dixon would be hiding from him forever. So, the solution had become clear. He needed Nation to be killed.

As Paul talked, Brian calmly listened and politely nodded in all the appropriate places. But internally, he was thunderstruck. He had come to realise precisely what was going on. The unbelievable coincidence had just become even more ridiculous. It was simply absurd, but it was happening. Mike had hired Brian to kill Paul. Meanwhile, Paul was hiring Brian to kill Mike.

CHAPTER NINE

Brian's meeting with Paul Dixon had knocked him for six. The coincidence was incredible and he had to take some time out to digest it all.

He had listened to Dixon's story quietly and studiously, and when the man had finished his tale, Brian had said he would be in touch within the next twenty-four hours to let Dixon know if he would take on the job. Obviously, Brian had not let on to the accountant that he had any existing relationship with Mike Nation, so Dixon had departed none the wiser and was undoubtedly hoping for positive news from Brian in the coming hours. It all meant that Brian needed to consider his options. He needed time to think.

Of course, there were still his other jobs to complete. Consequently, straight after the Dixon meeting, Brian chose to pay a visit to Gary down at the wholesale food market to resolve the whole halibut situation. The market was only a five-minute walk from Hill Street, and with so much on his mind, he needed to bring at least one of his tasks to a swift conclusion.

At the market, Brian found Gary at the trade counter of Nation Wholesale Foods and instructed him to sell the halibut to Rosie rather than Glynn Purnell. It wasn't what the *Yummie Brummie* was going to want to hear, but that was tough; this was a directive from on high. Brian warned Gary that if the instruction wasn't followed, he was liable to have a rather nasty work-related accident involving a meat slicer and his penis. To emphasise the point, Brian switched on a nearby slicing machine, borrowed a very phallic salami sausage from the counter display and began carving the meat into perfect discs. He was a bit of a fan of salami so he considered nibbling at one of the slices, but he ultimately decided that that would just look weird given what the sausage represented. Nonetheless, the message was hammered home and the demonstration was more than enough to secure certain guarantees regarding the eventual destination of the fish. With that done, Brian turned his mind to the absurd complexity of his other issues.

He had taken a call from Sammy while he was down at the market, and she had let him know that she was on her way into town. The two had planned to meet up in Colmore Row to debrief each other on recent events and then wander over to Rosie's restaurant together. Brian wanted to pass on the fish news to Rosie personally, and it transpired that Sammy was heading that way anyway. Brian decided to use the time, while waiting for Sammy, to settle into a coffee shop opposite the cathedral and try to draw some conclusions regarding his predicament. He ordered a black Americano and, having failed to resist adding a muffin to his order, he picked a free stool in the coffee shop window and sat facing the cathedral park opposite.

He liked to people-watch while he thought through his problems, and from his perch in the coffee shop, he could gaze out at the bustling crowd happily going about their daily business in the warmth of the early afternoon. Office workers were munching on burritos for their lunch in the cathedral square, while shoppers dragged their heavy bags up to the bus stop queues beyond. It was a relaxing scene, and Brian could have lost himself in the moment quite easily, but he knew it was time to focus.

To the matter at hand, then, and the fundamental question that needed answering: Which job did he take? Put another way, who did he kill? Nation? Dixon? Or perhaps even both? And if it was both, did the order matter? He worked through the various hypothetical timelines based on each of those scenarios, and he quickly figured that there would be no opportunity for 'double-dipping'. It was clear that he couldn't physically fulfil both contracts since someone had to die in the first place to trigger a payment. Which meant they would be insufficiently alive to pay up when their own contract was fulfilled. No one was going to pay Brian before their particular deed was done, so there was no way of getting paid twice. Ok, fine. That made sense. Therefore, the question became, which contract gets honoured? Who dies?

Brian first considered the arguments in Nation's favour, i.e. the case for killing Dixon. Well, the justification for siding with Nation was obvious. First of all, Mike had got his request in first. 'First come, first served' and all that. Plus, of course, Nation was a repeat customer. He had been doing business with Brian for years, which meant there was probably an element of loyalty owed there, in as much as 'loyalty' was even a concept in Brian's line of business. But it also couldn't be overlooked that if Nation died, so did the pipeline of new billable work that Nation would no doubt have for Brian and Sammy in the future. It would leave a big old hole in the pair's finances. And finally, of course, when it came to the deed itself, Brian didn't really know Dixon from Adam, nor did he owe him anything. Taking on Nation's job would be an emotionless solution, all told.

Pretty compelling arguments, Brian had to admit. But on the other hand, was there any logic in fulfilling Dixon's request and killing Mike Nation instead? Well, for one thing, Brian had found himself rather taken aback by Dixon's vivid descriptions of Nation's resolute evilness. The lengths the man went to in order to turn a pound, from bribery to blackmail, were overwhelming. The sheer number of businesses that were currently being pressurised into conducting Nation's illegal trades was shocking. Dixon had somehow managed to convey the real-life repercussions that dozens of hard-working people were experiencing just to wash the dirty money of Nation's underworld buddies and earn Mike his twenty percent slice of the pie.

Brian realised that this was a fairly emotive point of view, all told, argued by a proud Brummie on behalf of the city's small independent businessmen and women. He needed to think more objectively, so he considered the reasoning for a moment more. It was true, he conceded, Nation was indeed a rotten crook, but Brian had always known that was the case, on one level or another. Ultimately, emotion doesn't pay the bills, money does, and Nation was a good source of income whatever Brian thought about the man's scruples and morals. This was not a business where one could let feelings get in the way.

Fundamentally, Brian concluded that there was only one logical conclusion to be drawn from it all; he had to get Nation's money back and then execute the hit on Paul Dixon. And if he could use this mad coincidence to his advantage to gain access to the accountant's house, so much the better.

Brian looked up from his now tepid coffee and saw Sammy waving at him through the coffee shop window. The half hour had flown by, but at least his mind was now clearer, and he had a plan to follow. Sometimes a problem could be solved with just a bit of structure to your thinking, he reasoned. Brian resolved not to tell Sammy just yet about the absurd coincidence that had occurred. He would rather see how things played out first before sharing the news with his young protégée.

He hopped off his stool and headed out to meet his partner in the street, realising that he was suddenly very much looking forward to seeing Rosie again. He couldn't help but think there had been a little electricity between the two of them when they had met at Mike's office, so he was eager to pass on the good news about the halibut.

He reached the roadside and the pair greeted each other, as they always did, with an awkward hug and a smile.

'Hiya, Bri. All good with you?'

'Yep, all good, thanks, all good.'

'Excellent. You look a little tired, though, Bri. When did you last get a decent night's sleep?'

'Oh, I don't know. I think it was the autumn of 1979,' he replied dryly.

They turned up Colmore Row and continued through Birmingham city centre towards The Balancing Act, Rosie's

Michelin-starred restaurant in Brindleyplace. As they walked, Sammy updated Brian on her meeting with Nation at Moseley Station the previous day and how he wanted his dirty accountant to find his final resting place deep under platform one.

The plan, while clearly driven by ego more than anything else, actually made sense to Brian, although, like Sammy, he hadn't really followed the bit about Mike wanting to perform a metaphorical bum flash in the general direction of Dixon's dead body. Nonetheless, he considered it a good strategy all told; after all, the convenient use of major infrastructure for a concrete burial chamber was hardly a new concept. Brian knew that it wasn't just urban legend that during the construction of the M6 interchange, Spaghetti Junction, in the late 1960s, the underworld of the day took full advantage of the massive building work. It would be true to say that a carefully selected number of the expressway's cement columns had ended up functioning as the eternal home of a number of unlucky souls. It was rumoured that when the Kray twins were sent packing in the Battle of Snow Hill around the same time, a number of the twins' lieutenants ultimately vanished deep into the massive structure. In Italy, the Sicilian mafia had a saying that a murdered adversary was 'sleeping with the fishes'. In Birmingham, they were 'holding up Spaghetti'. Well, fair enough. If that was Mike's wish, so be it. Best not to stare a gift tomb in the mouth.

'Oh, and another thing,' said Sammy, completing her updates. 'I've got to pick this Colonel bloke up from the airport in a couple of days and somehow get him to his hotel without stripping him naked and shagging him. Quite the challenge, don't you think?'

'I'm sure you'll manage,' replied Brian, and they shared a smile.

'How was your meeting earlier, with that potential new client?'

'Well, it was curious, to say the least. But I don't think we'll take that one on, to be honest. I'll tell you all about it some other time.'

'Whatever you say, Bri.'

They strolled through Victoria Square, near the Council Houses of Birmingham, and noticed that a large group of people had gathered around *The Floozie in the Jacuzzi* in the centre of the plaza. Press photographers were there, as were a couple of TV cameras.

'It's switching-on day,' Sammy announced.

The Floozie in the Jacuzzi was the city's nickname for a large fountain and waterfall feature that had been installed in the square back in the '90s. Unfortunately, ever since it had been installed, it had leaked. The leaks got so bad that at various points over its lifespan, the landmark had haemorrhaged water all over the city.

Ultimately, the council gave up patching it and turned the whole thing off. They swapped out the water for what Brian considered to be a lousy glorified flower bed, thereby denying the floozie her vast, bubbling jacuzzi. Ever since that fateful day, there had been a local but vociferous call for the water to be turned back on, and eventually the money for the repairs had been found. Today was the big day: finally, the floozie was getting her jacuzzi back.

Brian and Sammy saw several local dignitaries pottering about the square, including Phillip Bland, the metro mayor, and the council leader, Colin Smith. The two politicians hailed from opposing political parties and so, over the years, had developed quite the personal rivalry. Their dislike for each other had steadily grown, reducing each man to often extreme levels of pettiness. They had entered into some sort of competition as to who could deliver the most 'good news' stories in the city; as a consequence, the number of official openings in Birmingham had sky-rocketed as each man tried to 'out-open' the other. Opening a new park? Better cut a ribbon. Opening a new playground, in an existing park? Still worthy of a ribbon. Opening a new slide in an existing playground, in an existing park? Well, they could probably squeeze out a ribbon for that, too. Opening ceremonies had become two a penny in Birmingham as one man ventured to eclipse the other, but the only people really celebrating were the ribbon manufacturers, who were going like the clappers to keep up with demand.

This time, the honour fell to Colin Smith, the council leader, to cut the ribbon and turn on the tap, since it was the city council that had found the repair money. Not to be outdone, though, Phillip Bland, the metro mayor, had not only chosen to attend the ceremony regardless but had turned up in his customary hard hat and high visibility jacket combination, looking as if he had repaired the bloody thing himself.

The council leader was fuming. He had presumed that the event would be all his and that it was his turn to be in the spotlight. Instead, the photo-op was with the guy in the safety clothes, and Bland was milking the moment. Smith knew that Bland loved a high viz and hard hat as he'd pulled this trick many times before; it was almost as if he had some sort of fetish for the gear. Rumour had it Bland had once attended a black-tie event wearing a sombre, charcoal-coloured hard hat, and the council leader was sure the story was true. There was no love lost between the two men, and Smith made a mental note to take revenge on his nemesis for upstaging him on his big day.

Sammy noticed that Mike and Barbara Nation were also in attendance for the opening. Mike was munching on a packet of crisps and wiping his greasy orange hands across the breast of his blazer.

'That man never stops eating, does he?' she commented to Brian, pointing in Nation's direction. Brian followed her gaze and spotted Nation on the far side of the crowd. He lowered his head quickly. The last thing he needed was to run into Mike and be pushed for another update on the eight hundred grand, particularly after that morning's peculiar events.

'By all accounts, there's a big opening ceremony for Nation's stupid train line in a few days' time as well,' Sammy continued.

'I'm sure there bloody is,' Brian replied with a shrug, lowering his head further. 'Which one of those two bureaucratic buffoons has the honour of opening that one, then?'

'Apparently, neither of them. Rumour has it some old actor bloke is doing the opening.'

'Well, that'll no doubt infuriate them both. How satisfying! Who's winning in the ribbon wars, anyway?'

'Nobody really knows, Bri; nobody really knows…'

By the time they heard the warm applause and the splash of water behind them, the pair had passed the onlookers and were heading up to Brindleyplace.

CHAPTER TEN

Dixon had finally made it back home following his morning meeting with Brian, the hitman, and he had made the whole journey without vomiting, which he considered quite an achievement in itself. He pulled his sporty hatchback onto his Edgbaston driveway and turned off the ignition. He took a moment to compose himself. A decade spent working for a bent businessman like Mike Nation had not even remotely prepared him for the realities of meeting gangsters like Terry and Brian. They were a different breed altogether. Sort of amiable on the outside, but my God, you could tell there was a nasty streak buried deep inside.

Finally, he felt steady enough to step out of the car. He locked the door behind him and turned to the house, taking the three steps up to his front door gingerly. He was still a little unsure on his feet. He reached the keypad and entered the six-digit code that he had selected as the password for the month. Dixon tended to change his code every thirty days for security. The electronic lock clicked, and the door swung open. The alarm started beeping its customary countdown from across the corridor, and the little red light started flashing on the control panel.

He closed the front door behind him and almost fell backwards over a large packet that had been thrust through his letterbox while he had been out. Cursing, Dixon managed to regain his balance and then hurried across the wooden hallway to the alarm box. He presented his thumb to the sensor, the alarm beeped a confirmation that it had been deactivated and the red light blinked off. He headed for the lounge and made a beeline for the drinks table, where he poured himself a huge glug of whiskey and added a splash of soda from the dispenser. He chucked the aerobic mat onto the floor and collapsed into the large sofa at the back of the room. Exhausted, he closed his eyes.

Dixon noticed that he was trembling. The silence in the room was disconcerting. Not a single sound emanated from inside the house, and nothing could be heard from outside either, despite the family of blue tits dancing and chirping in the air above the driveway; the toughened glass made sure of that. The only thing Dixon could hear was the booming thud of his own heart, thundering along at what felt like two hundred beats per minute. He took a large gulp of his drink.

His mind turned to the morning's meeting. Frustratingly, despite all his travails, he still did not know whether he definitely had a solution to his Mike Nation problem. Why did the hitman Brian need to spend twenty-four hours deciding whether to take his case or not? What was the issue? Dixon thought he had told his story in as much detail and with as much composure as was physically possible, given he quite literally could have wet himself at any point during the conversation.

Dixon pondered the worst. What if he said no? What the hell was he going to do if Brian declined the contract?

Did Terry from the café know *another* hitman, he wondered? And even if he did, could Dixon even bring himself to meet Terry again to fix it up? It didn't bear thinking about. He took a second big gulp of the scotch and water. He felt his heart rate slowing. He touched his brow and was relieved to learn that his skin was returning to its normal clammy state, as opposed to the drenched surface it had been for most of the day.

His mind returned to the morning's meeting once again. What the bloody hell was that verbal bombardment about stupid buildings in aid of, he asked himself. It was all, 'bloody beautiful' this and 'pig ugly' that. Straight lines over here and shiny metal over there. My God, it was bewildering. Although, he did quite like that signal box, come to think of it. Brutalism, eh? He'd have to look that up at some point.

He drained his scotch, stood up and returned to the drinks table to pour another. When the glass was replenished, he went over to his desk and switched on the computer. He was about to check his email when he recalled the package that he'd had to clamber over in the hallway when he arrived home. He got up to fetch it but made a little detour to the downstairs toilet first, just to have a check. Once again, a little dribble was the best he could muster, probably about the quantity of a double measure. At least he found the bowl this time. Nonetheless, he cursed in frustration. Where was all his urine? The urges were getting ever more frequent, so it made no sense. He concluded that he had probably just sweated all the liquid out instead, given the levels of stress he had been under. It would all be better when the nasty business was over, he assured himself. He pictured himself lying on a beach on a Caribbean island, with a cocktail to one side of him and a big bag of money on the other. It made him feel a little better.

He retrieved the parcel and returned to his desk. The package was slightly bigger than A4 and had been carefully sealed in a courier bag. There was a large sticker on the front, with SBCC stamped on it, together with Dixon's address written in biro. SBCC – South Birmingham Cycle Couriers. Paul realised that it was a delivery from Mike bloody Nation. Only Nation was tight enough to use the most unreliable courier service in Birmingham.

He ripped open the top, tipped the contents onto the table and discarded the courier bag in the bin under his desk. He studied the pile of documents. There were three files in total, and Dixon instantly recognised them. He picked up the stack of folders and quickly flicked through them all. Inside the files were all the data that Dixon had put together for Nation over the last couple of weeks. Information on the various bank accounts that held the profits earned from the money laundering activities he had undertaken over the last ten years. On the front of the first file, Nation had scrawled 'With thanks.'

What did that mean? Had Nation not discovered anything untoward, despite having studied all the information he'd sent him? Was he perhaps even more stupid than Dixon had thought? Or was Nation just pretending that nothing was wrong while he considered his next steps? Perhaps Mike had a little more about him than Dixon had given him credit for. Either way, Dixon could take no chances. Nation had taken what he needed from the files and returned the documents, and it felt as though things were coming to a head. It all meant that he was now even more reliant on Brian contacting him tomorrow and giving him the thumbs up.

Meantime, there was nothing he could do about any of it now. So he tossed the files back onto the desk and was about to get up and head for the kitchen to fix a sandwich when something caught his eye. The edge of a single piece of paper was jutting out between two of the files. He hadn't spotted it when he had flicked through the documents; it must have been stuck to the bottom of one of the folders for some reason.

He placed the first file to one side and then picked up the middle folder. He turned it over to reveal the back of the single sheet. Carefully, he peeled the piece of paper away from the buff file. Red and brown marks dotted the back of the sleeve, and the stains smelled. Tomato ketchup and brown sauce at a guess. Dixon guessed that Nation must have been stuffing his face with a breakfast sandwich while he was studying the information. He grimaced at the thought. The sauce must have dripped onto the file, and when the sheet of paper was placed between the folders, the sauce acted like glue and stuck it to the back.

He turned the piece of paper over and studied it. At first, it just seemed to be a sheet full of doodles. Dozens of swirls and shapes and scribbles and random lines covered the sheet, completely at random. Dixon didn't understand. It must have been added to the courier package by mistake. It made no sense.

Then he realised that there was the odd word scrawled sporadically across the paper after all. He spotted 'TRAITOR' and 'SCUMBAG' written in capital letters on the upper part of the sheet, next to some rather aggressive scribbling. The penmanship indicated that Nation was probably angry when he wrote the words, as he'd ripped through the paper in some places. Dixon was growing concerned, but he continued to scan the sheet. Further down, in between a couple of very extravagant swirls, were the statement 'SORT IT' and next to that, the word 'DISAPPEAR.' The latter was underlined twice.

Once again, Dixon's anxiety levels rose and a deep sense of foreboding formed in his gut. Quickly, he reviewed the bottom half of the sheet. About three-quarters of the way down, he spotted his own name, 'DIXON'. But this was crossed through, twice, in heavy ink.

Slowly, he called out the words he had discovered so far.

'TRAITOR, SCUMBAG, SORT IT, DISAPPEAR, DIXON.'

Jesus Christ. It had to mean Nation was onto him. Nation knew it all. He'd discovered Dixon's con, and the accountant immediately recognised he was in the shit, right up to his neck. Rapidly, he scanned the final section of the paper for any further words. There was just one more, and he spotted it tucked into the bottom right-hand corner of the sheet, in capital letters, and underlined three times.

BRIAN

Oh no…. Oh God, no… Oh God, no, no, no… It couldn't be. But it had to be. It must be. There was no other explanation, no other explanation at all. It was all perfectly clear. Nation wanted him dead, and the bloke that Dixon had just met that very morning, the guy on whom Dixon was completely and utterly reliant to resolve his current predicament, that very same man had been instructed to kill him.

Dixon's mind collapsed into panic.

His first impulse was to run. The subconscious fight-or-flight instinct kicked in, and he wasn't going to fight a bloody contract killer. He could just grab the bag of money from under the mantelpiece right now, stuff another bag full of clothes, and go. Jump in the car and drive. Anywhere. It didn't matter where. But then Dixon remembered he'd already accepted as fact that Mike Nation would never stop looking for him. And now his boss had employed a fixer to do all the looking in the world on Nation's behalf. Running would never work, not in a million years.

OK, if not that, then what? What was Plan B? Maybe he could hire another contract killer somehow and just set the two on each other. Best hitman wins. But there was no time! Nation's guy was already onto him! It suddenly dawned on Dixon that he'd probably escaped this morning's meeting with his life only because it had been held in such a public place. For a fleeting moment, he wondered how confused Brian must have been when he saw Dixon turn up for the appointment. The absurdity of it all.

Can't run, can't hide, no plan B and out of time. Dixon's head swirled, he was losing his balance, he couldn't think, his head screamed with pain, he was pouring with sweat, his eyes stopped working, he couldn't even see…

And then something happened. The anxiety, the stress, the meetings he'd had, the gangsters, the café, the money, Mike bloody Nation, it all came crashing down on him in a torrent of emotion, and under the most intense pressure imaginable, his mind sheared in two and one half shut down completely.

Some kind of inbuilt self-protection mechanism triggered, and his personality was compartmentalised, ring-fenced, hidden away in the deep recesses of his mind. A different Paul Dixon took control of his body, and all was calm. His eyes started working again, and a numbness came over his whole being, almost drug-like. Quietly, he withdrew from the desk and slowly settled back onto the sofa on the other side of the room. Once there, he didn't move for minutes on end. He sat perfectly still, as if in a trance.

Finally, as the cogs of Dixon's brain turned over and over in slow motion, the decision was formed in his brand-new consciousness. It was a deeply unattractive option, but there really was nothing else for it. His new personality recognised that, as much as he didn't want to do so, he had to take matters into his own hands. Only moments earlier, the very concept would have made him sick to his pit, but his psychotic break had brought about a different identity, with renewed focus and fortitude. He now knew exactly what he had to do: he had to see Terry again, urgently. Dixon stood up, coolly collected his keys and headed for the car.

CHAPTER ELEVEN

The Balancing Act had first been awarded a Michelin star three years ago and it was understandably Rosie Bell's proudest professional achievement. Rosie and her team passionately guarded the precious star, and they had managed to retain the award each subsequent year. Rosie's food had gained international recognition, and there were rumours that she could very soon become the city's first two-starred chef. Rosie felt the pressure.

Brian and Sammy had completed their twenty-minute stroll and arrived at Brindleyplace, which was located behind the main nightclub district in Birmingham. The restaurant occupied a modern building overlooking the Old Canal, opposite the city's symphony hall and convention centres. The area was a popular destination for the locals, with several restaurants, bars and microbreweries lining the tow path running alongside the canal.

Neither Brian nor Sammy had as yet had a meal at The Balancing Act, but they were both cognisant of the buzz the place had generated in the city. Social media was awash with food bloggers praising the quality and style of Rosie's food, waxing lyrical about the new summer seasonal menu.

As they entered the restaurant, the head waiter greeted them with a smile and asked whether they had made a reservation. Brian explained that they were not there to eat but that had resolved Rosie's halibut situation and wondered whether she was free for a quick chat. The maître d' nodded and suggested the two take a seat in the bar area of the restaurant to the front of the premises while he headed back to check on Rosie's availability.

Brian and Sammy settled into comfy grey seats in the bar and surveyed the dining area beyond them. There appeared to be a circus theme to the décor that ran throughout the premises. Large black and white prints of fire-eaters, trapeze artists, high-wire artists and ringmasters adorned the dark slate-coloured walls on all sides of the restaurant, and an object which Brian could only guess was a tightrope walker's pole hung proudly above the large open kitchen. Brian made a mental note to ask Rosie why she had chosen the circus theme for her restaurant.

A large chef's table stood in front of the kitchen area, and Brian could see Rosie seated at one end of the table, talking to a young man in a suit seated next to her. The head waiter had reached Rosie, and she looked over in the direction of the bar area. She waved and got up from the table to come over and greet her guests.

Brian turned to Sammy. 'So, what were you coming over this way for anyway? What's the coincidence?'

Sammy winked at Brian. 'Boyfriend business, Bri,' she said with a grin.

'What, he works here? At The Balancing Act?'

'Yep.'

Brian scanned the room and caught sight of a young spotty-faced busboy clearing a table in the middle of the restaurant. 'Not him, surely?' Brian commented, looking at Sammy with horror.

'God, no! Jesus, Brian, he looks about twelve!'

'That's a relief. He's got a face like a welder's bench.'

'Brian!' she protested, slapping her partner mockingly in the chest. The two of them giggled immaturely.

Rosie had reached the pair and greeted them warmly, but they could tell that she was somewhat preoccupied.

'Hi Rosie, this is Sammy, my partner,' said Brian.

'Hi Brian, hi Sammy. Good to see you both. Look, I'm just finishing up an interview with that journalist over there. He's from the local paper; they're doing a piece on the restaurant. Do you mind holding on for two minutes so I can get it done, then we can grab a drink at the bar?'

'Sounds like a plan,' said Brian, and they watched as Rosie hurried back to the chef's table. At that moment, a rather handsome young man with short blonde hair appeared from the kitchen, wearing a white chef's jacket. He wandered up to the bar area and gave Sammy a peck on the cheek.

'Brian, this is Aleksandr. He's a commis chef here; has been since Rosie opened the place.'

Brian thought there was something familiar about Aleksandr's features and was puzzled.

'Hello, son. Have we met before?' he asked.

'Erm, I don't think so, mate.'

Sammy knew what Brian was thinking. 'Aleksandr has an elder brother, Bri, called Tomasz. He works over at Nation

Construction, so you might have bumped into him from time to time. They do look quite similar.'

'Ah yes, of course. Well, how do you do Aleksandr?' said Brian, standing up. The two men shook hands confidently.

'I'll be back in a minute,' Sammy said to Brian. She looped arms with Aleksandr and headed off to the staff area with a spring in her step. Brian settled back into his seat and helped himself to a couple of mini parmesan shortbreads from the table, and then looking around to make sure no one was watching, he helped himself to a couple more. They were really rather good.

Rosie had settled back into her seat in the main dining area and offered her apologies to the journalist for the interruption. She was getting a bit fed up with the interview, though; the guy seemed content with just reeling off all the usual obvious questions and dumb topics of conversation. Frankly, he was outstaying his welcome and Rosie was feeling irritable.

'Not a problem,' the reporter replied. 'Now, where were we...? Yes, just finishing off. So, there's been an explosion of fine dining offerings in the city over recent years. Do you find it an increasingly competitive area to operate in?'

Another lazy question, she thought. 'Well, yes, of course it's difficult,' she responded testily, before regaining a little more composure. 'I mean there are seven Michelin-starred restaurants here. Seven stars is a lot of stars. And there are not a lot of punters out and about at the moment. Money is tight for everyone.'

'It's six, isn't it? Six stars?'

Rosie rolled her eyes. 'Well, there's one over in Hampton-in-Arden. So, it depends on whether you count Hampton-in-Arden as being in Birmingham, doesn't it?'

'Ok, and is Hampton-in Arden in Birmingham?'

'No.'

'Erm, right, so it's six, then, surely?'

'It's seven,' Rosie snorted back. 'Because while it's not in Birmingham, it is *in* Birmingham.' Rosie felt herself lose her cool somewhat. 'You see, it's about catchment areas. It's the same clientele. Same customer base as mine. We are competing for the same people, the same taste buds. And anyway, if it wasn't in Birmingham, where would you say it is? Coventry? No one's going to get all dressed up and go out to dinner in Coventry, for God's sake!'

'I'm from Coventry...' the journalist stated in a monotone voice.

'Well, I'm sorry for your loss.'

The reporter was clearly vexed at the slur on his home town. 'I see,' he said quietly. 'Well, just one final thing then, Ms Bell. What is absolutely *not* in doubt is that you are the city's first *female* Michelin-starred chef. Does that bring with it any additional pressure, do you think?'

'Oh, come on,' Rosie huffed. 'Please! Let's not go there. It doesn't matter whether I'm a woman, a man, or a penguin. Winning a Michelin star is hard. Retaining a Michelin star is hard. Designing new dishes, constantly re-inventing your menus, keeping the ideas fresh and unique. There's pressure everywhere, regardless of your bloody sex! I mean, when was the last time you worked a seventy-hour week, eh? Come on, when?'

Rosie realised she had got carried away. She looked away from the table and off into the distance. The journalist hadn't expected the outburst and was offended at the personal slight. He slowly clicked the top of his pen, closed the pad of paper in front of him and turned off the recording app on his mobile phone.

'I see. Right. Well, thanks for your time, Ms Bell. I think I have what I need.' With that, he stood up, gathered his things and made for the exit door. Stoney-faced, he breezed past Brian and left the restaurant.

'Damn it,' whispered Rosie under her breath as she drained the glass of water in front of her. 'Stupid bloody woman,' she added, chastising herself. She gave herself a moment's pause to regain her composure, then stood up, adjusted her chef's jacket and returned to the bar.

Brian had seen the reporter leaving and was pleased to see Rosie wandering over towards him. His eyes lingered as she walked in his direction. Her shiny, light brown hair sat neatly atop her white chef's coat, and those piercing green eyes that he had first spotted in Nation's office seemed to glisten even more brightly in the cool restaurant light. He was pretty sure that he was becoming quite attracted to Rosie, although he would admit to himself that it had been a long time since he had experienced such an emotion, so he couldn't be certain. Dating had never really been his thing; he was totally out of his comfort zone. But he sensed that he wanted to get to know Rosie Bell.

'How did the interview go?' he asked as she reached the bar and took a seat next to him.

'Well, it was a car crash, I'm afraid to say. I just don't seem to be on my A game at the moment. I've got a few things on my mind, you know?'

'Well, if it's about the halibut, you needn't worry. It's all sorted,' Brian said proudly. 'Gary will drop the first delivery off tomorrow morning. Oh, and I promise, I didn't lay a finger on him.'

Rosie didn't seem to be paying attention, but after a moment, Brian's words finally registered. She turned to him and smiled before mumbling, 'Oh yes, no, that's great. Thank you for sorting that out.'

Brian felt underwhelmed. He thought the news would have been met with a touch more enthusiasm than that. There was clearly something more on Rosie's mind.

'Fancy a quick drink as a thank you, Brian?' she offered.

'That would be lovely, thanks. As long as you join me?'

'Sure, what do you fancy?'

'Dealer's choice.'

Rosie waved to the bar tender and called over, 'Two glasses of the Chablis please.'

The bar tender poured the wine and brought the drinks over. Rosie and Brian clinked their glasses and took a sip.

'Very nice,' remarked Brian, without a clue whether it was very nice or not. Wine was not his thing. 'So, why was the interview so bad?'

'Oh, I just managed to put my foot in it a couple of times. I think I'd pissed the reporter off by the end of it.'

'I see. What was the interview all about?'

'Well, I was hoping it was just going to be a straightforward puff piece about me and this place. You know, a bit about my life and my rather unorthodox background, and then my plans for the future and my hopes for the restaurant. That sort of guff. But as I say, I'm not sure it's going to be spun quite as positively as I'd hoped.'

'I'm sure you're worrying unnecessarily, Rosie. This place has such a good rep. All the foodies in the city rave about it. That journo bloke would be committing career suicide if he did anything other than print a glowing review.'

Rosie smiled sheepishly.

'So, what *is* your story, Rosie? What's so "unorthodox" about it?'

Rosie was loosening up a bit; she was feeling comfortable in Brian's company and the tension was evaporating from her shoulders. The Chablis was no doubt helping the mood of the moment, but she felt herself relaxing for the first time in ages.

'You sure you want to know?' she asked.

'Sure, I'm sure,' Brian replied.

Rosie studied him for a moment. What did she *really* make of him? He had a rather grumpy demeanour, for sure, but in an oddly engaging kind of way. His weathered, rough-around-the-edges face suited him well. He was clearly intelligent, despite the rather physical nature of his work.

Rosie was de-stressing further, so she decided to try and enjoy the time they were spending together, sitting there in the bar chatting away. She considered Brian's request to hear her story and decided why the hell not; it's not a bad tale to tell.

CHAPTER TWELVE

Rosie Bell had been brought up, as clichéd and unlikely as it sounded, in a travelling circus, one of the few remaining touring circuses still operating in England. Almost as soon as she could walk, she was hula-hooping, pogo sticking and balancing on the high wire, albeit a high wire that was just two feet from the ground. She recalled that throughout the early part of her childhood, she loved the life, moving from town to town, seeing the crowds pouring in and watching on gleefully as they cheered with joy and howled with laughter. She had grown up with the whole troupe and considered them all as one gigantic family. During those early years, she'd been allowed to try her hand at pretty much all the circus tricks, everything from fire juggling to acrobatics, though she was gutted at being banned from having a go at the human cannonball. Who wouldn't want to fly?

She relished learning all the skills in the production, but it was her parents' artistic speciality that inadvertently propelled her into the restaurant business. They were the knife throwers of the troupe, and they were experts.

Her parents had developed their routine over many years, and what distinguished them from similar acts was their ability to throw many different types of knives and with many different throwing styles. They could alternate from half spin to full spin, and from classic throw to backhand, with masterful ease and speed.

In the beginning, Rosie remembered being scared to death by their act, watching wide-eyed as her parents practised day after day, throwing those deadly, sparkling missiles at each other. Each morning she would wake up and peer out of the caravan window to see one parent strung up on a rotating target board whilst the other flung the projectiles at the target – blindfolded. The lunacy! There were times when she would beg them to stop; she would plead for them to find something else to do. Rosie was petrified that something would go wrong, that one of them would get seriously hurt. But she gradually learned that their skill was ingrained, almost implanted in their DNA, and the never-ending practice merely sought to guarantee their safety.

Eventually, Rosie found herself practising with the knives. She was never the 'target girl'; aside from the human cannonball, that was the only other role she was forbidden from attempting. But she learned to throw those steel weapons through hour upon hour of practice. Her preferred throw was a backhand, the same action as tossing a frisbee, and she became adept at hitting her mark with a remarkable degree of force and precision.

She learned to respect the knives. She revered the workmanship involved in making the blades. She learned the importance of looking after them and treating them with reverence. But a by-product of this intrigue of hers was that she gained an increasing interest in using knives the way the rest of the world tended to use knives: in preparing food. She was still too young to be involved in any performance work inside the circus tent, so she started making meals for her mother and father while they trained and worked and honed their skills.

Rosie started off by copying her mother's meals because she was familiar with them, and even then she attempted only the easiest of the dishes. She followed the instructions rigidly, always chopping, cutting, slicing and dicing with care and precision. But, as with most eager yet young and naive cooks, her first culinary experiments were a bit of a disaster. She made all the typical mistakes that everyone has experienced over the years: overcooked rice; undercooked chicken; standard kitchen fare. Nonetheless, over time, she improved, grew more confident and started to think she perhaps had a bit of a knack for it.

One day, the troupe moved to a new location, and once they had arrived and started setting up for the week ahead, Rosie went for a walk. She found a car boot sale in the next field over. She wandered up and down the rows of neatly parked cars and finally, in the top corner of the field, came across a picnic table full of recipe books. Rosie had only fifty pence to her name, but the old lady behind the table must have taken a fondness to the teenage girl in front of her because she sold Rosie three books in exchange for her fifty-pence piece.

The books were all very different in style and influence. Rosie remembered that one was heavily influenced by Asian flavours, while another was distinctly Mediterranean, and the final one was classically French. She remembered reading those books from cover to cover, learning the recipes by heart.

When she was asked to do the weekly food shop, she would find as many of the ingredients listed in those pages as she could. Once back at the caravan, she would start cooking. The flavours were new to her parents, and at first they were not convinced they were enjoying the different styles of food. But Rosie persisted with the new recipes, and as she did so, her knowledge of food continued to advance. She explored different flavours and learnt more about taste and smell and depth. Her skills grew, and with them, the compliments of her parents. Soon she was cooking for the whole troupe, for every single member of her giant family, and they seemed to love it.

After she turned seventeen, Rosie realised it was decision time. She would need to either commit to the family business and embrace the skills and the training needed to become a performer inside the tent or do something else. Rosie knew that she loved the troupe, and she obviously loved her parents, but the lifestyle was beginning to feel repetitive. There were very few people her age in the circus family, and she wondered whether she was missing out on a more normal life. She felt the need to plant some roots somewhere and actually stay in the same location for longer than a mere week or so.

Rosie agonised over the decision until, eventually, the decision was taken away from her. The ringmaster called a meeting of the whole troupe, and as they gathered in the big top, he called Rosie up to the middle of the arena. He told her that the whole company, her entire extended family, had come to adore her food and they thought she had a future in the business.

They had all clubbed together and found enough money for the first six months' rent on a tiny flat in Birmingham. The ringmaster had an old friend who owned a small restaurant in the south of the city, and he had agreed to take her onto his staff. The man had good contacts at the local college of food, and he was sure that in time, if she was good enough, he could get an apprenticeship for her at the college. With that, the ringmaster presented Rosie with a tan leather storage case. Inside the case was a perfect set of eight gleaming Wüsthof chef's knives.

Rosie was overwhelmed and broke down in tears. Eventually, when she had pulled herself together, she looked out bleary-eyed at her huge, mad family of acrobats and clowns, strongmen and fire-eaters, and thanked them all for their kindness. She promised that she would never let them down.

A couple of weeks later, with her bags packed and her emotions in overdrive, she left the troupe and headed for the nearest station. A couple of hours later, she was at the bedsit and full of regret. She wanted to turn around and go straight back home, straight back to the family. But she had promised not to let them down and she intended to keep that promise, so she gathered up all her courage and unpacked her belongings.

The next day, she started at the small suburban restaurant. She listened and she learned, and she excelled. Rosie did so well in her job that she secured that apprenticeship in next to no time, and from there, she never looked back.

'And that, in a nutshell, is my story...' Rosie said proudly and drained the last of her Chablis. She called the bartender over and ordered refills for them both.

'That is fucking brilliant, excuse the French,' Brian said finally, having allowed himself a little pause to let it all sink in.

'Yes, I guess so. I think it's a nice story,' Rosie acknowledged.

'And it explains the theme of the restaurant. And the name. The Balancing Act. It's a salute to your circus past and to the family that helped you get where you are now.'

'Precisely,' Rosie replied eagerly, swirling her second glass extravagantly. 'But it's not just a tribute to those guys; I like to think it works on a couple of levels. Sure, it helps frame the whole carnival atmosphere that I wanted for the restaurant. But on top of that, as a chef, you're always acutely aware that you're only ever one really bad dish, one really bad review, from ruin. The tightrope we walk between pushing the boundaries of food and keeping it "safe" is quite the balancing act in itself.'

'Very clever,' said Brian admiringly. He was very much enjoying his time with Rosie and was encouraged to see that she was smiling right back at him. But at that moment, Rosie's brow furrowed a touch and a wrinkle of concern appeared on her face. Brian sensed there was more that Rosie wanted to say.

'… But the thing is, the circus business, just like the restaurant business, it's a tough one. The troupe is always struggling for money. You have to understand, I would have been nothing without that gang. And so, whenever I could afford to, I would send money back to the circus to help with the bills and stuff. I've always been kind of prudent with my money; the only real extravagance I have is being insistent on buying the highest quality ingredients for the restaurant. Other than that, and of course paying the team a fair wage, I try to be as careful as I can with my income.

'But word was getting round that the food here was pretty high calibre. Things were going well, and I found myself caught up in all the hype. I lost a little of my focus and that's when I made my first serious business mistake. Sod's law, it was a big one. You see, I bought a bar across the road from here. It made perfect sense. I figured people would eat at the restaurant and then enjoy evening drinks in the bar.

'But I over-extended myself financially when I opened that bar, The Rum Runner. The margins were always going to be tight, but I was convinced it would be ok. Then, of course, COVID happened, and money started disappearing. The furlough scheme didn't touch the sides, and I started bleeding cash. And because I had been sending money back to the circus troupe, I didn't have any savings to speak of. The whole bloody economy was shutting down, and, of course, the banks didn't want to know. I thought I was going to lose everything, Brian. Everything I had worked for and everything the family had helped me get.'

'Christ, Rosie. So, what happened?'

'I needed money desperately. And I'd heard of a man who was still prepared to invest in local businesses, despite the basket case of the economy.'

Brian's heart sank. Of course. 'Mike Nation?' he offered.

'Mike Nation,' Rosie confirmed, sadly.

'Go on. Finish the story.'

'Well, I approached him. I had no choice by then, Brian. You have to understand that I was all out of options. Anyway, Mike looked at my accounts and he agreed that the business was fundamentally a sound one, so he consented to lend me the money I needed. I thanked the Lord. The business was saved, and it was all down to Mike Nation. Little did I know what I had let myself in for.

'In the beginning, there were no issues. He said he didn't want to own my business, or even take a majority shareholding. He was just happy to loan me the money and be a silent partner. We agreed terms for his investment, which were steep, to say the least, but I was sure I could make the repayments, so I was happy.

'But after a while, things started changing. He wanted me to do things I was, let's just say, less than comfortable with. He got me to manufacture fake bookings for the restaurant, and I had to start putting money through the books that wasn't actually earned by the business. Once the statements were reconciled and I had got together the relevant receipts, I would be instructed to return the money to Nation's accountant. I knew what it was, Brian. I knew what was happening, but I couldn't do without his bloody money. I still can't, not at the moment. I'm just so overstretched...'

And just like that, Brian saw in full technicolour what Nation's scheming could do to a person. He was angry and he was conflicted. His mind wandered back to his musings in the coffee shop only an hour or so ago. He had recognised that he had always known what Mike Nation was, namely a bit of a shit, but until that morning, it had never really bothered him. After all, Nation had been a very good source of income for Brian.

But now, for the second time that day, he was hearing in explicit detail exactly what effect Mike Nation could have on people, both on their businesses and on their lives. He had naively assumed that people had brought these things upon themselves, through their own stupidity, or their own actions or inaction. But now he realised it wasn't quite that simple. People could purely be victims of circumstance and have no other way out but to turn to a man like Nation.

He felt uncomfortable. Maybe he had arrived at the wrong conclusion earlier when he had determined that the cards were falling to the disadvantage of Dixon? Perhaps it was Dixon's job that he should accept after all? Was he changing his mind? Brian chose to change the subject.

'It'll all bounce back, Rosie. Mark my words. The restaurant is already a complete success story. The bar will be too, I'm sure of it. And you'll get Nation out of your hair before too long. Keep the faith.'

Rosie smiled at him and finished her glass of wine. Brian was convinced that her emerald eyes brightened again, just a little.

'And anyway,' continued Brian with excitement, 'the bar, you called it The Rum Runner! I'm guessing you named it after the original one?'

'Oh yes, absolutely! I read all about it!' said Rosie enthusiastically, pleased that he had made the link to the historic venue that once stood only a couple of hundred yards from where they sat. 'I learned that all the big celebrities hung out there, back in the day. The TV stars, the reporters, the musicians, all the big names. I just had a feeling we could replicate that energy, get that same vibe back, but in a new venue.'

'It sounds like a wonderful idea,' said Brian, glad that the mood was lifting.

'Duran Duran was the house band at the original place! Duran bloody Duran! Can you believe it?'

Brian could indeed believe it because The Rum Runner had featured in one of his books on Birmingham buildings, so he had read all about it.

'So I've heard,' Brian nodded. 'Of course, I never got to go myself; it was a bit before my time. But it sounds like it was one hell of a place. Cocktails and food, music and dancing. Beautiful. And can you guess what they did with the place, Rosie?'

'I have no idea...' she conceded.

'We knocked the sodding thing down, Rosie, that's what we did. We knocked the sodding thing down.'

'That doesn't surprise me,' Rosie replied.

Sammy was walking towards the two of them, having parted company with Aleksandr at the staff room door. She had overheard the end of Brian and Rosie's conversation.

'Oh my God, Brian, you're not still banging on about demolished buildings, are you? It's bloody progress, Bri! Honestly, get with the program! Time doesn't stand still, you know, pal.'

'It's history, Sammy. It's knocking down history, that's what it is. I mean, you wouldn't bulldoze Windsor Castle now, would you?'

'No, but I don't think old Charley and Camilla are that likely to nip into an old Brummie nightclub for a pint now, are they? Throw some shapes on the dancefloor? Can't see it, Bri. Let me give you a little piece of advice.'

'What's that, Sammy?' asked Brian, rolling his eyes while flashing Rosie a smirk.

'Read a different book...'

'Yeh, yeh, whatever you say. Anyway, what have you been up to?'

'Oh, nothing, we were just fixing to meet up for dinner tonight, that's all. You about ready to get going?'

The conversation had drawn to a conclusion, and much to Brian's disappointment, he realised that he couldn't think of any further reason to hang around at the restaurant. Anyway, he had eight hundred grand to find and people to kill, and time was not on his side.

'Yep, we best get on, then,' he began. He turned to Rosie and added, 'Of course, I've never actually eaten here before. I'll have to do something about that.'

'Well, in that case, here's my number. Why don't you give me a bell sometime? I'm sure I can find the time to rustle you up a dish or two.' Rosie surprised herself with her own forwardness; it was totally out of character. But she realised she had enjoyed the bit of time the two had spent together, and her reaction had been intuitive. She didn't have many people she could talk to regarding all matters Mike Nation, and she was grateful for being able to let off a little steam. But it was more than that. For some reason, she seemed to find this large, gruff man with his little cranky ways rather attractive.

Meanwhile, Brian just looked as though he'd won the lottery twice; he was absolutely bloody delighted. He earnestly copied the number down, and then he wrote it down again in case he'd made a mistake the first time round.

Sammy and Brian adjourned to the canal side at the front of the restaurant and headed back into town.

'Well, well, well…!' started Sammy while giving Brian a nudge. 'You old fox! Who would have thought it? An internationally renowned chef having the hots for a miserable old bugger like you!'

'Don't start, Sammy,' complained Brian.

'Are you going to phone her, then?' Sammy continued, undeterred.

'Maybe,' Brian mumbled. 'We'll see. But anyway, enough about me. How long you been seeing lover boy then?'

'Oh, I don't know, three months maybe?'

'Three whole months, is it? A new record for you, I'd have thought.'

'Shut up, Bri.'

'Where does he live, this Aleksandr?'

'Oh, just down the road, in Stirchley Village. He's got a flat there with Tomasz.'

'Stirchley *Village*! What do you mean *Village?* For God's sake. It's not a bloody village, Sammy, it's a suburb.'

Sammy knew she had triggered another of Brian's pet hates. She enjoyed watching him grumble on about his peculiar little bugbears, like his obsession with long-since flattened old buildings or inappropriate labels used by various parts of the city. Brian had a small army of these quirks, and playing along with them was one of the forms of banter the two had developed. Each played out their respective roles with great bravado.

'Well, that's what they're calling it now, Bri. Just like what they do with Moseley. They've called Moseley *Moseley Village* for years, as you well know. And now they're doing it with Stirchley too.'

'Well, that's because *they* are idiots, whoever *they* are,' Brian moaned. 'I know what a village is. A village is a bloody hamlet. A small collection of houses in the middle of nowhere, with a pub in the centre and a church to the side. What a village is *not* is a row of shops right slap bang in the heart of the second biggest city in Britain.'

'No, Bri, you're wrong,' said Sammy, having fun, intentionally trying to wind him up. 'You see, it's all about marketing. Moseley sounds like it's a suburb, whereas *Moseley Village* sounds like a destination. It's got pizzazz.'

'Do what?'

'Pizzazz, Bri. And they're all cashing in on it now. Not just Moseley or Stirchley, either. Even Edgbaston calls itself *Edgbaston Village* now.'

'Shut up! How can Edgbaston be a village? It's a got a bloody international cricket stadium!'

'Well, it is, Bri. Look it up...'

'Clowns....'

They laughed as they crossed the footbridge over the canal, walking side by side as they continued into town. Brian was glad for the distraction. He was always happiest when he was moaning about Birmingham; it was something that was innate to all Brummies. A very self-deprecating bunch of people, all told.

Even so, he couldn't help but let his mind drift back to Rosie. The little knife thrower from the carnival who had gone on to culinary stardom. He had only just met her, but he knew he was already very fond of her. And he knew something else as well; he did not like the consequences that Mike Nation's actions were having on someone as genuine as Rosie Bell. Not one iota.

CHAPTER THIRTEEN

It is a common and accurate notion that most chefs, even commis chefs at Michelin-starred restaurants, just don't fancy cooking when they get home, particularly if they have just spent the day working a full shift in a boiling hot commercial kitchen. It was for that reason that, a few hours after meeting at The Balancing Act, Sammy and Aleksandr were wandering down Stirchley Village High Street heading for a small artisan pizzeria that had opened near Aleksandr's flat about a year ago.

The couple had first met while having weekend drinks in a Stirchley pub back in the spring. They had some mutual friends who had introduced them to each other, and having had maybe one round too many, and having fallen out of the bar at around midnight, the two had arranged to meet a few days later in the new pizzeria. Their first date had gone rather well, and the little restaurant on the corner had become a firm favourite with them both. They had been back about a dozen times since.

The little bell that sat atop the restaurant door gave its melodious chime as the two entered the pizza shop.

'Hi Roberto, how's things?' asked Sammy as they entered the diner and pulled up a pair of stools at the counter.

'Heyy! Sammy! Alex! My favourite little love birds! You have come back to me at last!' replied Roberto, and he rushed over to embrace the couple warmly. Contrary to every assumption one would make when meeting co-owner Roberto for the first time, he was not actually straight off a flight from Naples. With his tanned skin, good looks and jet-black hair, he would tell his customers he was a born and bred Italian. In fact, he came from Dudley.

'The usual, my friends?' Roberto enquired, and when the pair nodded in confirmation, he called out a ridiculously cheesy 'Bada Bing!' and skipped away to prepare the two sourdough pizzas: nduja and chorizo picante for Aleksandr, Parma ham and rocket for Sammy, with a side of arancini for the two to share. 'In or out today, you two?' he enquired from the kitchen.

'It's getting late; we'll take them away today, thanks Roberto,' Aleksandr confirmed.

'But a couple of beers while we wait, when you get a chance,' added Sammy.

Twenty minutes later and having drained their beers, the two were ambling back through Stirchley hand in hand, heading back to Aleksandr's home with hot pizza boxes nestled under their arms. Aleksandr was renting a modern and spacious second-floor flat on a small, fairly new estate on the edge of Stirchley. He shared the two-bedroom apartment with his elder brother Tomasz, although Sammy was spending more and more time there as well. So much so, she had requisitioned a drawer in Aleksandr's room for some of her stuff.

As they reached the front door of the flat, they spotted a large, dirty pair of construction boots near the entranceway. 'The bruv is in, I see,' commented Aleksandr. They entered and waved their hellos to Tomasz, who was slumped in an easy chair flicking through the channels on the TV.

'Any pizza, bruv?' Aleksandr offered.

'No, I'm fine thanks, mate. I've eaten. Mom brought over a large pot of bigos earlier today, so I just had a bowl of that. The rest is in the fridge if you fancy some later in the week.'

'Bigos again. How lovely,' said Aleksandr sarcastically, shuddering at the thought of the traditional Polish stew of meat and sauerkraut.

There was a strong Polish community in the city, and the two brothers had been brought up as passionate members of that neighbourhood, primarily because their parents had deep roots back in the motherland. However, Aleksandr did not consider Polish cuisine to be exactly at the forefront of culinary excellence, and the never-ending servings of his mother's bigos in his youth still haunted him. He was convinced it was one of the reasons he had ended up in the profession he had chosen.

Sammy plated up the pizza in the kitchen while Aleksandr opened some bottles of beer, and finally the pair collapsed onto the sofa, joining Tomasz in front of the television. The three sat in relative silence while Aleksandr and Sammy hungrily devoured their pizzas and guzzled their beers. When they had finished and Tomasz had grabbed them all another round of drinks, Aleksandr finally struck up a conversation

'Hey, Sammy. Tomasz has a new lady friend in tow!'

Sammy made a playful howling noise, and Tomasz threw a cushion in her general direction.

'It's nothing serious,' he appealed, but neither Aleksandr nor Sammy was having any of it.

'Tell us more,' probed Sammy, enthusiastically.

'Nothing to tell, really,' replied Tomasz sheepishly. 'We've only been seeing each other a few weeks, so it's early days. We're just going to see how things go, taking things nice and steady. And that's all I'm prepared to say on the subject.'

'What's her name then, Tommy?' she asked.

'I'm not saying. I've told you, I've said all I'm going to say,' said Tomasz with finality.

'What? No name? You absolute throbber! Why's that then?'

'I'm just not telling you, ok? Not yet, anyway. Now change the bloody subject!' Tomasz gave Sammy a playful glare to emphasise the point.

'Whoever she is, Tommy is her toy boy, Sammy,' Aleksandr interjected. 'It would be fair to say the mystery woman is a smidgen older than my big bruv, or so I have been led to believe. Isn't that right Tommy?'

'Shut up, Alex,' pleaded Tomasz, but he went a little crimson in the cheeks.

Sammy helped him out by changing the line of questioning. 'OK, so no name and no age, fair enough. But where did you meet your very own Mrs Robinson, Tommy? Surely you can tell us that!'

'Sort of at work.'

Sammy spat a little mouth of beer over herself. 'At bloody work!' she said incredulously. 'You work on a bloody building site, mate! What are you on about? What is she, some new butch construction worker? Come to push you around a bit? Is that it?'

'Bollocks, Sammy, shut your face!' Tomasz scowled, and the three of them had a good laugh.

Finally, and much to Tomasz's relief, Sammy decided to drop the subject and the three of them returned to the telly. Tomasz had eventually settled for the channel showing the football highlights, much to Sammy's disappointment. So, she turned to Aleksandr and gently laid a hand on his arm.

'So, how was the shift at the restaurant? Busy?'

'Yeh, mad busy to be honest. The evening sitting was mental. We didn't have an empty table all night. Rosie's new menu is going down a storm.'

'That's great.'

'Yeh, it is. And you would have thought Rosie would be absolutely made up about it. But she doesn't seem quite herself recently. Something's going on, I'm convinced about it. To be honest, I'm a bit worried about her. I've asked her what's going on, but she doesn't want to talk about it; she changes the subject. But I know something is upsetting her, and whatever it is, it's causing her a load of stress.'

'I did wonder if something was up. She seemed to be deep in conversation with Brian at the restaurant earlier on.'

Aleksandr sighed. He was exhausted from the day's shift. 'I think I know who's to blame, though, and it's the guy who pays your salary. And yours, Tomasz. He's the bloody problem, I'm sure of it.'

He felt himself getting worked up at the very thought of the man. He looked at Tomasz and Sammy, one after the other. 'He's got his grubby, cheating fingers into the business somehow. I just know it. You can tell by the way Rosie behaves every time he comes in with his wife. Rosie does everything she can to avoid him, but he wanders round the restaurant like he owns the place. There's something going on, and it's got to be your boss's fault. To be honest, I don't know how you two can work for a scumbag like that.'

'Whoa there, Alex,' Sammy said forcefully, and shoved him away from her, moving to the opposite end of the sofa. 'He's not *actually* my boss, for your info, so don't you go yelling at me about him. Sure, I may run the odd errand for him from time to time, just as Brian does, but it's only a couple of jobs, and I can stop anytime. I'm fully aware that the guy is a bit of a tosspot, but I didn't make Rosie get into bed with him.'

'Yeh, but you do all this dodgy stuff for him. You bend the rules for him. And I don't know what he's up to, but whatever it is, he might lose us the restaurant. I just don't know how you can bring yourself to do it.'

'Bollocks! I do my work to pay my bills, Alex, like we all do, so piss off, mate! And anyway, who made you the morality police?'

Sammy turned her back on him, grabbed her phone and turned her attention to her social media, firmly emphasising that she was done with that line of discussion.

There was silence in the flat for what felt like a lifetime. No one knew what to say. This was not turning into the evening any of them had planned.

Finally, Sammy turned back to Aleksandr and spoke in lowered tones. 'Look, if I could help Rosie out, then I would, Alex. She seems like a really nice person. And you've always said how good she is as a boss and a mentor. And you don't need to remind me how much the restaurant means to you because I know. But it really isn't my fault. And anyway,' she added, 'I wouldn't know what I could do to help in the first place.'

Silence again.

It was Tomasz who eventually spoke next. 'I might.'

'Sorry?' said Sammy.

'I might know what to do. Or at least, I may know someone who might know what to do.'

'What does that mean?' Aleksandr asked, looking confused.

'I… Look, I had better not say any more. But hell, you're right Alex. Working on the building site, you get to hear rumours about Nation, stuff he might or might not be up to. The guy does seem to be a tosspot, but he's ultimately my boss and that is embarrassing. Having to work for a man like that, well, it's not great. But without the pay packet, I couldn't pay for my half of this place.' He waived his arms across the flat, then continued. 'Mike bloody Nation. He has his fingers in so many pies. He just doesn't know the damage he's doing to people...'

Tomasz trailed off as if he had said too much or spoken out of turn. But then he started up again. 'Look, Sammy, you said you would help Rosie if push came to shove. Do you mean it?'

Sammy thought for a moment. 'Well, yes, I think so, if I could.'

'And what about your mate? Your partner Brian? You said that he and Rosie were having a long conversation earlier. Do you think he would help her?'

'Abso-bloody-lutely right he would! No doubt about that; he's got the hots for her something chronic. The weird thing is, I think she quite likes him back. Very odd.'

'OK,' said Tomasz finally. 'Leave it with me. I can't say any more than that right now. But there may be a way to help us all out. And you never know, it might knock Mike bloody Nation off his throne for a bit...'

Later that night, Aleksandr and Sammy enjoyed some highly passionate and exhaustingly vigorous make-up sex, their relationship's first. And afterwards, they lay together in peaceful silence, staring up at the bedroom ceiling and watching the moonlight silhouettes creeping from the window.

Sammy considered whether the stupid row earlier had actually been worth it, just to enjoy Alex's enthusiastic reconciliation attempts in bed. But how ridiculous was it that their first argument had been over Mike bloody Nation? She found it maddening. And while she was on the topic of Mike Nation, what on earth was Alex's big brother Tomasz up to with his mysterious comments? She had no idea what he had been on about, but she guessed that she would find out in time.

CHAPTER FOURTEEN

The following morning Brian was up early and eating breakfast at the kitchen table of his Hall Green flat. Sammy hadn't come back the previous night, instead staying over at the boyfriend's place, which meant he was left alone to ponder his troubles.

He stared disappointedly at his food and wondered whether Michelin-starred chefs had marmalade on burnt toast for breakfast or rustled up something a little more exciting. He decided to ask Rosie the next time he saw her. He just couldn't get her out of his mind.

He had been reflecting on his deliberations of the day before, both at the coffee shop and over at The Balancing Act, regarding Nation's actions and the impact he was having on innocent people. However, that thought process had naturally led him down the path of questioning his own actions and his own decisions. After all, Brian's specific line of work would inevitably impact others along the way as well.

He knew that he had fallen into the world of fixing, protecting and killing because it was what he had learned to do in the forces. But he had also wanted to hit back at the world, the world that he blamed for his mother's death. He had been angry, blinkered, and he hadn't given a damn about anyone else.

But this all meant he had never taken the time to analyse the consequences of his actions and the after-effects of the jobs he had taken on. He had told himself that he needed to earn a living, and it made sense to do something he was good at. But a by-product of his endeavours was that people like Nation got their way, and normally at the expense of others. In effect, he was an enabler, and he was enabling people like Nation.

It was all rather unsettling and he resolved to ponder on these questions more deeply later. Concepts such as "moral codes" were not topics to be debated over a bad breakfast in the middle of a difficult job.

For now, Brian had more pressing concerns. For a start, he was acutely aware that Colonel John P. Kicklighter was flying into Birmingham the following day. He knew this because, despite the relatively early hour, Mike Nation had already called him about seven hundred times to remind him.

'I am not pissing around here, Brian. Seriously, pal, this is how Rome fell,' Nation had said with grave finality before ringing off for the last time. Contrary to Mike's warning, Brian was fully aware that Rome did not, in fact, fall because it failed to find eight hundred thousand pounds worth of dodgy cash to put towards a retirement village in Arizona. But Brian sensibly chose not to point that out at the time, deciding instead that discretion was the better part of valour.

The problem for Brian was that he was yet to resolve his conundrum about who to kill and who to bill. The logical solution that he had settled on at the coffee shop still held true. Nation the repeat customer was the rational choice. But Rosie's difficulties with the man were haunting him somewhat.

Putting that aside for the moment, he recognised that he still didn't know for certain where the bloody money was either, although he was pretty damned sure it would be in Dixon's fortress of a house somewhere.

His mobile phone started buzzing from the other side of the table so he spun the handset round to check the caller detail on the screen. It was Terry. Not another new client. surely, Brian thought. He simply didn't have the time for this. If it was a new referral, he would have to see how much work Sammy had on at the moment, and if she could make room, he would pass the job on to her.

He accepted the call, put it on loudspeaker and placed the phone back on the kitchen table so he could continue with his crappy marmalade on toast.

'Hello, Terry, how's tricks?' he enquired, chewing a mouthful of food.

'Mustn't complain, Bri; mustn't complain. Still stuffing myself full of Alli's dreadful sausage sandwiches, so I probably don't have long for this world, to be fair.'

Brian heard a distant 'Oi, fuck off, you,' emanating from the other end of the phone, and he guessed that Terry was in the café again, doing his best to wind Allison up.

'Good stuff, mate,' Brian replied. 'So, what's up? Not another new client, is it? I've got a lot on at the moment.'

'No, Brian, it's not about a new client; it's about an existing one. Or at least I thought he was an existing client, but I'm guessing you turned him down, and I was just wondering why. It's that Paul bloke that I set up for you yesterday.'

'I haven't turned him down, Terry. I just haven't made a decision on that one yet. But don't worry, you'll get your usual intro fee, even if I do knock that one back. Anyway, what makes you think I didn't take the job?'

'Well, I just assumed you'd said no, which is why he'd decided to take matters into his own hands, that's all.'

Brian was confused. He put the toast back down on the plate, brushed his hands together and picked up the mobile phone, flicking the speaker function off as he did so. He got up from the kitchen table and paced towards the lounge.

'What do you mean, taking matters into his own hands? What are you on about, Tel?'

'Yesterday afternoon, Bri, he came back over to the café. I was halfway out the door on the way home; he only just caught me.'

'And…?' said Brian impatiently.

'Well, he seemed a little different this time. As if a bit of steely determination had been injected into that skinny, sweaty monstrosity of a man. He seemed, I don't know, more alert all of a sudden. Very different to the feeble mess that chucked up all over Kings Heath the last time I saw him.'

'Chucked up? What are you on about, Terry?'

'Oh, didn't I mention it? Yeh, he was sick outside the café on his first visit. The guy was a nervous wreck. Anyway, he didn't seem the same man yesterday evening.'

'Look, where are you going with this Terry? As I say, I've got a lot on…'

'Well, he wanted to buy a gun…'

135

There was silence on the line.

Terry continued. 'Bri? Brian? Are you still there?'

Brian found his voice. 'What do you mean, he wanted to buy a gun? A real gun?'

'Of course, a real gun, Bri. What are you on about? I'm not running a branch of Toys R Us, am I? He said that he needed to buy a gun and he needed to buy it quickly. He asked if I could source him one. I said of course I could source him one, but it wouldn't come cheap. He didn't seem to care; he just needed one straight away. So I went back to my place, dug out a little revolver from the stash, sorted him out a dozen bullets and met him back in Kings Heath within the hour. By which time he'd got the cash together, so we did the deal.'

'Tell me you didn't sell that weirdo a bloody gun, Tel! Jesus Christ alive…'

'Course I did, Bri. A little Colt thing. Small-calibre revolver. He doesn't look like he could handle a big old bugger, so I gave him a compact snub-nosed job. Dirty Harry this guy is *not*, am I right, Bri? But you can see why I thought you had turned the bloke down, can't you? I'm pretty sure he wasn't just buying it for protection.'

'OK. Right. Well, thanks for letting me know, Terry. I'll see you later in the week to pass on your cut. And Terry, if you see Dixon again, don't sell him anything, ok? Just stall him and contact me, alright?'

'Whatever you say, Bri. Catch you soon.'

Brian rang off and threw his mobile onto the sofa. He had been pacing up and down the length of his lounge for the whole conversation and found himself at the window, so he stared out on the communal gardens, deep in thought.

What the hell was going on? What was Dixon playing at? Why had he suddenly decided to get a gun *before* Brian had even contacted him about taking the job?

He could only assume that Dixon had resolved to get rid of Mike Nation himself for some reason. Unless the guy had panicked at the thought of Brian turning him down, decided there was no way out of his predicament and was just going to top himself? That seemed unlikely, but either way, Dixon had obviously come to the conclusion Brian was not taking the contract. What had made him come to that decision?

Something was up. Something had happened that Brian wasn't aware of, and he didn't like losing control of the situation. He knew from experience that as soon as you lost control, bad things tended to happen. Now there was a loaded handgun in play, and to make matters worse, the guy who had it was the man Brian was supposed to kill. Not ideal. Not ideal at all. He needed to contact Dixon. He needed to meet up with him, if only so Brian could regain control.

He determined that the best course of action would be to tell Dixon he would take his job on. Granted, that remained pretty bloody unlikely, despite his own internal conflicts, but at least it should buy him some time. He'd tell Dixon he would accept his assignment but that he needed to meet up with him to finalise some details.

Brian retrieved his mobile from the sofa and swiped to the text function. He found Dixon's number and typed.

Have decided to take the contract, but I need more info. Let's meet up. Corner of Livery St and Colmore Row, 3pm this afternoon.

He hit send and then waited. A minute passed by, then another, and another. At last he heard the ping of his phone. He looked down to see the reply. One word.

OK.

CHAPTER FIFTEEN

The lunchtime sitting had finally wound down in The Balancing Act and Rosie was in her office, working through the accounting program on her laptop. She was manipulating the restaurant takings once again, just as Nation had demonstrated to her all those months ago. In one column Rosie artificially inflated the reservation numbers, in another she exaggerated customer bills, and the combination of the two led to inflated profit estimates making way for the dodgy money Nation's accountant had sent her way. It was so depressing.

'Dickhead,' she whispered under her breath, and she imagined punching Nation right in the middle of his stupid, fat, orange face. That made her feel a little better.

When the numbers finally balanced, she couldn't help but smirk. Not quite the balancing act she was referring to when she had proudly named her restaurant, she thought. Next, she flicked to the accountancy tab for The Rum Runner and ran through the figures in each of those columns. All the numbers in this spreadsheet were very much real, and unfortunately, they did not make good reading. The bar was still failing to pay for itself, despite a cost-cutting exercise Rosie had recently undertaken. She wasn't going to get out from under Nation's control any time soon, it seemed. She sighed gloomily, and realising she couldn't concentrate properly, she hit the save button and closed the laptop; she would have to come back to that later.

Rosie got up from behind her desk and wandered out into the restaurant. She walked into the open kitchen where Aleksandr was helping with the post-lunchtime clean-up.

'Good shift today, Alex. Well done, mate.'

'Thanks, chef,' replied Aleksandr proudly, but he could sense once again that there was something else on Rosie's mind. 'Is there anything I can do for you, chef? You look bothered.'

'What? Oh, no. Thanks anyway, Alex. That's good of you. Are you rostered for tonight's shift as well?'

'No, chef, not on tonight.'

'Well, you get off then, and have a good afternoon. Thanks again for your efforts today.'

'Yes, chef, thanks.' With that, Aleksandr made for the staffroom to get changed.

Rosie spotted the tan leather storage case on the workbench to one side of the kitchen. Her precious Wüsthof knives. Ever since she had been presented with the treasured gift all those years ago back in the big top, she had used the knives pretty much every single day. She unravelled the leather and studied the eight knives, one by one. Individually, she gently ran a finger up and down the edge of each blade to check the sharpness. First the paring knife, then the chef's knife, the nakiri knife, the utility knife, the santoku knife, the bread knife, the carving knife and finally the cleaver. From the moment she had started using the set, Rosie had ensured they had only ever been professionally sharpened, to maximise their long life.

Aleksandr had got changed and popped his head round the corner on his way out. He saw her stroking the silverware. 'I can run them up to the Jewellery Quarter and get them sharpened this afternoon if you like?'

'Thanks, Alex, but no, I'll do it myself. I could do with some fresh air to help clear the head, blow the cobwebs away.'

'OK, well, see you then,' said Aleksandr and headed for the door.

Rosie wrapped up the leather bundle and secured it with the little leather ties attached to the flap of the case. She placed the leather holder into her rucksack and slung it over a shoulder. Finally, she checked with her sous chef that everything was in hand, in readiness for the evening sitting. The numbers for dinner were good once again and she should have been delighted, but the cloud of Mike Nation hung heavy over her head. Her number two assured her that it was all under control, so she set off for the Jewellery Quarter in the city.

The walk would take her about twenty minutes, and as she strolled through the city centre, Rosie relished the sensation of the heat from the summer sun beating down upon her face. The country was having an unnaturally good holiday season, and she was pleased about that, at least.

Her mind turned to Brian and to the feelings she seemed to be developing for the man. Was it really attraction? It probably was… sort of. She couldn't explain what it was about him that so enamoured her of him, but she couldn't deny there was a connection. Maybe his strength was his appeal? She had never really needed anyone to look after her; after all, she considered herself a strong and independent woman in her own right. But eventually, everyone comes to realise they could do with at least one person in their life on whom they can rely for support. Currently, she was having to work her way through the muddy waters of her relationship with Mike Nation all alone, and she recognised it would be nice to have someone in whom she could confide. Rosie found herself hoping that Brian would use her phone number, and sooner rather than later.

She reached the small industrial district of the Jewellery Quarter where a wonderful array of talented craftsmen had plied their trade for centuries. From precision engineers and toolmakers to painters and, of course, the jewellery designers and retailers from whom the area took its name, skilled craftsmen worked away, perfecting their talents and training the next generation. During the industrial revolution, Birmingham became known as 'the city of a thousand trades'. The area flourished as the workshop of England, and that beating heart of history was living on strongly in that district of the city.

A short distance from the main crossroads in the centre of the Jewellery Quarter, Rosie arrived at the familiar commercial unit and went inside. The owner recognised her immediately and greeted her warmly. She unpacked the leather sleeve from her rucksack and passed the knives to the trusted man. Rosie asked if she could wait in the workshop while he worked on the blades, and the owner said that, of course, that was fine. He would start the job straight away and the knives would be ready in about twenty minutes. She settled down on a small stool in the corner of the unit and watched as the man started up his water-cooled sharpening belt, settled in behind it and carefully got to work.

At the same time, Paul Dixon was preparing to leave his Edgbaston home to make the meeting that Brian the assassin had fixed up. Brian the hitman, who had been contracted to kill Dixon. Brian the hitman, and Dixon the man with the target on his back. Except, unbeknown to Brian the hitman, Dixon knew that his adversary wasn't in possession of all of the facts. For a start, Brian the hitman didn't know that Dixon was onto him. Secondly, Brian the hitman didn't know that Dixon had a loaded gun in the side pocket of his jacket. And finally, Brian the hitman most certainly didn't know that Dixon planned to put a bullet in his head and then hunt down Mike bloody Nation and blow that dirtbag away as well.

Dixon grinned, a changed man. Only forty-eight hours earlier, the concept of him murdering two people in cold blood would have been laughable. Back then, he had timidly and pathetically thrown up outside a bloody greasy spoon café just because he had needed to have a coffee with a damned middleman. But look at him now! Armed and dangerous, and focussed on the task at hand. He realised his prostate hadn't played him up for hours, not since the day before. Perhaps his whole body was adapting in line with his newfound conviction. Maybe this spark of self-confidence was improving him physically, as well as mentally. Dixon felt alive for the first time in years.

He checked himself in the full-length mirror in the hallway. He wanted to make sure that the gun was not visible through the pocket material; he didn't want Brian the hitman to gain any sort of advantage over him. Once satisfied, he pushed a bony hand through his hair and stared at his reflection, composing himself, readying himself.

So it had come to this, he told himself. Ten years of stealing. Ten years of skimming off the top. Ten years of shafting the nastiest little crook he had ever had the displeasure to meet. Ten years on, eight hundred thousand pounds later, Dixon had reached the point where he had a bag of money in his chimney, a gun in his pocket and the resolve to assassinate two human beings.

Things had not turned out quite as he thought they would, although it would be fair to say he hadn't given it much consideration until recently. If he had done, he was damned sure he wouldn't have considered this scenario as the likely outcome. But you play the cards you are dealt. And he was ready.

Dixon pressed his thumbprint to the alarm panel in the hall and the little white box beeped back. The red light on the top of the panel started flashing; the countdown had begun, in more ways than one. He made his way through the front door, securing the electronic lock behind him. He climbed into his car, started the engine and pulled out of the driveway, heading off towards his destiny.

CHAPTER SIXTEEN

It was approaching three o'clock in the afternoon and as usual, Brian had arrived for his meeting half an hour before the allotted time to check on security and conduct a little surveillance. For twenty minutes or so, he had carried out a reconnaissance of the immediate area around the corner of Colmore Row and Livery Street, which had been his chosen location for the rendezvous with the accountant. As ever, the setting was nice and public, with plenty of shoppers and office workers mulling around the precinct. Having completed his recce, he was satisfied that all was in order, and so he was happy for the meeting to go ahead as planned.

Brian's plan was simple. He would convince Dixon of his commitment to taking on the contract of killing Mike Nation. In doing so, by persuading Dixon that his offer was credible, he hoped to be able to raise the topic of the handgun at some point. He would emphasise how things, in his experience, tended to turn out badly when guns played a part, and so handing it over to him was a condition of Brian's acceptance of the job. He would suggest they go together to retrieve the weapon, hoping that it was at Dixon's house as it would mean he would have easy access to the premises. Once Dixon was unarmed, Brian could make a judgement as to whether to execute the accountant there and then.

A multi-storey car park was located on Livery Street, and Brian chose to position himself halfway up the access ramp to afford himself an excellent view of the junction of Colmore Row and Livery Street. Brian watched and waited, frequently checking on the time. At precisely three o'clock, he spotted the skinny rake of a man reaching the intersection and observed him checking the screen of his mobile phone. The accountant was wearing the same black trousers and shoes as he had at the previous meeting, but the jacket was a different shade of grey. Or was it blue? Brian couldn't be certain from his vantage point.

After a couple of minutes, Brian headed down the ramp and casually sauntered up the road to meet Dixon. The pair shook hands, and Brian noticed that the man's grip seemed a lot more confident than when the two had first met.

'Shall we take another stroll, Paul?' asked Brian.

'By all means.'

They turned and started down Livery Street, away from Colmore Row and back towards the multi-storey.

'So, as you may have guessed, Paul, I have been doing some thinking around the proposal you put to me, and I'm pleased to say I've decided to take on your job,' Brian lied.

'Well, that is excellent news, and quite a relief,' replied Dixon calmly. Inwardly, he wondered how much bullshit he was going to have to swallow before he got round to putting a bullet in the hitman.

'Good. Now then, I've been doing a bit of research into this Mike Nation bloke. I'd not come across him before, so I've been doing a little digging.'

Never heard of him? What a load of crap, thought Dixon.

'It seems he's got a head office in the Moseley area of Birmingham – is that right?'

'That's correct,' replied the man with the gun, choosing to play along for now.

'Good. So, the extra information I referred to in my text. What I need you to do is to tell me, in as much detail as you can, everything you know about Nation's movements and habits. Things like what time he arrives at his office, when he leaves the office, where he goes for lunch, that kind of thing. Can you do that for me?'

'Sure thing.'

'Excellent, so let's get into the specifics…'

The men continued the walk down Livery Street, deep in conversation.

A quarter of an hour earlier, Rosie had thanked the owner of the small metalworking business for his time and his workmanship. She had collected her leather pouch of knives together, placed them back into the bottom of her rucksack and set off towards town. She had settled on the route she would take for the walk back to The Balancing Act since there were a few options open to her. The chosen course took her across St Paul's Square to the south of the Jewellery Quarter, before going up Livery Street to Colmore Row and then on to Brindleyplace. She was enjoying being out and about, and the path she had picked was the prettiest she could think of. Rosie found that her spirits were lifting somewhat under the sun's rays. It was at moments like this, she told herself, that it was good to remember the world was not all badness and ruin out there.

Back at Livery Street, Brian was wrapping up his list of completely pointless questions that he had been posing to Dixon, all to fake a demonstration of allegiance to the man and his contract. Mission accomplished and it was time to broach the subject of the revolver.

'There is one other, small thing, Paul, that I feel we need to discuss.'

Dixon wanted to scream but just managed to keep it in. He, too, had spent the last ten minutes equally pointlessly listing what little he knew of Nation's movements, knowing full well that the hitman would have a much better idea of what Mike bloody Nation got up to from one day to the next. Far more than he ever would. The seemingly never-ending stream of nonsense was doing Dixon's head in, and he considered whether, when all was said and done, he might actually *enjoy* shooting this total charlatan.

'What small thing is that, Brian? Is it the payment? Because you know I'm good for it. I can get the money for you at any time.'

Brian hesitated while he considered Dixon's words. *Get the money at any time*, he had said. Brian had a flashback to the phone call he'd taken from Terry that morning. *I met him back in Kings Heath within the hour, by which time he'd got the cash.* That's what Tel had said. That confirmed it. Brian was sure the eight hundred grand must have been converted into cash, and assuming he was right, it was bound to be in his stronghold of a house. This could all be over in a matter of hours.

'Well, Paul, I tend not to worry about things like that. You see, people more often than not pay their dues to contract killers on account of the fact they're contract killers...' They both faked a chuckle. 'That said, it may be prudent to discuss the payment terms in a minute. And it would perhaps be beneficial for all if we concluded the handover of the money today. However, first of all, I wanted to discuss something else with you. I wanted to talk to you about the small matter of a gun. I understand you have purchased a snub-nosed revolver, and I admit that concerns me a little.'

Dixon froze. How did he know? Then the penny dropped: the middleman must've blabbed. Damn it, of course he would have spilled the beans. He should have assumed as much; that was careless. Oh well, it was now or never. The moment had arrived. Come on Paul, time to get this show on the road.

Dixon wanted to make sure there was sufficient distance between himself and the hitman to ensure Brian couldn't react and grab at the gun, so he edged backwards by just a couple of small steps to get out of range. He checked that no one was about to walk past them on the pavement, and having given himself the all-clear, he slowly reached into his jacket pocket and calmly, deliberately pulled out the revolver and pointed it directly at Brian's chest. He kept the revolver tight to his body to keep it hidden from public view as best he could.

'Woah there, fella!' exclaimed Brian, with genuine surprise in his voice. He knew that Dixon had *bought* a gun, but why the hell had he *brought* it to a rendezvous with a hitman? Was Dixon suicidal after all, he wondered?

'What's going on here, Paul? What are you up to?'

Dixon didn't reply.

'Put the damned gun down, Paul! Are you mad? You know what I do for a living; you know who I am!'

'Oh, I know who you are, alright. You're a lying piece of shit,' Dixon stated in a hardened, monotonous voice.

'I'm sorry?' said Brian, still absolutely stunned to be in this situation.

'I said you're a lying piece of shit!' repeated Dixon, this time in a louder, more agitated tone.

Brian was utterly confused. They had just spent the last quarter of an hour discussing how he was going to kill someone on Dixon's behalf. Brian was the good guy here! Why the hell had the accountant pulled the gun?

The pair found themselves standing at the entrance to a stairwell which led up to the various floors of the adjacent multi-storey car park. Dixon knew they had to get out of sight, and fast.

'Get up those stairs,' Dixon said, waving the gun in the direction of the stairwell.

'Look, let's just talk about this,' Brian appealed, starting to feel some genuine concern.

'*Get up the fucking stairs!*' Dixon hissed.

Rosie was strolling purposefully up Livery Street on her way back to the restaurant, her rucksack bouncing across her shoulder blades as she went. Her rejuvenated mood had prompted a couple of new menu ideas in her mind, and she was excited to try a couple of things out when she got back to base.

She glanced up the hill and was delighted to spot Brian standing on the other side of the road, next to the car park. What a wonderful surprise, she thought. Perhaps this could turn out to be a very good day after all. She began waving and was about to call out Brian's name when she realised that he was in mid-conversation with another man whom Rosie did not recognise. The discussion seemed to be very intense, and it looked as though the skinny bloke was shouting something at Brian.

As she made her way up the road, the creepy other man came more into view. His stance seemed peculiar, holding one arm tight against his body. She looked more closely, and to her absolute horror, she realised that he was holding a gun to Brian and he seemed intent on using it.

Brian turned towards the entranceway as instructed, and Dixon prodded the barrel of his revolver into the hitman's spine, indicating that he should climb the stairs into the car park. Brian complied, and he stretched out his arms in the surrender position as he ascended the muggy stairwell. He had well and truly lost control of the situation. He wished that he had brought Sammy along as backup, lurking nearby somewhere in the shadows, ready to intervene. But how was he to know the meeting would go so pear-shaped?

Dixon had already decided that they were heading for the penultimate deck of the multi-storey. He knew the top floor had no roof, so if they climbed to the highest level of the car park, all the office workers in the surrounding tower blocks would have a clear view of the two of them. The floor below, however, would be completely obscured from the surrounding offices while still benefitting from being one of the quieter, uppermost levels. Dixon didn't want to be disturbed while he was taking the hitman's life.

Rosie's fleeting cheerfulness changed to dread as she watched the man with the gun force Brian into the car park. He was in deep trouble, that much was as clear as day. She knew she had to help, but how? Should she call the police? Possibly, but what if Brian was engaged in something less than legitimate, something that the police should not find out about? That was a distinct possibility, given the nature of Brian's work. And anyway, it didn't seem as if time was on her side.

On the other side of the road, Brian and the gunman had disappeared into the stairwell. Rosie desperately looked up and down the pavement in the hope someone else had seen the altercation, but the people passing by all had their faces buried in their mobile phone screens. No one was reacting to the events across the street. It seemed there was nothing else for it: Rosie had to follow them into the stairwell.

The two men had reached the next-to-last floor of the structure, and as Dixon had surmised, there were very few cars parked on the higher levels of the multi-storey. They were all alone. Dixon instructed Brian to walk to the far end of the car park then turn and face him. Brian cooperated while his mind churned over and over, desperately trying to come up with a plan. He couldn't think of anything.

Dixon cleared his throat. It was time. Time for the great reveal.

'I know who you are,' he started. 'I know you work for Mike Nation. And I know that he has hired you to kill me.'

Brian was stunned. How the hell had Dixon found that out? What the hell was going on? How could he possibly have learned that? Had Nation *told* Dixon about the hit? Surely not! Why on earth would he do that? But the only people in the whole world who knew about the arrangement were Nation, Sammy and Brian himself. And he was certain Sammy would never be loose-lipped about such matters. It meant the leak had to be all Nation's.

'You're trying to work out how I know, aren't you?' continued Dixon, relishing the moment.

'I really don't know what you're on about,' replied Brian, opting to go for the very last strategy in the playbook, the play dumb approach.

'Oh, but I'm afraid you do, Brian. You see, the moron that is Mike Nation scrawled the outline of the entire plot across a single sheet of paper. My name. Your name. And how I was going to disappear. And the idiot *posted the thing to me*! The fool might've just as well drawn me a bloody map. Unfortunately for you, the note arrived before you had time to carry out your instructions. Quite obviously, when I learned the truth, I realised I needed to take matters into my own hands.'

'No, look, wait, I can explain,' Brian pleaded, but to no avail.

'The time for explanations has long since passed, I'm afraid, Brian. It's time to say goodbye.'

Paul cocked the hammer of the revolver, rested a finger lightly on the trigger and pointed the gun at Brian's head. He realised he had never in his life fired a gun, but he'd seen it done enough times on TV. Point and shoot. Nothing to it.

Moments earlier, Rosie had reached the same level of the multi-storey and had quietly positioned herself about a dozen yards away, tucked down behind a parked car. She had heard the last part of the conversation in its entirety, and so she knew she had to act. She was out of time and out of options, but she knew she had to do something to try to save Brian. Carefully, she slipped the rucksack from her shoulder and reached in for the leather wrap. In one move, she deftly unravelled the knife case and unholstered the cleaver. The beautiful, shiny, perfectly manufactured cleaver that had, only half an hour earlier, been professionally sharpened and meticulously polished.

Silently, she got up from behind the car and took two soundless steps towards the men a few feet away. She planted her feet, just as she had done all those years ago when she'd practised her knife throwing at the side of her parents' caravan. She calmed her breathing, slowed her heartbeat. She was back at the circus now, back at the big top. Practice after practice, throw after throw. It was innate, in-built, automatic. She took her old, familiar frisbee-throwing backhand stance, withdrew her arm, bent her knees, and turned the knife blade in her hand. She aimed. And she threw. Hard.

Just as he was about to pull the trigger to end the hitman's life, Dixon thought he spotted a gleaming shard of light out of the corner of his eye. Momentarily he was distracted and he glanced, ever so briefly, to his side to see what it was. What he saw was a pristine, shiny cleaver hurtling through the air towards its target.

The cleaver flew straight and true, and it passed right through Dixon's neck without even slowing down. The force of the impact caused the accountant's head to completely detach from his body, and it launched skyward like a rocket, somersaulting through the air. Dixon's last-ever vision was of his own torso, and the parked cars, and the car park floor, all incomprehensibly appearing above his eyeline as his cranium spun up and around in an arc, before reaching its peak and then plummeting back towards the ground. The head plonked onto the bonnet of a Nissan Micra with a tinny bang and then skipped forwards onto the floor.

Blood started pumping from the top of the torso, which was still standing erect, motionless and headless, with hand outstretched and the gun still pointing in Brian's direction. The crimson liquid seeped down Dixon's neck and onto his favourite jacket, staining the material a dirty russet brown. It seemed the sun was finally setting on the hippopotamus, and Dixon would have been horrified, had he been alive to see it.

Finally, after what seemed like an eternity, the upright body subsided and it toppled backwards, slumping onto the car park surface with a thud.

CHAPTER SEVENTEEN

Sammy was out and about running errands. She was planning to hook up with Aleksandr later on in the day, and she was looking forward to it. He wasn't working that afternoon, so the couple had decided to catch a film at the cinema, followed by drinks. Sammy fancied cocktails at The Phoney Negroni in Moseley and was going to suggest the idea when they met up. She was thinking she might even squeeze in a quick haircut beforehand if she had time. Sammy wasn't one for booking hair appointments months in advance and lounging in a salon for hours on end, but a quick cut and dry wouldn't go amiss. It made sense to make a bit of an effort because, last night's daft argument aside, things seemed to be going rather well with Aleksandr. And that was no bad thing. And anyway, putting aside the disagreement, the make-up sex was superb. She grinned broadly at the memory. They should row more often…

At that moment, her mobile phone rang.

'Bit busy, Bri…'

'It's important, Sammy. Where are you?'

'Eh…?'

'Where *are* you?'

'Poundland.'

'What?' said Brian, confused.

'I'm in Poundland. You asked where I was, it being so important and all. Well, that's where I am. Just picking up some women's bits, if you really must know. Is that important too?'

'No, look, where are you geographically, I mean?'

Sammy groaned like a teenager. 'Kings Heath, Bri. Why?'

'Are you in the van?'

'What?' It was Sammy's turn to be confused.

Brian sighed. 'Damn it, Sammy, are you in the van? Yes or no?'

'That rusty old banger? No chance. Why would I be in that bloody thing?'

'Look, I need you to get to the lock-up, pick up the van and meet me in town. As soon as you can. It's urgent.'

'You're joking, right?'

'Why would I be joking?' Brian really didn't have time for this.

'You want me to come into town? In the van?'

'Bloody hell, yes! Right now, Sammy!'

'No chance…'

'Why the hell not?'

'Clean air zone charge, Bri. I'm not going to go and get that shit bucket and drive it all the way into town, just to give the shitty city council eight bloody quid clean air zone tax. I told you we should've got a newer van, but oh no, you had to buy it on the cheap off Mike bloody Nation, didn't you? Bollocks to that. I'll cycle in; it'll be just as quick, anyway. Be there in thirty minutes.'

'No, no, wait...'

Sammy had hung up. Brian swore under his breath. He needed urgent assistance, but he tried to stay calm and hit the re-dial button.

'Look, I'm on my bloody way, Brian,' Sammy complained.

'*Sammy!* Listen to me very carefully.' His voice accentuated the importance of the message. 'Please, do not speak. Just listen. I'm in the multi-storey car park on Livery Street. I'm here with a dead man. A corpse. Decapitated, as it happens. His head is currently residing in the bottom of a rucksack I've borrowed. Meanwhile, I've stuffed the rest of him under a Kia Sportage. The owner of the car could come back at any time, and if they do, they will regrettably get a rather morbid surprise when they reverse out of the parking space on their way home to cook little Harry some tea. We're a bit buggered, Sammy, and we need some extraction transport for the corpse – both bits – right now. Please get the bloody van and get here ASAP. Oh, and bring gloves. Now, do you understand?'

'Christ almighty, what the hell have you done? Ok, on it, Bri. I'll be there as soon as I can. Oh, erm Brian, you said '*we're* a bit buggered... Is there someone else with you?'

'Just get here Sammy.'

Brian hung up and, having done all he could do for the time being, he returned to Rosie.

Moments before the call, Brian had delicately helped Rosie over to the corner of the car park and had gingerly sat her down on the floor. She had looked petrified, and he thought she was probably in shock.

Moments before that, Brian had run to Rosie, grabbed her, buried her head in his chest and told her not to look at the carnage surrounding them. They hadn't moved for a full two minutes until Brian eventually let her go and walked her to the secluded corner of the building.

And moments before that, just before Brian had gone to Rosie, held her tight and hadn't wanted to let go, Brian had noticed that Dixon's skinny little head, having just that second bounced off the bonnet of the Nissan, was trundling towards the edge of the car park. The perimeter barrier wall had large openings at regular intervals at its base, and the head was going towards one such gap. It was about to roll off the edge and plop down onto the pavement below.

Brian had reacted in a heartbeat and made a full-length dive just as the head toppled over the edge. He thrust out a hand and at the very last moment clasped a few strands of hair on the top of Dixon's head. For a moment or two the head just dangled there, swaying in the wind, before Brian managed to carefully haul it back up. He buried it deep in the bottom of Rosie's rucksack, then shoved the body out of sight, before turning his attention to the stunned, motionless woman in front of him.

Now, with the head in the bag, the body under the Sportage and Sammy on the way, all that mattered was Rosie. Brian sat next to her and put his arm around her. They sat in silence.

Brian couldn't think of anything worth saying. Finally, he turned to look directly into Rosie's emerald green eyes. 'You saved my life,' he said quietly.

'I'd… I'd just got them sharpened…' she stammered.

'Well, they're certainly bloody sharp,' confirmed Brian.

'I don't think I'll ever forget that image for as long as I live,' Rosie said with tears in her eyes. 'My God, I've killed a man. Brian, I've killed a man! What have I done? Oh my God, what am I going to do?'

'You're not going to do anything, Rosie. I'm going to take care of everything. None of this will ever come back to you. That, I promise you. I will sort it all out. Everything is going to be fine.'

Brian kept looking up from their position, checking for shoppers who might be returning to their cars. So far, they had been lucky. They were still alone on that level of the car park.

'But… But I've killed him! The police? What are they going to say? I mean, he's been, he's been, I mean I've, I've *beheaded him, Brian!*' Rosie was moving from shock to hysteria.

'Rosie, please try to stay calm. The police are not going to be involved. They will never find out. The head and the body will just disappear. I promise.'

'I don't understand. There will have to be an investigation. I need to be punished. I mean, his family! His family, Brian! They'll have to know. They'll want to know where he is.'

'It's ok. It's all ok. He didn't have a family, Rosie. There's no family to inform. Please listen, you don't need to worry.'

Rosie paused for a moment, then turned to look directly into Brian's eyes. 'And how would you know that?' Despite her emotional plight, she recognised that his last comment was an odd thing for him to say. She worked out that Brian must have known the dead man. Of course they knew each other; she recalled the two of them having an argument on the pavement. And then, in a rush, the memory of the revolver came flooding back to her. '*And why was he aiming a bloody gun at you in the first place, Brian? Who the hell is he to you?*' she demanded.

Brian gently took Rosie's hands in his own and resolved to tell her as much of the truth as he dared. 'He was a very nasty man, Rosie, and you don't need to feel any guilt or pain over what has happened. Not in the slightest. The man worked for Mike Nation. He'd been doing so for years. But it wasn't just any old role he played inside Nation's grubby empire. He was the money launderer. He was the one that washed all that cash, through all those businesses, and earned Nation his nasty little cut from the process. He cleaned all that money for Mike's underworld contacts, and he did so by using and abusing so many decent, independent businesses throughout the city. Including yours, Rosie. That man was a major part of all the pain you have been experiencing these last few months. Frankly, if anything, you should be glad he's dead.'

There was silence as Rosie absorbed all the information. Brian continued. 'I didn't know it at the time, but he had come here to kill me today, Rosie. He had ripped Nation off and he had backed himself into a corner. He was here to kill me, and you saved my life.'

Rosie remained mute, listening intently, so Brian went on. 'I will never be able to thank you. Not properly. But I promise you two things, Rosie. First, you will never, ever, ever have to take the blame for what happened here. That will never happen. And second, I owe you my life, so I am going to do everything in my power to get your life back for you. I am going to get you out from under Nation's control. I don't know how yet, but I will find a way.'

The two looked at each other in silence; then Rosie buried her head into the gruff old man's chest once again and allowed herself a little moment of emotion.

The stillness of the car park was shattered by the sound of squealing tyres and a heavy-revving engine reverberating across the building. Brian leapt to his feet and checked that the body of Paul Dixon was still suitably camouflaged by the chassis of the car. Once satisfied, he took guard as the vehicle approached. It rounded the bend of the ramp and appeared at high speed from the other end of the car park. It was Sammy in the van. Thank Christ, Brian thought. He ran to the middle of the car park waving at the vehicle. Sammy spotted him and flashed the headlights twice. Brian pointed to the far corner of the car park, directing her to her destination as if he were an airport worker on the apron.

Sammy reached the rear of the car park, slammed on the brakes, pulled the handbrake with a yank and jumped out of the driver's seat. She ran round to the back of the van and flung the rear doors open wide.

'Hi, Bri,' she called out then spotted Rosie in the shadows, sitting on the floor with her arms hugging her knees. 'Oh, erm, hi Rosie,' she added and gave Brian a very confused look.

'Rosie isn't here, Sammy, ok?'

'Gotcha, Bri. No problems. Right, so where are we?'

'He's under that one… And in that one…' said Brian, pointing simultaneously to the black Kia Sportage and the blue rucksack. Brian joined Sammy at the car and stooped down by its side.

'Gloves,' he called to Sammy, and she threw him his pair, then put her own on. When Brian had done the same, he reached underneath the car and grabbed a good fistful of the bloodstained jacket. He yanked hard and freed the body of the accountant from its hiding place.

'Christ alive!' exclaimed Sammy, seeing the headless corpse for the first time.

'Feet,' said Brian, pointing to Dixon's legs and continuing with his urgent, single-word instructions.

Brian linked his arms under the dead man's shoulders, heaving the corpse off the floor. Sammy did as she was instructed, grabbed Dixon around the ankles and lifted. Between them, they quickly carried the body over to the rear of the van and thrust it through the back doors. Brian ran over to where the rucksack lay on the floor and threw it into the van's rear compartment in one motion. Sammy slammed the doors shut and locked them.

They took a breath, hands on knees, panting heavily. Brian noticed that there was a small pool of blood seeping from the underside of the Sportage where the torso had pumped out its final heartbeats. 'Got any water in the cab?' he enquired.

'Yep,' replied Sammy. She opened the passenger side door, reached inside and grabbed some water from the centre console bottle holder. She lobbed the bottle over to Brian, who undid the screw cap and proceeded to squirt the clear liquid around the pooling blood, diluting and dispersing the red gooey puddle as he did so.

Brian and Sammy stared at each other for a moment. 'Sammy, I owe you one,' Brian said finally.

'Bloody hell, Bri, a bit more than *one*, I think, mate!'

'Yeh, I guess you're right there,' he replied with a grimace. 'OK, listen, here's what I want you to do.' Then he lowered his voice, conscious that Rosie was still nearby. 'The headless corpse in the van is our friend the accountant. Now, we both know precisely where Dixon is going to end up being buried. But that is most definitely a nighttime job. So, I need you to take the van back to the lock-up and secure it there for now. For God's sake, stick to the speed limit; you do *not* want to be pulled over on this little journey.'

'No, I do not.'

'I need to take Rosie home. I need to make sure she's alright, so I need to leave the journey back to the lock-up with you. Is that ok?'

Sammy glanced at Rosie, who looked pale and unblinking as if she was stuck in a trance. She hadn't moved an inch while the two had conducted their militarily precise operation.

Sammy nodded her agreement and began to speak but was interrupted.

'No questions, Sammy, please. I'll explain it all later. I'll take Rosie home. I'll meet you at the lock-up at nightfall. We'll take Dixon over to the station shortly thereafter and get him into his box. Ok?'

Sammy nodded again, realising that a date night with Aleksandr was well and truly out of the window now. She'd have to make something up as an excuse. 'Yeh, I guess so, Brian.'

'Thanks,' said Brian, and offered her an indebted smile, tapping the side of the van to send it on its way.

Sammy was halfway to the driver's door when Brian had a flash of inspiration. 'Hang on a moment,' he called after her. She popped her head round the side of the van again.

'What's up, Bri?'

'Have you got a bag, Sammy?'

'Eh?'

'A bag. Do you have one?'

'Well, I've got a Sainsbury's carrier. Will that do?'

'That's fine. Chuck it over here, would you? And unlock the back doors again for a second.'

She did as Brian had requested. Brian ran back over to Rosie's location and reached down to scoop up the leather knife case. He quickly opened it up and took out the cleaver that he had retrieved, cleaned and replaced while they were waiting for the van.

'Back in a minute,' he said to Rosie reassuringly and jogged back over to the rear of the vehicle. He checked the coast was clear before re-opening the doors.

'What's going on, Bri?' asked Sammy, but in the absence of a response, she just watched her partner at work.

Brian jumped into the back of the van and grabbed one of Dixon's arms. He laid it flat on the floor of the van and worked his way down to the hand. Slowly, he separated out all the fingers of the hand, carefully spreading them as wide as he could. When he was ready, and with one swift, clinical swing, Brian chopped off Dixon's thumb.

PART TWO

CHAPTER EIGHTEEN

Sir Johnny Weaver, legendary actor of stage and screen, was in an exceptionally good mood. He was slurping a Darjeeling tea and munching on a bourbon biscuit, but between bites he couldn't help but wear a smile that beamed from ear to rosy-red ear. He was at his large Victorian home in Sutton Coldfield to the north of Birmingham, and he was in the airy and spacious coach house situated across from the main dwelling, on the other side of his long gravel driveway.

Over the preceding decades, Sir Johnny had converted the coach house into a giant playroom, the centrepiece of which was a gigantic model train set crammed full of tunnels, bridges, trees, houses and little model people. The tiny, landscaped details were flawless, and the imitation locomotives, passenger carriages and freight wagons spun round the railway track in perfect choreography. Sir Johnny was busy driving his *Mallard* locomotive around the main loop, his engineer's hat balanced precariously on his head.

Sir Johnny had been with his little steam engines for about an hour, and as always, he was enjoying the thrill of controlling the trains down the tracks, pausing at danger signals and speeding into little train stations. It generated a childish exhilaration within him.

But despite the fun, he found that his mind kept wandering back to the telephone conversation he had enjoyed a couple of hours earlier, a call that he had made to his good chum and three-time Oscar winner, Dame Flora Trent. The two friends had first met on set in 1974 while they were filming the Hollywood classic *Slow Train to St Louis,* and they had remained very close ever since.

The reason Sir Johnny had made the call was that he had received two pieces of very exciting news, news that was so thrilling he had almost burst with joy. He had been eager to share the gossip with his dear pal, so he had spent most of the evening on the call, excitedly passing on all his stories.

The first piece of important news was local in nature. He was delighted to report that with great fanfare and huge acclaim, a Taco Bell had opened up just down the road from him, in the centre of town. It was easily within walking distance, and he was very much looking forward to giving it a try. Dame Flora hadn't known what a Taco Bell was, so Sir Johnny had explained that it was a bit like a McDonald's, but for Mexicans. Dame Flora had pointed out that Sir Johnny was neither a Mexican nor in Mexico, and she wondered whether there was a big enough population of Central American expatriates in Sutton Coldfield to support the opening. But she had gone on to say that she was delighted for him, nonetheless. She had certainly sounded delighted, but you could never really be sure with Dame Flora; she was such an excellent actor.

But secondly, and much more important than the Taco Bell announcement, was that Sir Johnny had received wonderful personal news. He had been given a formal invitation, that very morning, to the grand opening ceremony of a brand new railway line in his beloved home city of Birmingham. Sir Johnny was to be the guest of honour, and as such, he would both 'cut the ribbon' at the platform's edge and then ride on the footplate of a real steam engine as it made the inaugural journey from the suburbs into the city.

'On the footplate!' Dame Flora had exclaimed with excitement. 'Just like in *Slow Train to St Louis!*'

'Exactly like it!' Sir Johnny had replied happily. Dame Flora was *definitely* pleased at this piece of news; there could be no doubt about it. He could hear it in her voice, and nobody was *that* good an actor, he thought.

They had laughed together and reminisced about their time in California, working on the film shoot for the movie in which they had both played starring roles. They recalled the time they flew up to Carmel with Roger Moore and dear old Patrick, the love of Sir Johnny's life, at the end of filming. The four of them, drinking champagne and eating shrimp in a little restaurant overlooking the Pacific, without a care in the world... Such a tragedy Patrick had been taken from Sir Johnny in the '80s, all because of that dreadful virus. Sir Johnny had been in relationships since then, of course; he was, after all, an outrageous flirt. But he had never properly loved again.

'Patrick would have just *adored* seeing you riding on the footplate, dear! Make sure you wear your engineer's hat!' Dame Flora had said.

'He most certainly would have, old girl! But I think, rather than wearing the engineer's hat, I'll wear the full cowboy outfit from *Slow Train*, just for old times' sake. What do you think? That would get the crowds talking! I still have it, you see, and can you believe it, I can still get the bloody thing on! Yes, that's settled: we'll revisit *Slow Train* one last time!'

Dame Flora had thought the cowboy outfit was a wonderful idea. The friends promised to make arrangements to meet up soon and then said their goodbyes. After the call, Sir Johnny had grabbed the very same engineer's hat his friend had mentioned, plopped it onto his head and made his way outside and across the driveway to the coach house with a spring in his step.

Sir Johnny Weaver was a bit of an acting icon. Famed for his Hollywood films and his West End shows, he was considered a local treasure. He was getting on a bit now, but he carried his eighty years with vigour. He was recognised as a jewel in the British acting industry crown, particularly having moved, as he had done in his later years, towards playing characters with a mischievous nature to their charm.

He had shot to fame in the early 1970s in the ITV drama *Stone Dead*, in which he played lead character DCI Lee Stone. Working the mean streets of London, Stone had to solve a different murder each week, including, infamously, in one Christmas special, the savage death of one of the Queen's corgis. It turned out the butler really did do it.

He had been rather dashing in his youth and had famously been considered for the role of Bond when Roger Moore got it. Sir Johnny – just Johnny then – had ultimately been considered too young for the part at the time. He was again considered for the role when Moore retired, but by then he was viewed as too old. 'Such is life, old boy,' he would explain with a wry chuckle to those interested in the unfortunate episode.

His good friend Moore would tell him the part was never for him anyway. 'Bond would never say, "Yam got a loissunce tow kill," old bean,' Sir Rog would often remark with a grin, playing up to Johnny's West Midlands roots. Sir Johnny would tell him until he was blue in the face that that was a Black Country accent; meanwhile, he was a born and bred Brummie. But it made no difference, and it didn't matter, anyway; they both had always enjoyed telling the tale.

It would be true to say that pretty much everyone loved Sir Johnny. But what Sir Johnny loved the most was trains. He had quite literally spent thousands of pounds and invested thousands of hours constructing his model train set, and it was now his pride and joy. He spent as much time in that coach house as his busy schedule would allow.

His love affair with rail could be traced back to that first Hollywood hit, *Slow Train to St Louis,* in which he had played a train engineer on the footplate of a steam locomotive running between the Missouri city of St Louis and the frontier towns of the American Wild West. He had loved being in the movie, of course, but even more, he had fallen in love with the steam engine that was such an integral part of the story. Ever since that moment, he had been hooked and had become quite the famous fan of all things trains. Sir Johnny had no idea how the apparatus actually worked, of course, and he had no real desire to learn, either. The technology wasn't what fascinated him. To Sir Johnny, it was all about the way they looked and the way they sounded, the noises and smells of the engines, and the sheer grandness and scale of those massive locomotives. His well-known love for steam engines meant that the honour being bestowed upon him by his home town had touched him immensely, and he was extremely enthusiastic about his big day out.

It was getting late, and it was growing dark outside. Sir Johnny heard his tummy rumbling and he realised that he had skipped supper. The packet of bourbon biscuits was empty, and he decided that he had better grab something more meaningful before bedtime.

He very deliberately slowed down all his moving locomotives and then switched the points on the trackside. One by one, he guided the trains into their stabling shed and parked them up until they were all safely secured. He powered down the track and took off his engineer's hat, hanging it on a peg behind him. From the adjacent hanger, he recovered his tweed jacket and slid it on before heading back to the main house.

Once back inside, he fixed himself a sandwich and settled into an armchair in the drawing room. To his side was an occasional table, and on the table was the formal invitation. He picked it up and read it once again, probably for the hundredth time that day. Sir Johnny smiled, closed his eyes and dozed off, dreaming of driving his grand locomotive across the old Wild West.

CHAPTER NINETEEN

Shock affects different people in different ways, although it is true to say there are some symptoms, both psychological and physiological, that are more common than others. Emotionally, the sensation of numbness and feeling detached from one's environment are two such symptoms. Victims of shock tend to become unresponsive; they won't engage in conversation and become withdrawn and distant. But there are very real physical effects too. Blood pressure drops, heart rate rises, and sufferers tend to feel extremely lightheaded and often seriously nauseous.

As long as the shock is not acute, those latter physical symptoms can be treated pretty effectively, and that was precisely what Brian was busy attending to, having finally managed to get Rosie away from the car park and back to the sanctuary of her home. The more psychological effects, on the other hand, would be a different matter altogether, as Brian knew only too well.

On the remote level of the multi-storey deck, Brian had managed to glean from Rosie the location of her house and had subsequently succeeded in escorting her to his car as quickly as possible. He had at first considered leaving Rosie momentarily in order to retrieve his vehicle and then returning to pick her up; that would certainly have been the quickest way of getting Rosie home, after all. However, he had immediately realised that it would be unwise to leave Rosie alone for even one second, and so he had, instead, stayed by her side and calmly steered her to his car.

When they finally arrived outside her house, Brian located Rosie's keys, unlocked the door and ushered her inside. Together they headed for the sitting room where Rosie settled down on the sofa while Brian tracked down a blanket to help make her more comfortable. She was still feeling traumatised and faint, so she lay down along the full length of the sofa, and Brian raised her feet, propping some cushions underneath her legs to help get the blood flowing back to her vital organs.

The warmth of the blanket, the effects of the raised legs and the comfort of a sugary cup of tea slowly had the desired impact on all those physical symptoms, and Brian was glad to see colour returning to the woman's cheeks. Quite what the psychological consequences of the day's events would be, and how profound an effect they would have on Rosie's wellbeing, only time would tell.

After a while, Rosie was feeling well enough to sit up and talk. Absurdly enough, she had initially wanted to set off to work because she was, after all, supposed to be in The Balancing Act for the evening sitting. Instead, Brian had persuaded her to contact Aleksandr for help. She eventually sent him a text telling him that she had come down with some sort of bug and that she couldn't make it to the restaurant that evening.

She asked whether he would cover for her. Aleksandr, who was supposedly going on a cinema date with Sammy later that evening, was nonetheless concerned enough to confirm that he would, of course, help out. Aleksandr had then phoned Sammy, apologising profusely for having to cancel their date night, saying that Rosie needed his help and he just had to go to work. Sammy had been remarkably understanding, which was a great relief to Aleksandr. In truth, Sammy was just thankful not to have to come up with a reason for cancelling the night herself. She was, of course, going to be otherwise engaged as well, busy burying a decapitated corpse under a suburban train station. As one does.

Brian and Rosie talked the afternoon away. Rosie asked question after question, and Brian told her everything he knew about the man who was Paul Dixon, everything he had learned from that very first meeting with the accountant back on Hill Street. Was it really only yesterday that Brian had first met Dixon? It felt a world away.

Brian figured that the more "evil" he could make Dixon sound, the more relieved Rosie would be of her feelings of guilt. He chronicled, in as much detail as he could, the many small, independent businesses that Dixon had damaged at the behest of Mike Nation. He recounted examples of the dodgy deals Nation and Dixon had put together over the course of a decade working together, and of all the money they had extorted on the way to making Nation his big pile of dirty money. Brian described the complete apathy with which Dixon seemed to conduct these murky acts, painting him very much as the villain of the piece while he did so. He presented Dixon as a callous man who had most likely been spending the previous day planning Brian's murder. He was a man who had coldly succeeded in tracking down a gun dealer of dubious repute in order to buy a gun and use it on Brian. All of that, Brian proposed to Rosie, added up to just one logical conclusion: the man simply got his comeuppance.

He assured Rosie that there was no need for any sorrow, no need for any remorse. And most of all, he guaranteed her that there was absolutely, resolutely, unquestionably no way anyone would ever find out what had happened in that car park. He told her it would be best to imagine that it had never happened at all. It was just a nightmare, a figment of their wild imaginations, a pure invention. A vivid one to be sure, but nothing more than that.

It seemed as though the effects of the trauma were lessening with each passing minute. Rosie was mending, Brian was sure of it. He recognised there were likely to be longer-lasting consequences, of course, and how they would manifest themselves was impossible to tell. But those first few hours were crucial for stabilising Rosie, so Brian made sure he stayed as long as was needed. As they talked the evening away, the bond between the two of them grew ever stronger.

It was almost dusk when Brian finally left Rosie's side. She had fallen asleep on the sofa, so Brian quietly let himself out, having left a note next to her telling her to call him at any time of the night or day should she need him. He also mentioned in passing that he had borrowed a thermos flask from the kitchen and would return it as soon as possible; he hoped that would be alright.

He'd stayed much longer than he had intended to. There was an important errand he had wanted to run before meeting up with Sammy at the lock-up. But there was no time for that now, so it would have to wait until morning. No matter, staying at Rosie's side was the right thing to do, and anyway, the thermos had bought him more time.

Outside, he quickly shot a text over to Sammy.

En route to the lock-up. Fifteen minutes out.

He jumped into the car, fired up the engine and speedily pulled out into the road.

CHAPTER TWENTY

A quarter of an hour later, Brian pulled up outside the rented lock-up situated on a small industrial estate to the south of the city. The sun had just set, and the humid summer night was rapidly drawing in. He was pleased to see Sammy already at the meeting point. She was leaning on a nearby wall playing with her mobile phone, having padlocked her bike to the lamppost a few feet away. She looked up from the screen and wandered over to the open driver's side window.

'Alright, Bri. Is Rosie ok?'

'I think so. Difficult to tell, but she's a bloody strong woman. I think she'll be fine.'

'Good, glad to hear it. Now, more importantly, *what the absolute fuck*, Bri? Decapitation? What the hell were you playing at? Please, do tell me, when precisely did 'beheading a mark, in front of your girlfriend, in a public car park, in the middle of the day' become a sensible, go-to strategy? I mean what the hell were you thinking? And what about the bloody money? How the hell are we going to find it now?'

Brian realised that, of course, Sammy had jumped to the conclusion that *he* had done the killing himself. A perfectly logical assumption to make; after all, he was being paid to kill the guy in the first place. This was good. He decided the best course of action was to play along with the ruse.

'Well, quite obviously, I hadn't planned it like that Sammy. Christ!'

'So what happened then, for Christ's sake?'

'It's complicated.'

'Well, *un*-complicate it then!'

Brian thought for a moment. 'Ok look, I'll tell you the story once, then we move on, ok?'

She nodded.

'Good. So what happened was this. I just happened to bump into Rosie while I was in town. Sod's law, Dixon ambushed me while I was with her. You see, he'd found out about the hit. He was onto me, and he had bought a bloody gun, Sammy. I was in a bit of a tight spot all told. Fortunately, Rosie had her kitchen knives on her. I managed to knock the gun from Dixon's hand and while he made to go after it, I went for the knives. I won the race, thank God, but I didn't realise quite how sharp the blades were. I went for his neck and the next thing I knew, his stupid, scraggly head fell off. I had to stuff it in Rosie's rucksack. Obviously all very distressing for her. Anyway, there we are. The full story of the rather eventful death of Paul bloody Dixon. Now, can we move on?'

Sammy studied her partner seated in the car and considered his story. It sounded plausible, just about. Bit bloody unlikely though. 'How did he know about the hit?'

'It was Nation. He dropped the ball, the idiot. He accidentally let the cat out of the bag. Now, *no* further questions, all right?'

She thought for a moment. She knew Brian too well by now; he was definitely leaving something out. But she realised there was no point in pushing the topic right then. There were jobs to do, bodies to bury and all that. She would return to the discussion at a later date.

'Right-oh,' she said finally and changed the subject. 'Let's get on with it, then. How do you want to play this, Bri? Are we both going in the van?'

'No, you take the van, and I'll follow you over there in the car. If you stick your bike in the back now, then when we're done, we can both just get back to the flat from there. I need an early night; got to get up early in the morning and get something done. That ok?'

'Whatever you say, partner,' said Sammy as she unlocked and then opened the roller door of the lock-up, revealing the dirty old white van inside. 'But if this shitty cart horse breaks down on me on the way to the station, you were driving it, got it? I'm telling you, Nation stitched you up selling you this piece of garbage.'

'No problem, understood,' Brian replied with a smile.

Sammy wheeled her bike over to the van and opened the rear doors. Immediately, she bent double, gagging for breath. 'Jesus Christ, he's been cooking in here all day. The guy stinks like a sewer! No wonder you want me to drive, you bell end!'

Sammy composed herself, then chucked her bike in the back, jumped into the driver's seat and reversed the van onto the estate. Brian pulled in behind her and the pair set off in convoy, making the short distance to Moseley Station.

The two kept rigidly to the speed limit, and the journey passed without incident. A few minutes later, Sammy flicked the indicator lever and turned the van onto the slip road in front of the station where she was confronted by a pair of locked gates a few metres ahead. She pulled up to one side of the slip road, allowing Brian to park alongside her. He hopped out of the car and walked round to the boot to retrieve his lock-picking kit, stuffing it in his jacket pocket and then joining Sammy at the locked gates. He leaned down and studied the entrance.

'Three bloody padlocks? Seems a bit overkill, doesn't it?'

'Yeh. Dogging,' said Sammy.

'I beg your pardon?'

'Alex's brother Tomasz, you know, the one who works here? He told me they had a dogging problem. Had to beef up security. Strengthened the perimeter fencing, improved the locks, that sort of thing. Put them back a day or so.'

'Charming,' said Brian.

'Yep. Seems, the good people of Moseley are not averse to watching some naughty business in a station car park. So, there you go.'

'How very bohemian of them.'

'Very,' agreed Sammy.

Brian opened up the lock-picking equipment and set to work on the padlocks while Sammy kept watch. Her attention was drawn to the massive sign above the portacabin.

'Bri, that slogan… *We build more than for any other reason…*'

'No idea, Sammy. No idea at all…'

'Well, it's a good job Mike isn't on the city tourist board, that's all I can say. Imagine it. *Birmingham. More canals than for any other reason!*'

'Very catchy.'

It took just a matter of minutes for Brian to release each of the three mechanisms, and when the last one popped open, the gates swung ajar with a rusty, high-pitched squeal.

'Shall we get both bits of Dixon, then?' asked Sammy.

'No, let's leave them, I mean him, in the van for a moment. We'd better make sure his big tin box is definitely down on the platform. We obviously don't want to drag him, or them, or whatever the pronoun should be, all the way down there if something's gone tits up. So I'll stay up here and guard the body; you nip down to the platform to make sure everything's ready for him.'

Sammy nodded. She took the lock-picking tool from Brian and moved stealthily across the car park, under the twilight sky. She reached the main station door where, as expected, she found another padlock securing the entranceway. Sammy made equally short work of that latest lock, and once it was unlatched, she slipped quietly into the station concourse, heading for the steps to platform one.

Brian, meanwhile, had returned to the van and had climbed into the driver's seat. He turned his nose up and pulled a face. He had to agree, the pong from the back was really bad. The abnormally warm summer temperature had been magnified by the metal van, and the combination had served to speed up the whole decomposition process. Dixon had been roasting nicely in his oven for a full day and was by now most certainly 'done'. Brian thought back to the thermos he had borrowed as soon as he had reached Rosie's house and thanked the Lord for his earlier brainwave.

At that moment, a police car idled up the street and turned into the station slip road. The vehicle's headlights flashed.

'Balls,' Brian whispered under his breath. He waved to the two policemen in the patrol car and jumped back out of the van, attempting to keep to the shadows. The copper in the passenger seat climbed out and walked up towards the van, while the officer in the driver's seat turned to a small dashboard laptop and started typing in some details. Brian assumed he was doing a registration check and realised the clapped-out vehicle that he had bought from Nation would almost certainly still be registered to Nation Construction. Maybe he could use that to his advantage.

'Evening, sir,' began the approaching policeman. 'Anything I can help you with tonight?'

'Thank you, officer, but no. We're from Nation Construction. Security. We had a report of another possible break-in on the construction site here, so we're here to check it out. You'll probably have heard that we've been having a few "issues" recently, so to speak.'

'Jesus, not again? What are they like?' asked the policeman flippantly.

'Takes all sorts, I guess. But it looks like it's a false alarm this time. The padlocks were secure when we got here. My partner is just down on the platform level now to check there's no one there, but it looks like everything's fine.'

The officer began walking round the van, inspecting each of the doors as he did so. He noticed the peculiar odour emanating from the back.

'I see. So, you're not dumping anything, then? No rubbish in the back of the van you were planning to fly-tip? We've had a lot of that recently, you see, and there's a bit of a smell, sir.' He tapped the rear doors of the van, indicating the source of the smell.

'No, nothing like that officer. We were just shifting some waste compost for the station landscaping earlier today. That's what you can smell,' explained Brain, while pulling the most honest of all his faces.

At that moment, Sammy reappeared from the station forecourt and noticed the patrol car. She gulped. Brian spotted her and quickly called out to her, loudly enough to ensure she could hear.

'Any sign of anyone? I was just telling the officer here that we'd received a report of a potential breach of the car park again, but it all seems secure up here.'

Sammy caught on immediately. 'No sign of anyone down on the trackside, either. Looks like it's all clear.' Her heart was racing. If the cops got a look in the back of the van, they were screwed. She kept her head down and out of view

The other policeman got out of the car and joined his colleague. 'It's registered to a Derek Penrice, and a business called Nation Construction,' he said to his partner.

The first policeman nodded. That seemed to correspond with the man's story. 'And you are Penrice, then; is that right, sir?' he asked Brian.

'That's me,' lied Brian. He knew they were about the same height and had a passing resemblance, so he decided it was worth a gamble. Anything to get rid of the coppers. Sammy just stared at the ground.

The policeman seemed to be assessing the situation. 'Well, everything seems to be in order. But do you mind if we have a quick check of the rear compartment before we get going?'

Brian's heart sank. The game was up. No way were they coming up with a rational explanation for having a decapitated, rotting corpse in the back of the van, regardless of how good it might be as compost.

At that very moment, a crackle came over the police radio asking for urgent assistance at an ongoing burglary in Kings Heath. All available units were instructed to respond. Sammy and Brian held their breath.

'We'd better take that one,' remarked the first cop to his partner. 'OK,' he said, turning back to face Brian. 'If you get any further trespassing reports, Mr Penrice, you know where we are.'

'Yes, thank you, officer,' replied Brian and waved as the two policemen got back into the patrol car and reversed out of the slip road at speed. The car paused as the driver flicked on the blue lights before screeching off into the distance.

'Bloody hell' said Sammy, while the dust from the spinning tyres slowly drifted back down onto the car park surface. Brian nodded his agreement.

They took a moment to regain their composure, but eventually Brian asked, 'So was it down there?'

'Yep, all good, Bri. Or should I say Mister Penrice? Anyway, big old hole, tick. Big old box, tick.'

'Good, let's get on with it then, in case those two come back.'

In tandem, the pair threw open the rear doors and put on their protective gloves once again. Having done that, they used a tarpaulin from the back of the van to cover the body, and Brian picked up the rucksack with the head in it and put it across his shoulders. Repeating the technique they had used that morning, Brian grabbed Dixon under the arms while Sammy took the feet, and together they steered the body out into the open. Sammy nudged the doors shut with her hip and they quickly covered the ground between the gates and the station. Once inside, they paused for a breather in the security of the waiting room darkness before completing their journey down to the platform edge.

The pair struggled over to the awaiting steel box halfway up the platform and carefully lowered the corpse into its steely depths. Sammy removed the tarpaulin and put it to one side, while Brian opened the rucksack, turned it upside down and allowed Dixon's head to plop into the box, re-joining its body for the first time in hours. The head landed face-up, and it seemed as though it were staring right back up at the two of them, studying them, judging them through its stony, lifeless eyes. Sammy shuddered. Brian cautiously and quietly closed the lid of the steel box and secured it with a waiting padlock.

The two repositioned themselves at opposite sides of the box and grabbed two corners each.

'Ready?' asked Sammy.

'Ready,' Brian confirmed.

Steadily they lifted the box, edged their way over to the hole in the platform, and lowered the cold steel coffin into the awaiting tomb below.

CHAPTER TWENTY-ONE

It was five o'clock in the morning when Rosie finally awoke from her hallucinatory and agitated slumber. She found herself half lying on, half falling off her sitting room sofa, tangled up in a blanket. Her sleep had been badly disturbed for obvious reasons, and, on a number of occasions, she had got up and stumbled to the downstairs toilet in fear of being sick.

Nonetheless, as the hours slowly passed, her feelings of shock and repulsion at what she had done in the car park only hours earlier turned into feelings of shock and repulsion for the very man she had killed. The words Brian had spoken the previous evening had resonated with her deeply. She knew the main reason he had said those things was to try to relieve her feelings of guilt, rather than expecting her to believe every word. And yet Rosie concluded that all the points he had made were valid.

She reminisced about her life with that vast, crazy family back at the circus, and she longed to see them again. She thought of the money she so desperately had wanted to send them to help them through those tough times. That money, *her family's money,* had been compromised, poisoned and stolen by the accountant, that money-laundering rat. He had stolen from her family, and he had undoubtedly stolen from other people's families too. She found that the disgust she now felt for Dixon had reached the same level of intensity as the disgust she held for her own earlier actions, and to her surprise, the two were cancelling each other out.

Rosie spotted Brian's note on the table in front of her, and when she read it, she was comforted further. She was sure she could trust him. She knew he would make sure no one would learn of their secret. She would need to lean on Brian in the coming days; Rosie knew that much was inevitable. But at the same time, she felt that she was coming to terms with what had happened the previous day, and she thought that she might just get through the whole awful ordeal after all. Brian was right: Dixon deserved to die. And now he was dead, and she was glad about it. Schadenfreude.

Feeling dehydrated, and not remembering when she had last had a drink, she untangled herself from the blanket and made for the kitchen, wondering why on earth Brian had needed to borrow her thermos. She poured herself a glass of water and drained the lot in one go. She poured a top-up and started shuffling, bleary-eyed, back to the sitting room.

When she reached the hallway, she spotted a small piece of paper, folded in half, lying on the doormat under the letterbox. Rosie dragged herself over to the front door and stooped to pick it up. She unfolded the sheet, and squinting through her sleepy eyes, she made out a short message written in neat and precise handwriting.

I may be able to help you with your Mike Nation difficulties. Please meet me tomorrow morning at 11.00, by the bandstand in Cannon Hill Park. And please come alone.

There was no name or signature on the note, and it wasn't possible to tell from the handwriting whether the author was male or female.

The information contained within the short memo was curiously non-specific. Rosie hadn't a clue what was meant by 'helping' with her difficulties, and in any event, she found it a little disturbing that some stranger knew about her problems with Nation in the first place. As far as she was concerned, the only people who were aware of her dealings with the man were Brian and Nation himself.

It crossed her mind that the whole thing could even be some sort of a trap, although she couldn't conceive why that would ever be the case or who would want her entrapped. One thing was for sure, though: she was going to need Brian's help. Good job he owed her one.

CHAPTER TWENTY-TWO

A t about the same time that Rosie was pondering her curious, unsigned note, Brian's alarm started bleeping from the bedside table of his Hall Green flat. He groaned. His back hurt from all the dead body lifting he had been doing recently, and he had only managed to get about five hours' sleep despite his best efforts. When this was all over, he promised himself he would sleep for a week. Nonetheless, he knew he needed to get moving before rush hour hit and the roads and the pavements got busy. He had a very important task to undertake, and he wanted to keep out of sight as much as possible while he carried it out. No time for marmalade and burnt toast today.

Half an hour later, Brian reached the suburb of Edgbaston and he pulled up one block away from Dixon's house, in the same side road he had used on his previous visit. He grabbed the thermos, locked the car and headed for Dixon's home.

It was bin day in that area of Birmingham, so dozens of grey and blue wheelie bins had been haphazardly parked at the kerbside outside each house all the way along Brian's route. He casually sauntered up the street, swerving round the waste rubbish as he did so, until he reached his destination. Repeating the tradecraft from his last visit, he hesitated at the bottom of the drive to check that the street was deserted before nipping into the driveway and deep under the protective cover of the ash tree.

Brian hurried over to the base of the tree and was relieved to see the small remote camera he had placed on the trunk a few days earlier still in situ. Once again, he lifted himself off the ground using the lower branches as a lever and reached up to the camera. He detached it from the trunk and lowered himself back to the grass, then plugged the device into his mobile phone using a small USB cable. When the camera registered, he swiped to the application on his phone. The app took a while to transfer the data but eventually it displayed six files, indicating that there were half a dozen different movements captured by the camera over the preceding forty-eight hours.

Starting at the most recent file, Brian hit the play button and an image appeared on his screen. It was Dixon leaving his house, as it turned out, for the very last time. Brian watched on as he saw the accountant, wearing that familiar grey-blue jacket of his, calmly walk to his car and get in. The vehicle slowly reversed onto the road and Dixon drove off towards his own oblivion.

It gave Brian pause for thought. He knew that what he was watching was Dixon, gun no doubt already in pocket, leaving his house with the sole intention of meeting and then executing him. It was chilling, but other than being a somewhat haunting final image of the ex-accountant, the short film offered nothing of use to Brian, so he deleted the footage and skipped to the next file.

This time the screen was dark; it was late evening and the lack of light made it difficult for the camera to make out much detail. Brian saw Dixon appear once more, but this time he was arriving rather than leaving; Brian watched the man getting out of his car and walking up to the front door. Brian guessed that he was returning home having met up with Terry to buy the gun.

On the screen, Dixon had reached the door and tapped in his entrance code. Brian could tell that it was a six-digit passcode, but due to the poor-quality lighting, he wasn't one hundred percent sure of the actual digits. If he were to guess, he would have gone for 6-4-2-1-8-1, but he couldn't be certain. He hoped that there would be something more useful in the other files. Brian skipped past the next piece of footage, which was once again a film of Dixon leaving the house and therefore of little use, before finally finding what he was looking for. A clear, daylight view of Dixon arriving home. Brian observed Dixon at the front door tapping 6-4-2-1-9-1 into the electronic keypad. Brian's guess had been one number out. On the phone screen, the front door unlocked and swung open into the hallway.

Brian stuffed his phone, the digital camera and the USB lead into his jacket pockets. Phase one completed; he had the door code. Now for phase two of the operation. He grabbed the thermos that he had borrowed from Rosie and unscrewed the top. He tipped it upside down and poured the ice and water that he had placed in the container onto the gravel driveway.

Once the thermos was emptied of all the liquid, he shook the thermos gently. Eventually, a small piece of orange plastic appeared, and Brian yanked out the Sainsbury's carrier bag. He unfolded the bag and reached in for Dixon's thumb.

Back at the multi-storey the day before, Brian had had a moment of realisation. Dixon's corpse was going to be sitting in the heat of the van, inside the lock-up, for at least the remainder of the hot summer's day. He had wanted to preserve the integrity of Dixon's thumb as best he could and had rationalised that the best course of action was to remove the thumb there and then and get it on ice as soon as possible. That had been precisely what he had done, and that was why he had needed to borrow the thermos at Rosie's house. Ever since he had placed the thumb inside the container, Brian had made sure he periodically topped up the ice, ensuring the digit remained undamaged.

Brian now had the passkey and the thumb, so he was ready to search the house. He climbed the three steps to the front door and approached the keypad. Carefully, he inputted the six-digit code and heard a mechanical click. The door swung open. Immediately he heard the beeping of the alarm, so he moved swiftly into the hallway and closed the door behind him. He scurried across the polished floorboards to the other end of the hall and pressed Dixon's thumb onto the sensor.

Nothing happened. The alarm continued to beep and the little light on the panel continued to flash. Shit, thought Brian. Perhaps the thumb was too damp? Some of the melting ice had seeped into the Sainsbury's bag and dampened the digit; in fact, it was dripping wet. Brian wiped the thumb on the base of his shirt and tried again. He held the thumb in place for what seemed like a lifetime. He had no idea how long the countdown was before the alarm was triggered, but it would be only a matter of moments. If the alarm went off, he would need to make a run for it. The seconds ticked by, and with heart racing, he pushed the thumb a little harder against the sensor, while slowly rolling it across the detection area. Frustrated, and convinced that time was almost up, he was about to give up and run for it when finally, the alarm bleeped in acknowledgement and deactivated.

Brian gave a sigh of relief. He placed the thumb back into the orange supermarket carrier and stuffed it into his jacket pocket next to the camera, then placed the thermos down on the hall table.

He decided to have a little poke about before commencing a more thorough investigation, so he headed into the lounge at the front of the house. Brian's first impression was that the room screamed 'single man'. It was devoid of personality, lacking any sign of an individual touch, and it felt about as warm and welcoming as a mediocre city centre hotel lobby. Everything appeared grand but was entirely impersonal. There were no photographs on the walls, no flowers in vases, no plants on the floor.

The room looked just as it did when Brian had stolen a look through the bay windows earlier in the week. The large light fitting dangled from the middle of the high ceiling. The four-seater sofa sat empty on the back wall, except for the exercise mat propped to one side. There were a few occasional chairs dotted across the room, two of which were facing the impressive fireplace. And in the bay window there was the big old oak desk, on top of which sat Dixon's personal computer.

The little white LED light to the side of the computer pulsed slowly, indicating that the PC was not off but merely asleep. Brian approached the desk and rolled the mouse across the mouse mat. The centre of the three display units flashed on to reveal the locked screen; the system was unsurprisingly password protected. Brian wondered for a moment. Surely not? For the second time in a couple of minutes, he typed in the 6-digit code he'd seen Dixon use at the front door, 6-4-2-1-9-1. He hit enter. A password error message appeared. Well, it was worth a try, he thought.

Brian thought back to the limited information Nation had emailed to him at the beginning of the whole affair, including Dixon's place and date of birth. He gave them a go, but neither was accepted. Acknowledging that they were long shots, Brian unplugged the hard drive and placed it next to the front door as a reminder to take it with him. Then he turned back into the hallway to begin his full inspection.

Over the years, Brian had developed a standard protocol for building searches. They needed to be methodical and thorough, and he always started at the top of the building and worked down. By doing that he benefited from getting a decent overview of the property layout on his way up, before conducting a more forensic examination on the way down. To that end, Brian had a quick look into each room as he climbed the two flights of stairs to the uppermost floor. Once there, he commenced his detailed investigation.

On the second floor of the building, there were two small attic rooms and a laundry room. The attic rooms were completely empty, while the laundry room had a washing machine, a tumble dryer, a sink and very little else. It didn't take Brian long to clear those rooms, before dropping down to the much larger first floor. There, he found three double bedrooms, two en suite, a smaller bedroom and a separate shower room. He conducted a careful examination of each room, searching under beds and inside chests of draws, cabinets, closets and cupboards; with each item of furniture, he was sure to check that there were no false bottoms or secret hideaways. He inspected toilet cisterns, airing cupboards and storage units. He checked for any potential fake walls and unusual stud partitions, and he thoroughly examined all soft furnishings that could potentially hide a private compartment. Everything was turned upside down.

Having satisfied himself that there was nothing to be found, Brian returned to the ground floor to search the kitchen, the breakfast room, the huge dining room with a long, ornate, mahogany dining table which had probably never been used, and finally the downstairs loo. Every panel, every cupboard, every door was examined, but to no avail.

The only room left was the lounge, so Brian re-entered the room and began his final examination. He chose to start with the old oak desk in the bay window. There were three drawers on either side of the central seating position and Brian investigated each in turn. He found that five of the drawers were empty and was quickly able to confirm there were no false bottoms in any of them. He turned his attention to the final drawer, where he found three buff folders and a single sheet of paper. The paperwork gave off a strange smell, similar to that of a cooked breakfast. He dug the folders out of the drawer, placed them on the desk and studied the loose sheet. He saw dozens of doodles and a few capitalised words, and it dawned on Brian what he was looking at. He read out the bold words in order. TRAITOR, SCUMBAG, DIXON, DISAPPEAR, SORT IT, BRIAN.

'Fucking idiot…' Brian murmured out loud, picturing Nation scrawling all those words on the sheet of paper while seated at his office desk, before couriering it over to the very person he wanted killed.

Brian put the sheet on the desk and continued the search. He looked under the settee, across every shelf in the bookcase, deep into the fireplace, up into the chimney breast and behind the mirror on the wall. Nothing seemed out of order. There was no sign of a hidden compartment and no sign of the money. Brian felt exasperated; he didn't understand it. He had been convinced that the cash would be in the house somewhere; otherwise, the security of the place seemed completely over the top.

He was so desperate to be right that he repeated his entire search a second time, moving from room to room in the same order as before and with the same methodical process. It took him a further hour to complete the second inspection. Nothing.

Depressed, Brian slumped into the four-seater in the lounge and rubbed his brow. This was disastrous. With Dixon being cold, dead and buried, tracking the money down would be even more difficult. No one to follow, no one to track, no one to lead Brian directly to the cash. And Brian was acutely aware that Colonel John P. Kicklighter was arriving that very afternoon. Mike Nation was going to lose his shit.

He was just pondering what the next plan of action should be when his phone rang. It was Rosie. Brian's heart skipped and he accepted the call hastily.

'Everything ok?'

'Yes, thanks, Brian. I'm feeling a lot better.'

'Great to hear.'

'Brian, I think I need your help. Something rather peculiar has happened.'

'Peculiar how?' asked Brian with concern.

'Well, it's about Nation and the crap he's been pulling on me and the business. It seems that someone else knows about it. You see, I've had a note through the door. Hand-written. It's not signed, and I have no idea who it's from. Whoever it is, though, they reckon they may have information that could help me with my Mike Nation problem. They say I'm to meet them in Cannon Hill Park tomorrow, and that I need to come alone. What do you make of it?'

'Interesting,' said Brian, mulling the whole thing over. 'Well,' he said finally, 'one thing's for certain: you're not bloody well going alone.'

Rosie smiled at the other end of the call but said nothing.

'However,' continued Brian, having thought a little more, 'I *do* think we should go. I can't think why it would be some sort of trick; that wouldn't make any sense. So, we lose nothing by making the meeting. But caution is the order of the day. Give me the details, and we'll meet up ahead of time to come up with a plan.'

'Thanks, Brian.'

'I promised to help, and I meant it, Rosie. But to be honest, it might end up helping me out too.'

'How's that?'

'Well, it seems you're not the only one to have a Mike Nation problem coming to a head. You see, there's some money I needed to find for him. I had a couple of clues as to where the cash might be, but it turns out my last lead died… I mean, erm, the lead went cold. *Went wrong.*'

Christ, Brian, what are you saying? Rosie really didn't need to know the lead died because Rosie herself killed it! He reprimanded himself for his choice of words, but fortunately Rosie didn't seem to react; instead, they discussed the details of the meeting in the park that was set for the next day. They agreed to get together an hour before the 11 a.m. rendezvous to come up with a plan, and with that set, they rung off.

Brian leant back into the sofa in the Edgbaston home. He would love it if he could help Rosie get out of Nation's clutches, but ultimately, if he couldn't find the eight hundred grand, he might need an escape route himself.

He got to his feet and, concluding that nothing more could be done at the Dixon house, he made to leave. He picked up the thermos from the hall table, together with the computer hard drive he had left at the foot of the front door. Leaving the alarm unset, he exited the premises and heard the large electronic locks secure themselves behind him. He took out his mobile phone and typed 6-4-2-1-9-1 into the contacts app under the name 'ACCOUNTANT' in case he needed access to the house in the future.

At the bottom of the drive, Brian could see a refuse lorry making its slow and steady progress up the residential street. As he passed the next wheelie bin on the kerbside, Brian calmly and inconspicuously slipped the Sainsbury's bag into the rotten-smelling depths within.

CHAPTER TWENTY-THREE

The traffic was light as Sammy rode her bike from the Hall Green flat over to Nation House in Moseley. The sun was out once again, just as it had been for a seemingly endless number of days in a row, yet Sammy's mood did not mirror the weather. She was contemplating why it was that, despite all her training and hard work over the previous half a decade, it was she who was tasked with getting Mike bloody Nation's Mercedes washed and then conducting glorified chauffeur duties for some dumb Yank. She energetically pedalled across South Birmingham towards her destination feeling frustrated, convinced that her skills merited far more responsibility and respect.

Sammy recognised that, of course, compared to her old life of years ago, she should really be thankful for the world she had built for herself. And she knew deep down that the catalyst for her black state of mind was that day's date more than anything else. After all, she had read at length about the 'anniversary effect' and how a person's mood and feelings can be dramatically influenced around dates that mark significant events.

Today was precisely one of those days. Today marked the anniversary of *that* day. That day four years ago when her mother's new partner, fuelled by booze and furious at his own miserable life, did what he did to her. Today was the anniversary of Sammy deciding that the only option open to her was to pack that little red rucksack with whatever she could squeeze into it. Today was the anniversary of her running away.

She had never told anyone the reason she had ended up alone and homeless, deciding that it was her secret to keep. Instead, Sammy wanted to move on from the past and become a new person.

For those few early months, life was awful, and the bitter winter was becoming unbearable. Cold, vulnerable and penniless, she felt her very existence drifting away. But then Brian came into her life, and the new Sammy was born.

Over the subsequent months and years and with Brian's help, she had developed abilities she'd never thought she would master. Now, she was earning a reasonable income, she had a roof over her head and she had a small but close-knit group of friends. She even had a steady boyfriend, much to her surprise. And of course, most important of all, she had Brian. All in all, it was a miraculous transformation from the little girl trapped alone, marooned on the freezing streets of the city, and for that, she would forever owe a debt of gratitude.

But the anniversary always darkened Sammy's mood. Past events echoed into the present day and cast a melancholy shadow over her. Everything seemed unfair, annoying or infuriating on anniversary day, and at that moment, she just couldn't shake the nagging frustration that she was being under-utilised, that she kept being handed all the menial tasks. The business was supposed to be a partnership now, after all.

That all said, Sammy had to acknowledge that she'd been entrusted with helping to bury a decapitated corpse under a station platform last night, so there was that, she supposed.

Trying to snap out of it, Sammy sped past The Phoney Negroni and a minute later pulled into the car park of Nation House. She ambled into reception and saw the ever-faithful Beryl manning the fort, seated behind her desk and typing away on her keyboard.

'Hi Beryl, how are you?' she asked

'Hello, dear! How lovely to see you. Mike mentioned you would be popping in. I'm very well, thank you. You're here for the Mercedes, yes?'

'Yeh, that's right,' grumbled Sammy, resigning herself to the mundane tasks awaiting her.

'Righty-ho, love. The keys are hanging up over there.'

'Thanks, Bezza,' she replied and wandered over to grab them. They said their goodbyes and Sammy set off for the Nation House car park.

She reached the Merc and stared at the mucky vehicle parked in the corner. It was in desperate need of a wash. She peered inside and saw that the interior was filthy, with empty crisp packets, chocolate bar wrappers and coffee cups littering the back seat of the car.

'For God's sake, Mike, you absolute doorknob,' Sammy complained loudly, fuming at the scummy state in which Nation had left the vehicle. It wasn't so much in need of a clean as complete decontamination. Her mood darkened further as she slid into the driver's seat and sat on a half-eaten biscuit. Sammy held her breath, counted to ten, threw the remnants of the biscuit out of the window and put the key into the ignition.

She turned the engine over and the petrol gauge indicator sprang up before falling back to rest over Empty. The petrol warning light pinged on.

'Aargh!' Sammy shouted at the top of her voice. Now she was really angry, and had the car door not been shut, her scream would have reverberated across Moseley Village. She put the car into gear and pulled out aggressively into the road.

An hour later, the car was full of petrol, the interior had been valeted, bottles of water sat in the rear drink holders and the exterior paint was sparkling clean. Sammy's mood did not sparkle, though. It had blackened still further because she was running late. Coventry Road, the main thoroughfare to Birmingham Airport, had been closed due to a car accident, so Sammy had no choice but to join a myriad of other vehicles trying to plough a furrow through the rat runs and back roads of East Birmingham. She was starting to feel stressed. Perhaps she couldn't be relied upon for even the most menial of tasks after all, she thought.

She accelerated and braked vigorously, tailgating the car in front as she desperately tried to make up time. At one particular junction, she misjudged the changing traffic lights and had been forced to brake so forcefully that her own open bottle of water tipped from its holder and landed on her trousers, drenching her legs.

'*Aargh, piss off!*' she yelled once again as she frantically scrambled to retrieve the bottle from underneath her seat. She screwed the lid back on and threw it into the side compartment angrily.

'Worst. Day. Ever,' she said slowly.

The short-stay car park at the airport was located a five-minute walk from the main terminal building, and Sammy pulled into a space at two minutes to midday. The flight was due in at twelve o'clock, so time was very tight. She grabbed a crumpled piece of paper from the glove box and with a biro scrawled 'COLONEL KICKLIGHTER' across one side. She stared at the sign. It looked crap, she knew, but it would have to do. Slamming the door shut, she sprinted across the car park and into the terminal building. She made it to the arrivals area at a minute past twelve. She put her hands to her knees and panted in relief.

Having taken a moment to compose herself, she looked up at the arrivals board for the flight from New York, where The Colonel had changed planes. The first five entries were typed in green and all had the word 'Landed' next to their city of origin. The sixth entry down was the flight from New York, but this line was winking in yellow and had the information 'Delayed, now due 13:45 hrs' annotated to it.

Sammy's dejected mood turned thunderous. She trudged off to a nearby café and settled in with a coffee and some paper serviettes with which she patted her still-damp thighs.

Two hours later, the New York flight finally landed, and a depressed and angry Sammy repositioned herself in the arrivals area, battered paper sign in her hand, waiting for her client.

At the same time, the towering Colonel John P. Kicklighter disembarked the aircraft, marched past the international departure gates, breezed through customs and charged into the baggage reclaim area, all with the confident swagger uniquely characteristic of the American military. He collected a large grey suitcase from the conveyor belt and effortlessly hauled it along behind him as he marched through the terminal towards the arrivals hall.

Most people considered The Colonel to be a rather intimidating man. His very demeanour oozed power and dominance. Standing a full six feet five, he looked taller still when he was wearing, as he always did, his obligatory Texan cowboy hat. Close-shaven, his jaw was so square and his head so gigantic that he resembled an Easter Island statue.

Underneath the hat, The Colonel was wearing his full military dress uniform, replete with all the medals and decorations that had been awarded to him during his distinguished service. He always travelled in uniform, particularly when journeying overseas, as he felt the regimental gear asserted the full power and authority of the U.S. Army wherever he found himself. His journeys were less of a visit, more of an invasion.

The Colonel glanced across the arrivals hall and spotted his name scrawled on a crumpled piece of paper being held up high by a slightly scruffy if athletic-looking young lady. He barrelled over to the lady with the sign in double-quick time, his suitcase swinging wildly behind him.

'Hi,' said Sammy. 'You're The Colonel, I take it?'

'Sure am, li'l lady,' he replied.

Sammy cringed at the phrase but managed not to react, despite her dreadful and deteriorating mood.

'I take it Mikey sent you?' The Colonel added.

'He did. He says that I'm to take you to your hotel straight away. Unless, that is, you want to go anywhere else first. Mike will join you this evening in the hotel restaurant for dinner.'

'Hotel's fine. Plan sounds fine, little darlin', said The Colonel.

Sammy flinched again. The condescending American was already getting right on her wick, but she knew she was on best behaviour. She glanced at the amount of metal dangling off The Colonel's breast pocket. 'You must've set off every metal detector between here and Texas with that lot,' she commented. The Colonel ignored the remark, so she dropped the subject and nodded towards the direction of the exit doors.

'Would you like me to take your suitcase, Colonel?' she offered as they walked.

'Y'all seem a little too small to be dragging this big thing around; I'll be just fine,' he responded.

Sammy rolled her eyes. 'OK, good. Well, do you want to grab a bite to eat or a drink before we head for the hotel?'

'No, I'm fine, honey. They feed you *good* in business class.'

'Right you are.' Sammy felt the hairs on the nape of her neck jangle. She did not like The Colonel one bit.

They reached the car, loaded the suitcase in the boot and The Colonel chose the back seat. Sammy put the car in gear and made a beeline for the hotel. She wanted to get there as quickly as possible without looking unprofessional. She was feeling unbelievably tense, and the arrogance of the man was not helping.

After a while, The Colonel piped up from the back seat. 'So, you work for Mike Nation, then, do you, young lady?'

Oh, great – small talk. 'Well, I'm not on the payroll. But he calls upon my services from time to time.'

'Services, you say. I see. So, you're not just a simple taxi driver, then, I take it? I imagine you do a little bit of evr'thang; that it?'

'Something like that, yes.'

'Makes sense. You seem too pretty to just be a cab driver, little lady.'

Forget sleeping with the bloke. Managing to get to the hotel without killing him might be more of a challenge. 'The name's Sammy, Colonel. Feel free to call me Sammy.'

'Well, right you are, Sammy, partner.'

Sammy glanced at The Colonel's massive rectangular head in the rear-view mirror. How did it all fit on his passport photo? It must take up two pages, she thought. She doubted he could fit into a photo booth in the first place; it was absolutely gargantuan. God, she hoped he would shut the hell up. She was so agitated; what an appalling day she was having.

But Sammy was in no such luck. The Colonel continued his patronising spiel, wandering through various bits of pompous nonsense as the journey went on. Sammy felt perspiration drip down her back, and her pulse was racing. The Colonel droned on.

'Of course, I doubt you get involved in the business side of Mike's work, Sammy. I find that doing deals and negotiations, working on finance and projects, these things aren't really in a typical lady's repertoire, would you say?'

Sammy was breathing heavily. She bit her lip to make sure nothing came out of her mouth. The man was possibly the most arrogant, patronising jerk she had ever had the misfortunate to meet. He and Nation were a marriage made in heaven. She desperately tried to ignore him and concentrated on the road ahead. Almost there.

'We're doing a deal tonight, in point of fact, li'l pardner. A big ol' deal, a real game-changer. But of course, not really for you to know about these sorts of things, I'm guessing. Is that right, honey?'

At that moment, Sammy cracked. The sheer patronising bullshit she had been taking from him, on top of the dreadful day she had been having anyway, all suddenly conjoined and erupted.

'*Well, there won't be any bloody deals if he doesn't have the bloody money, will there*?' she snapped before immediately regretting it.

Straight away, she changed the subject. She pretended nothing had happened, but she knew it was too late. Sammy could see through the rear-view mirror that The Colonel had registered the words. And yet, he said nothing.

The journey continued in a bit of a haze for Sammy, as if she was on autopilot, and a quarter of an hour later they arrived at the Grand Hotel in the centre of Birmingham. The Colonel thanked his driver politely, plucked his big grey case from the boot and strutted into reception.

Throughout the remainder of the drive, The Colonel had continued to spout his gibberish, and Sammy vaguely recalled a number of daft questions he had posed her, which she had done her best to answer. But she wasn't concentrating. She knew she'd cocked up; she knew she had let something slip. She just didn't know how much trouble she was now in.

Later on, up in his hotel suite, The Colonel unpacked and neatly folded his casual clothes into well-ordered piles on the cupboard shelves. He decided to put on the TV news while he got changed ahead of his meal with Mike Nation, so he grabbed the remote control and hit the power button. A list of twelve menus appeared on the TV screen. Confused, he pressed 'Guide'. Then 'Source'. Then 'Content'. Then 'Apps'. Then 'Home'. Then 'Info'. Then 'Menu'. Then he hurled the remote control across the room and gave up. Hotel TVs were the pits, he thought.

Instead, he lay back on his bed and closed his eyes. What had he made of that little lady on the drive over from the airport? She had clammed up a bit after she had made that throwaway comment about the money. And later, when he had made the very reasonable inquiry about where he could purchase a side-arm for the rest of his stay, she had been rather rude. He hated being unarmed, and he never travelled in the States without his weapon. How dumb could a country be that it didn't even allow its residents to defend themselves, he wondered.

Anyway, that comment about the money... It had obviously been unintentional on little Sammy's part, but surely there couldn't be anything to it? No way would Nation have dragged The Colonel's ass all the way to little ol' England to finalise the Golden Valley deal if he didn't have the funds in place… Or would he?

The Colonel's mood darkened. It seemed that the upcoming evening's get-together might regrettably turn out to be less of a celebration and more of an interrogation. And hand to God, if Nation had lied to him, there would be hell to pay.

CHAPTER TWENTY-FOUR

The portacabin shook as Derek Penrice, foreman of Nation Construction and Mike Nation's trusted right-hand man, pounded his fist onto the desk in frustration. He had just wasted another thirty minutes arguing with that bloody architect, Stephanie Sutton, about the quality of the materials they had been using in the development of Moseley Station. She was getting more vociferous in her arguments, and Derek was worried that things could easily get out of hand. The last thing he needed was the threat of another delay; Nation would hang him up by his short and curlies.

He was fully aware that the grand opening was in just four days, when the steam train full of local celebrities was set to depart from Stirchley Station, further down the line, and pass through Moseley on its way into Birmingham. Derek knew that there was no way the journey would be permitted if any of the stations along the route had its safety certificate revoked. He felt under pressure.

Penrice had only recently arrived on site, having spent the morning at the other two stations, Stirchley and Kings Heath. He thanked God there were no issues at those sites.

Any other problems and his blood pressure would explode, and he really wanted to avoid taking up permanent residence in Strokestown.

That damned woman had complained about the safety issues at all three of the sites; however, she had been particularly vocal about her concerns at Moseley. Unlike the other two, the Moseley Station building had been designed to straddle the tracks because the railway was in a cutting. This meant that the station building also doubled as the pedestrian bridge, allowing access to the platforms on either side of the railway. It made sense as a design, but it meant that the load-bearing components needed to be much more robust, a great deal stronger than the requirements for simple, single-storey structures like the other sites. And it was just those load-bearing issues that Stephanie bloody Sutton had been bitching on about for half an hour.

He simply didn't have time for it all, and frankly, she was probably only moaning because she was a nasty old racist. She had to be because she obviously had a problem with Far Eastern concrete and steel, the prejudiced old crone. But still, he'd better have another word with Mike about her; best to make absolutely sure there was nothing to worry about.

Derek rubbed his throbbing brow and got up from his seat. He needed to catch up with his site manager about the final bits of snagging, so he stepped out of the portacabin into the sunlight and made his way over to the main station building. He passed Tomasz on his way and asked him if he knew where the site manager was. Apparently, he was down on platform one.

As he entered the station building, he spotted one of his men installing a new departure screen on the ceiling of the waiting area. He nodded to the man on the stepladder, and as the labourer waved back, Derek noticed that a few metres away from the worker on the side of the building, a rather large crack had appeared, stretching from halfway up the wall all the way to the roof. Derek was certain it hadn't been there the day before, so it must have opened up overnight. He went over to inspect the damage. It was pretty deep, but Penrice convinced himself that it was probably just a settlement crack, which occurred in most new buildings when all the weight of the new structure finally settled into its foundations. Nothing to worry about, he told himself. It just needed a quick plaster and another paint job, that's all. Derek made a mental note to get his plasterer back over that afternoon to sort it out.

He turned and headed for the platform one stairwell. As he rounded the corner and took the first step down the stairs, he thought that one of the steel girders holding up the main building seemed ever so slightly bent out of shape. Obviously, that couldn't be possible. Steel girders were as strong as, well, steel girders. Realising that the station lighting was not on, and given that the natural sunlight was not particularly strong in that area of the station, he concluded it was just a trick of the shadows. Anyway, his eyes were not as good as they once were, either. He'd have to bite the bullet and get some glasses at some point, he decided.

Derek reached the bottom of the steps and turned onto the platform. His site manager was hanging up a 'Moseley' sign on one of the lamp posts.

'Alright, son?' he called over.

'Alright, Derek,' returned the site manager tiredly.

'How's progress? Everything on time?'

'No problems, boss.'

'Good. Oh look, there's a bit of settlement cracking upstairs in the main building. Can you get the plasterer to come back and sort it out ASAP?'

'Yep, no problems, boss. By the way, that steel box you wanted, the one that's been lying about the place the last few days, it's been all locked up and put in the hole you got us to dig out. Thought you'd want to know.'

'Has it, indeed?' commented Derek, and he wandered over to the hole in the platform. He looked down and saw the steel box, securely locked, fitting snuggly into the chamber below. 'Well, that's a bit of good news. Can you arrange for the thing to be filled in, pal? Get it all concreted over. And maybe do that ASAP as well, eh?'

'Sure thing, Derek,' the site manager said with a nod.

Derek took a few steps along the platform to make sure that he was out of earshot, then dug into his pocket and retrieved his mobile phone. He dialled Mike Nation's number. After a few rings, Nation picked up.

'Derek, my good man! Still building more than for any other reason, I trust? To what do I owe the pleasure?'

'Hi, Mike. I've got some good news. It seems your package has been delivered, if you see what I mean. I've just got to Moseley Station and the box has been locked up and put in the hole. I presume you want me to concrete it over?'

Nation jumped up from his chair and did a little jig in the middle of his office before getting puffed and retaking his seat.

'Is that so? Well, that's tremendous news, Derek! Tremendous! You know what this means, mate? He's dead!

That loathsome little pirate, that prostate-buggered piss-emperor, he's finally bought the farm! Well, well, well, good old Brian. And perfect bloody timing, what with The Colonel arriving in town today. That's excellent. Yes, Derek, concrete the thieving snake over, will you? Confine him to his pit of hell, there's a good lad. Oh, but Derek, one more thing. I need to be able to tell exactly where the cheating good-for-nothing is buried, ok? For the butt cheeks and everything. So, leave me a small clue, maybe a little cross in the cement, will you?'

'Erm, butt cheeks, boss?'

'Never you mind, Del. Just leave the mark, ok?'

'Whatever you say, Mike; will do. Oh, but there's another thing. In less good news, the bloody architect has been banging on about the Far Eastern stuff again. Are you sure she's not going to kick up a stink?'

'You leave her to me, Derek, my man. As I've said before, she can whinge all she likes, but she is fully aware of the interests I have in her business, and those interests mean that despite her barking and growling, she is most certainly not going to make things difficult for us. Don't you worry about Stephanie Sutton.'

'Whatever you say, boss. I'll just ignore her, then. The daft racist.'

'Say what, Derek? Racist?'

'Oh, sorry, ignore me. Just thinking she was probably a racist, that's all.'

'Whatever you say, Derek. Just get these last few things sorted, and then get the men off that bloody site, alright?'

'Sure thing, boss.'

Back at Nation House, Mike Nation leaned back into his comfy leather chair and swung his chubby little legs up onto the desk. He had been eating a bag of crisps, and he noticed that some crumbs had escaped and settled onto his tie. He picked them off with his thumb and finger, then tipped them into his mouth. Then he reached over to grab another packet and opened it. His favourite: ready salt and vinegared.

Good old Brian, he thought again while munching on his snack. A large, satisfied smile appeared on his pumpkin-coloured face, and some half-chewed crisps escaped out of the side of his mouth. He concluded that Brian and Sammy must have recovered the eight hundred grand and then bumped the snake off last night. And what with The Colonel being picked up by Sammy right now, and with dinner booked for that evening to conclude the Golden Valley deal, it was perfect timing! Thank the Lord for that, he thought. What a relief.

He closed his eyes and let his mind drift. He found himself at Golden Valley Retirement Community in Arizona, and he was standing proudly on the beautifully manicured lawns in front of the perfectly landscaped water features. It was ninety degrees in the shade, and he was in a polo shirt and shorts, with a glass of champagne in his hand and Barbara by his side. Then Barbara was gone, and Angelina Jolie was by his side. Well, why the hell not? It was his daydream. How wonderful. It was all coming together…

But then the daydream was momentarily paused to make room for some more rational thought. Nation opened his eyes. Something was a bit off. Something didn't quite add up. Why hadn't Brian contacted him personally with the good news? Why hadn't Brian phoned him the very moment the cash had been found and the deed had been done? After all, Mike had left strict instructions for him to do so. It was peculiar. He decided he had better get hold of Brian directly, to make sure that the money had indeed been retrieved.

He grabbed his phone and fired over a text. In it, he mentioned that Derek had been in touch and had advised him that the steel box was in position and the concrete was to be poured that day, sealing the little prick into his grave. Nation confirmed that he was delighted with the news that Dixon was dead, and he thanked Brian once again for his services. However, he did just want to confirm that this all meant there was some equally good news regarding the eight hundred thousand cash. Nation asked Brian to contact him urgently to verify its recovery and to arrange delivery of his money.

A few miles away in a Hall Green flat, a mobile phone pinged to indicate the text message had reached its intended recipient. That recipient opened the text and read the note in full, then slowly placed the phone back down beside him.

'Balls,' Brian whispered to himself.

CHAPTER TWENTY-FIVE

A few hours later, Nation was staring at the full-length mirror in the bedroom of his Solihull home. He was getting ready for his big dinner date with Colonel John P. Kicklighter later that evening. Best shirt, best blazer, best gold cufflinks, best pants. He had yet to choose his trousers as he wasn't sure which best shade of grey to go for. He held a couple of pairs up to his body and fixed on the reflection in the mirror, his bare orange legs shining brightly back at him. He finally went for the slate grey pair and haphazardly put the trousers on, stumbling across the room as he did so.

He desperately wanted to make a good impression. He needed the night to go perfectly. The following few hours were to be a celebration, an evening of merriment and revelry crowning the finest deal he had ever made or would ever make again. A lifetime spent working his fingers to the bone, and finally, all the effort had paid dividends. His life was about to change, and all thanks to The Colonel.

But there was a problem. It had been six hours since Nation had texted Brian from his office, and he was still waiting for some sort of response. It was unnerving, and his concerns were playing on his mind as he prepared for his big night out. For that reason, about an hour earlier, he had decided there was nothing else for it but to phone Brian and get the truth. But Brian had failed to pick up. He had tried three more times and sent two further texts. Nothing. Finally, Nation had resorted to threats. He had left a voicemail saying that if Brian did not phone him back within the hour, they would never do business again.

The strategy seemed to work. Finally, Nation's mobile rang. He looked away from the full-length mirror where he was adjusting his tie and grabbed his device from the dressing table. Seeing Brian's name flashing on the screen, he immediately hit the accept button.

'Brian, what the *fucking fucking fuck*?' he complained.

'Look, I'm sorry, Mike, I know you've been after me all day, but I didn't want to get back to you without anything to report. I've been working around the clock to find the eight hundred grand. I've turned over every stone, left no angle unchecked. I've searched his home, I've checked his banks, I've been desperate to get some good news for you. But I'm sorry to report no sight of the cash as yet.'

Nation let the news sink in for a moment and then exploded. '*No sight of it*? What the hell do you mean, *no sight of it*? I need that money, Brian! You know I need that money, and you know I need it now! There was a *deadline*, Brian!'

Nation was losing it. 'What the hell is going on here? I'm seeing Kicklighter within the hour! What the hell am I going to tell him? This is a total shitshow, Brian, that's what it is. I don't understand it. Derek says the box is sealed and in the hole. I presume that means Dixon is dead. Or have you screwed that up too?'

'No, Mike, Dixon is dead. He's in the box.'

'But if you haven't found the money, why did you bloody well kill him, Brian? You were supposed to disappear him *after* you'd found my damned cash!'

'Hold your horses, Mike. *He* tried to kill *me*! He'd been tipped off! And *by you*, I might add! He knew I was contracted to kill him, and so the idiot came at me with a gun. I had to kill him – it was self-defence!' Brian would take Rosie's secret to his grave. Mike would never know who actually killed Dixon.

'Don't be ridiculous, Brian. I never tipped him off! Why the hell would I do that? Do you think I'm a moron?'

'What I *think*, Mike, is that you may have inadvertently couriered over to Dixon a piece of paper with doodles on it. And on that sheet of paper, there were words describing how a man called "Brian" was going to "sort" a "traitor" of a man called "Dixon" by making him "disappear". You realise I'm quoting directly from the page here, Mike. I saw the bloody thing with my own damned eyes!'

There was silence for a moment as Nation realised what he had inadvertently done. Eventually, he responded, and his tone was much more conciliatory.

'I see. Well, that does sound all rather unfortunate. I shall endeavour to remind Beryl not to post kill lists to the very people I want taken out. That is not ideal, I do appreciate that. All very regrettable, and I apologise if I caused you a small difficulty.'

Only Mike Nation would call this shambles a small difficulty, Brian thought, but he chose to keep silent.

'Look, Brian, don't get me wrong. I shed no tear for the prick. He's dead, and I'm happy for that. He can rot beneath my station for the next two centuries for all I care. But that does not change the fact that I need my bloody money back.'

'I know that, Mike, and I'm doing everything I can to find it – everything. As I said, I've searched the man's house from top to bottom. Twice over, in fact. Unfortunately, there was nothing of note to find. So I took his computer home with me and I finally cracked the password protection a few hours ago. I've spent the rest of the afternoon looking at the files and trying to make sense of the transactions the guy was making.

'Now, I'm no finance expert, but I think I've found a pattern. It seems he was making regular withdrawals from a select number of bank accounts over the last few months, and I think they must relate to the missing eight hundred thousand. If I'm right, it means the money must be in cash form, and this is good news, Mike. It means it's not stuffed in an offshore bank account somewhere; it's in real hard readies, which means it can be found and retrieved. So now it's just a case of working out where the man hid it.

'I'm following up a couple of ideas, and I'm in the process of tracking down his car. He must have driven it into town and parked it up somewhere before he tried to take me out. The solution could be as simple as popping the boot open. But regardless, as soon as I get a lead, I'll let you know, ok, Mike?'

Nation considered Brian's comments for a moment. It did all make sense. If the money really was in cash form, that probably was good news. It meant it was likely still nearby, hidden in Birmingham somewhere, and it was just a case of finding the location.

'Ok, Brian, fair enough; you follow up on your leads. But as soon as you find anything, make sure you let me know. You have to understand, if the money isn't found, my only plan B is to really put the screws on some of the businesses I have interests in. The Balancing Act, for instance. I may have to drain the restaurant dry to raise the funds.'

Nation let his last comment linger. Brian wondered why Mike had made specific reference to The Balancing Act. It seemed deliberate. Did Mike know that Brian had developed some feelings for Rosie? Was this some kind of passive-aggressive threat? It was disconcerting, and Brian did not take kindly to threats. Threats to Rosie and her business were unacceptable. But for now, he decided to let it lie.

'Understood, Mike. I know the importance of finding it.'

'Good.'

'Meantime, what are you going to say to The Colonel later on?'

'Well, Brian, I'm going to do what any good Christian would do in such a situation. I'm going to fucking lie to him.'

CHAPTER TWENTY-SIX

According to one of Brian's books, the Grand Hotel in the centre of Birmingham is a grade two listed building which can name Winston Churchill and Charlie Chaplin among its famous and historic clientele. It's a beautiful 1870s structure in the French Renaissance style, blossoming with stunning architectural features both inside and out. It's therefore fairly unsurprising that on a number of occasions throughout its history, Birmingham council's city planners, in their infinite wisdom, almost knocked the sodding thing down.

Fortunately, that eventuality has been permanently averted, and it is now recognised as the flagship hotel of the city. It is also where Mike Nation booked rooms for Colonel John P. Kicklighter for the duration of his stay in Birmingham. First impressions are everything in business, as Nation knew only too well.

It was an hour after his phone call with Brian that Nation's taxi pulled up outside the hotel, and he clambered inelegantly out of the rear passenger door. The house restaurant at the Grand Hotel, Isaacs, is styled around a high-end New York diner, which Nation knew would be perfect for the big Texan, so he had booked an 8 p.m. table for two. He checked his watch and, noticing he was early, decided to grab a drink in Bar Utopia, the pub situated opposite the hotel. He was as nervous as hell and needed to try and calm himself down.

He settled into a small booth in the bar, ordered a beer and tried to get his thoughts clear. He was sure the best course of action was to bluff that the full four million was in place, but he realised that he also needed to convince The Colonel to stay on in Birmingham for a little longer than planned to give Brian more time to find the missing eight hundred thousand. If he succeeded and The Colonel obliged, Nation could start using the money he did actually have to cover all the early expenditures. Kicklighter need never find out about the slight financial mishap.

Nation resolved to use the opening ceremony for the railway line as the reason for extending The Colonel's stay. He remembered the conversation the pair had had back in Florida when Kicklighter had told Nation his favourite actor was Sir Johnny Weaver. That was perfect. Sir Johnny was cutting the ribbon at the opening ceremony. Surely The Colonel wouldn't resist the chance of meeting his Hollywood hero?

With renewed confidence in his plan, Nation finished his pint and headed for the hotel restaurant over the road. He strolled through the lobby and followed the imposing staircase down to the basement diner where he was escorted to the table by the head waiter. Colonel John P. Kicklighter was already there, his imposing frame dwarfing one side of the table for two. He had changed out of his military dress and was instead wearing the uniform of all American men over the age of fifty: a pink polo shirt and tan chinos. His Stetson hat was balancing precariously on the corner of the table, and he was using it to prop up the restaurant menu.

'Good to see you, Mike!' shouted The Colonel when he spotted Nation walking through the restaurant. He jumped to his feet and vigorously shook Nation's hand.

'Great to see you too, Colonel,' replied Nation. A cheerful smile planted on his round face hid the excruciating pain he was feeling from The Colonel's powerful grip.

'I'm glad you picked a steakhouse, Mikey. A Texan man loves his red meat, as you well know! I was kinda worried you'd book us somewhere fancy, what with you Brits being obsessed with your la-di-da poncy food these days.'

'God, no, you're speaking to the converted here, Colonel,' replied Nation as the pair settled into their seats. 'All those posh places, they make you feel like you're doing a bloody exam half the time. I mean, you decide to go for an Italian and you're not even allowed to do your own pepper! What's that all about? All a bit pretentious, to be honest. Not for me. You don't get a guy hovering over you with a massive pepper mill at a Toby Carvery, do you?'

'Who's Toby Carvery?'

'Not who, Colonel, what. It's a restaurant chain. You get beef *and* turkey. And you can eat roast potatoes until you throw up. Utterly brilliant.'

'Sounds wonderful.'

'Oh, it is! Although I must admit, I do have a minor interest in a Michelin-starred restaurant nearby. But that's just diversification. Always a good business model, wouldn't you agree?'

'Very true, Mikey.'

Everything seemed to be going swimmingly, so Nation relaxed a little. 'I assume you had a good journey over from the States?'

'No problems there, buddy. I only fly American carriers, as you well know. Biggest and the best. You can't go wrong if you pick the biggest and the best. Especially if you're turning left when you get on board, if you get my meaning!'

The men chuckled together.

'And the car? The one I arranged for your transfer from the airport – I trust that was comfortable?'

'It was just fine, Mike; very considerate of you. She's a strange girl, though, your l'il lady, Sammy. I was asking her about guns on the way over. I wanted to know where I might get hold of one, on account of security an' all. I never go anywhere Stateside without a firearm, you see. But she just looked at me funny.'

'I see. And then what happened?'

'She called me "an absolute Kleenex" and changed the subject. I mean, what's that all about?'

'Well, the thing is, this is England, Colonel. We don't really *do* guns this side of the pond. A bloke's more likely to own a castle than a gun over here. We've got castles coming out of our arseholes. Go round a corner and bang, there's another bloody castle, right in front of you. But guns? Not so much. She probably thought you were having a little joke. Anyway, shall we order?'

'Sounds good. Let's order a bunch of steaks and then get down to business.'

The Colonel called the waiter over to the table. 'I'll take a ten-ounce sirloin, rare, *and* a twelve-ounce ribeye, medium. I'll take some fries and some wedges. And one each of the sauces. And a side of sweetcorn. That should do me for now, son. Unless you'd recommend anything else?'

The waiter stared at him in disbelief. 'I'd suggest a paramedic,' he murmured under his breath.

'Speak up, boy!' hollered The Colonel.

'I said your order is *epic*, sir. I think you've covered it off nicely.'

'Good, good! A man's gotta eat, am I right, Mikey?'

Nation was glowing with admiration. 'Too right, Colonel. Same for me, lad,' he said triumphantly and handed his menu card back to the waiter.

The Colonel picked, rather predictably, a bottle of the Californian red, and with orders taken, the men settled back into their seats ready to conclude the Golden Valley deal.

'So, let's talk turkey, Mike. Everything in order at your end? All funds good to go?'

'Absolutely,' Nation lied. 'Everything's in place. I'm ready to push the button.'

The waiter returned with the bottle of wine and presented the label to the pair. Kicklighter nodded and pointed to his glass. He swirled and sniffed and took a little swig, nodding his approval. With both glasses topped up, the waiter scuttled off back to the kitchens.

'I see,' replied The Colonel, finally. He inspected the ruby liquid in his wine glass and took another sniff. 'Well, isn't that just funny...' he added, in a rather off-hand manner. He took a large gulp of wine and casually placed his napkin on his lap.

'I'm sorry?' said Nation.

'I said, isn't that just funny...'

'What's funny, Colonel?'

'That after all this time, and with the trust we had built up between us, and ahead of this huge deal we are about to complete...' he paused for effect, '...you take me for an idiot.'

Nation was gobsmacked. What was happening? Why was The Colonel suddenly acting like this? Maybe it was jetlag.

'I... I'm not really following you, Colonel,' Nation stammered.

'I said,' continued Kicklighter, 'that after all this time, you take me... for a goddamned idiot.'

'I don't understand...'

Kicklighter exploded. '*You're short,* Nation! I know it! Your li'l lady let it slip on the drive over. You've come up short. You don't have all the funds in place! I mean what the Sam hell, Mike? What's going on here? What gives? And don't you lie to me, partner. People who lie to me tend to end up rather less alive than they were *before* they lied to me.' There was a pause, and Nation fidgeted nervously in his seat while The Colonel gave him a cold, dead-eyed stare. 'I suggest, Mike, you tell me everything.'

Fucking Sammy, thought Nation. He was going to bloody well kill her.

'Ahh. Yes. Well, you see, there is perhaps a very minor setback, but it's not a significant issue, I can assure you. I might potentially be a tiny bit deficient in the funds department as of right now, driven by a very small cash flow problem I seem to be experiencing. But that problem is being resolved as we speak.'

'How short?'

'It's being resolved...'

'*How short,* Mike?'

Nation took a breath, then finally said, 'Eight hundred thousand pounds.'

Kicklighter exploded again. 'What the goddammed hell! Eight hundred thousand pounds? What are you saying here? Are you trying to do a joke, Mike? Are you trying to be a comedian? 'Cos if so, sweet Jesus, I've gotta tell you I've seen funnier hurricanes.'

'Look, it won't be a problem, Colonel, honestly. I have a man on it. I just need a few days.'

'A few days? Why a few days? Do you think I'm a fool? I'm not a damned fool, Mikey...' The Colonel's face was reddening. He was clutching a fork in one of his massive hands and waggled it aggressively in Nation's direction.

'No, of course I know you're not a fool... It's just...' spluttered Mike.

'You are eight hundred thousand pounds short, Nation. That not *just* anything!'

'But if...'

'That's like *a million dollars* in actual, proper money.'

'But...'

'Hang on a minute,' snapped The Colonel. He banged his fork back on the table and reached for his mobile phone, then scrolled to the calculator app.

'But...' pleaded Nation once again.

'Shut up, Mike.'

The Colonel typed the numbers carefully and then applied the exchange rate he had used at Dallas Fort Worth Airport the day before.

'I'll tell you how much it is, Mike. It's one million, one hundred and four thousand dollars.' He rammed his phone screen into Nation's face. 'Read the screen, Mike! One stinking million, one hundred and four thousand stinking dollars.'

There was silence for what felt like an age. Diners on neighbouring tables began coughing and murmuring nervously, pretending not to notice the blazing argument in the middle of the restaurant. Finally, Nation bravely interrupted the quiet.

'Look. It's just a minor setback, it really is. And I am assured the money will be recovered any moment now.' His lies sounded unconvincing, even to himself.

'Tell me, Mike, why has it taken you so long to realise that you are so short? Why am I only hearing about this now, having flown halfway round the goddammed world?

'Well, it's taken me a little while to consolidate all the various funds together, you know, into one place. And it was only when I'd done that, that the problem showed its head.'

'But we've been working on this deal for weeks! Hell, Mike, if you kept all your money in one place, you'd *immediately* know how much capital you had. Why didn't you bring your finances and all your accounts together in one go?'

'It's not good business practice, Colonel. It looks, well, it looks suspicious. It's better to slowly consolidate rather than all in one go. It's like ten-pin bowling; you don't try and knock your skittles down all at once.'

'But you literally *do*, Mike. That is precisely the point of the stupid game. Jesus Christ.'

'Well, yes...'

'Look, cut the bull, Mike. I'm wheels up out of BHX at sixteen hundred hours the day after tomorrow, whether the contract's signed or not. So give it to me straight: is this deal collapsing or can you guarantee me that you can get the funds? Are you certain you just need a little more time?'

'I assure you, Colonel, and I would never lie to you... Well, ok, I will never lie to you *again*. I guarantee that the full four million pounds will be in place in a few days. It's not a question of if, it's a question of when. And when is just a matter of days.'

The Colonel sat back in his seat and thought for a while.

Nation added, 'Look, why don't you stay here just a little longer? You don't *have* to fly home in two days, do you?'

'Well...'

'You could see it as a little English holiday. Stay for a while! Enjoy the city, enjoy the hotel, enjoy the facilities!'

'If I do, you'd be paying...'

'I'm paying, Colonel. And anyway, there's another very good reason to hang around just a little while longer. My firm has just completed the construction of a brand new train line. It's my pride and joy. Well, until we complete the Golden Valley Retirement deal, of course. There's going to be a grand opening in a few days and lots of big-wigs and celebrities will be there. Now, I remember you telling me how much you like *Slow Train to St Louis*. Well, get this... Sir Johnny Weaver will be there at the opening! In full *Slow Train* costume! And not only can I get him to meet you, but I can get you on the footplate of a steam train with him, riding into Birmingham on the inaugural journey. How would you like that? Riding a steam train with Sir Johnny just like in the movie! And by the time the ceremony comes round, I am sure all the money will be in place. So, what do you say?'

The Colonel's mood brightened a little. 'I get to meet *the* Sir Johnny Weaver?'

'*The* Sir Johnny, yes.'

'And I get to ride a steam train with him, just like in *Slow Train*?'

'Just like in the movie.'

'And you will definitely have the money by then?'

'Definitely,' Mike lied again.

The Colonel stroked his huge chin and contemplated the proposal. He goddamned loved Johnny Weaver, that much was for sure, and it sounded like a once-in-a-lifetime chance to meet him. There was no harm in delaying his journey back to Texas by a couple of days, he reckoned. Finally, he leaned forward onto the dining table.

'Alright, Mike. Let's take the steam train with Sir Johnny, and let's watch your little railroad get opened. But you had better have the money by then. Because, Mikey, people don't screw The Colonel over twice.'

'Understood, Colonel. Message received, loud and clear.'

Mike Nation silently blew out a strained puff of air, slumped back into his seat and dabbed his brow with his napkin. At that moment, the four steaks, the fries, the wedges, the sweetcorn and the sauces all arrived at once, and they wouldn't fit on the table. The waiter quickly pushed the neighbouring one over to make room. The pair tucked in, eating largely in silence, although Nation had by now completely lost his appetite. He knew the evening was a total write-off. His wonderful celebratory dinner had turned into a complete and utter disaster. He was crestfallen, and he was furious.

At every turn, his fixers were letting him down. Brian couldn't find the money, and Sammy had dropped him right in it. What was the bloody point in having fixers that didn't actually fix anything and just ended up making things much worse? No bloody point, that's what. He wondered what the correct name was for a person who appeared to be the opposite of a fixer. He settled on a 'bollock-upper'. When he was done with his meal, Nation was going to contact his chief bollock-upper and give him a piece of his mind.

CHAPTER TWENTY-SEVEN

It was 10 a.m. the morning after Mike Nation's disastrous meal with The Colonel, and Brian was heading to meet Rosie just outside Cannon Hill Park, a popular two-hundred-acre green space lying a couple of miles south of the city centre.

The midnight tirade that he had experienced a few hours earlier, having taken a call from a slightly drunk but no less furious Nation, was still ringing in his ears. Mike had called him from his homeward-bound taxi and had slurred his way through the details of Sammy's slip-up, demanding some kind of retribution. It was really out of character for Sammy, but Brian couldn't defend her mistake. One of the first rules of their profession was that all client information was held entirely confidentially. She knew the directive, and yet she'd ignored it, and it was difficult to excuse.

Meanwhile, Brian had made no progress on the money front, either. The search of Dixon's house had been fruitless, and accessing Dixon's computer had only demonstrated that the money was now almost certainly in hard cash. It gave him no indication as to where, and worse still, Brian still couldn't find Dixon's car. It was all getting a bit desperate.

Earlier that morning, he had spoken with Sammy to try to understand why she had made the error. By all accounts, it was just down to her having a very bad day. Nation's insolence around the state of the Mercedes combined with Kicklighter's condescension had triggered her reaction. It wasn't anywhere near enough of an excuse, and Brian was left with a nagging impression that there was more to it than Sammy was letting on. Nonetheless, his partner had admitted to the mistake, and Brian had intended to berate her more severely over the amateurish cock-up but had stopped short because Sammy had come up with a very good idea for finding Dixon's car.

Some time ago, as part of her skills training, Sammy had undertaken some IT security exercises. One of the tasks Brian had set her was to try to hack certain aspects of Birmingham City Council's databases. Not only had she been supremely successful at her assignment, but she had also decided to leave a back door into the system so that the two of them could gain access at a later date. Sammy suggested she search the council parking ticket database using Dixon's registration number. The accountant would have parked up his car for the final time almost two days ago, and if it was in a council car park, it was bound to have been given a fixed penalty charge by now. If she searched the penalty notice section of the database and found the relevant registration number, they would have the location. Brian had to concede that it was a brilliant idea, and so he had asked her to execute the plan straight away. He needed her help, so any reprimand over the previous day's actions would have to wait.

Brian pulled into the car park at Cannon Hill Park and spotted Rosie hovering near the entrance. She was early, and

Brian guessed that she was probably nervous. He got out of the car and greeted her.

'Hi there, bab. How are you?'

'Fine thanks, Brian, I think. So what's the plan?'

'Right, well, the instruction was to meet at the bandstand at eleven, which gives us plenty of time. So we'll head over there now and we'll scope out the area. We'll make sure nothing is amiss, and then I'll pick out a place to hide. Don't worry, I'll have you in my sights at every moment of the meeting.'

'Ok, but what if the other person wants us to walk away from the bandstand and head back into the park?'

'I'll just drop in behind the two of you and follow. I'll stay some distance away, but you will never be in danger, and you'll never be out of my sight.'

'Fine. Great. That works for me,' Rosie responded, anxiously but firmly.

They set off into the park and headed for the bandstand on the opposite side of the grounds. The pair made small talk as they strolled across the lawns. Small park birds soared and swooped through the peaceful summer sky, while the fat geese waddled their way across the grassy terrain in search of discarded bread and snacks. The sound of young families merrily splashing about on the boating pond nearby sporadically cut through the harmony of the birdsong. The world was carrying on around them.

They passed the tennis courts and the crazy golf course, and after a short while, they reached the ornate bandstand situated to the south east of the park. Rosie took a seat and tried to keep her nerves in check while Brian conducted a quick inspection of the immediate area. The octagonal stage was still used for live performances and it was, logically, situated in a large open space that could be viewed easily from all sides. To its west and north was acre after acre of neat and freshly mown lawn, but on the southern and eastern sides, extensive areas of woodland lay about fifty metres from the stage.

Satisfied that there was nothing untoward in the immediate vicinity, and having found a place to take cover in the wooded area beyond, Brian returned to Rosie's bench opposite the bandstand.

'OK,' said Brian, checking his watch, 'let's grab a quick coffee, and I'll get into position ten minutes ahead of time.'

They made their way to the park's tea room a short stroll from the bandstand and ordered their drinks. They took a table in the shade of the terrace and sat quietly, absorbing the calm of the morning.

'This meeting. It's going to work out ok, isn't it?' asked Rosie.

'It will, I'm sure of it. There's no logical reason why someone would want to lure you here for any nefarious reason. I imagine you'll be met by some kind of whistle-blower. Someone clearly knows something about Nation or his businesses, and they want to share that information. The only question is, why share it with you?'

'I have no idea,' replied Rosie. 'And what if I feel as if I'm in trouble?'

'Don't fret. There's nothing to it; it'll be a walk in the park. It's, well, it's quite literally a walk in the park,' Brian replied before immediately regretting it.

Rosie couldn't help but smirk, despite trying to look stern. Brian, who knew the gaffe was entirely unintentional, wondered why he kept saying the most stupid things in Rosie's company. But he finally answered the question. 'Look, if you do feel concerned, if, at any point, you think you need some help, then we'll have a signal. Do you have a handkerchief on you?'

'Yes.'

'OK, so if, at any time, you feel you want my assistance, just blow your nose. I'll be with you in a flash.'

'Great, ok' said Rosie, feeling more confident with the backup plan.

The moment came when Brian needed to set off and position himself at his observation post, concealed deep within the woodland area of the park. Sometime later, Rosie followed the same path back to the bandstand, trying as best she could to breathe calmly and keep control of her racing heartbeat. She reached the stage, took the same bench as before and waited.

The minutes rolled slowly on as countless numbers of people passed by the bandstand. Some were jogging round the park, others were kicking footballs with friends, while still more were walking their dogs and taking in the morning air. The meeting organiser could have been any one of these people, Rosie thought, and she anxiously searched for Brian's face in the woodland beyond for reassurance. She knew he was in there somewhere, but she couldn't spot him at all. She started feeling exposed, isolated. All of the challenges she had confronted in her life she had faced head-on and with a steadfast resolve. But these last twenty-four hours had been something else.

She was just beginning to wonder how long she should wait when she heard a soft female voice from behind her.

'Rosie Bell?'

CHAPTER TWENTY-EIGHT

From his vantage point in the woodland, Brian had observed the woman in the dark blue business suit approaching Rosie's location. He had assumed that the smartly dressed lady was the meeting organiser while she was still some way out as her mannerisms betrayed her. The woman had been walking unusually slowly and cautiously while staring intently at Rosie's back. But at the same time, she was obviously trying to assess the immediate vicinity, searching to see whether there was anyone else planning to gatecrash her meeting. Brian had the nagging feeling that he had seen her before, although if he had, he couldn't place where. He followed the woman's path steadfastly, ready to react at a second's notice if required. He doubted there would be a need, however, since the stranger seemed about as nervous as Rosie.

Over at the bandstand, Rosie turned around with a start.

'Yes, that's me,' she replied to the unknown woman.

'I thought it was you. I recognise you from your photo in the local paper. They did a write-up on your restaurant yesterday.'

Rosie had a flashback to the disastrous interview a few days ago and cringed. Fortunately, and to her great relief, the piece had nonetheless been kind.

The lady in the suit went on. 'Thank you for coming. Do you mind if we go for a walk?'

'Well, ok, if you wish.' Rosie stood up and faced the lady. She estimated that she was about her own age, and her first impression was that she didn't seem dangerous in the slightest. The stranger was hardly oozing confidence, and that had a calming effect on Rosie, dispelling much of her earlier concern.

'What shall I call you?' asked Rosie, as they turned onto the path that led round the park.

'My name's Stephanie. Stephanie Sutton.'

'Well, then, hello Stephanie. It's nice to meet you.'

They walked on for a few steps, at which point Brian left his hiding place and dropped down onto the path, about twenty metres behind the two women.

'Perhaps you could tell me why you put your note under my door, Stephanie?' said Rosie, feeling emboldened by the businesswoman's apprehensive demeanour.

'Well, it's my understanding that you're having some difficulties with a man named Mike Nation?'

'And why would you think that, exactly?'

'I've… well I've been informed as much. By a friend of mine.'

'And who is this friend, may I ask?'

Stephanie hesitated. 'Look, can I trust you, Rosie?'

'That all depends on what's going on here, Stephanie. But I'd like to think I'm a trustworthy kind of woman.'

'Well, I hope so. You have to understand I'm taking a bit of a chance, arranging to meet you like this. It's risky for me.'

'I'm afraid I don't understand. And to be honest, I don't know what I'm doing here. Look, perhaps you had better just tell me your story.'

'Ok, but where to start? The thing is, I'm sort of dating someone. Well, maybe not dating as such, but certainly *seeing* someone, at least. Actually, he's a bit younger than me. Someone by the name of Tomasz. He has a brother...'

'Aleksandr!' said Rosie, putting the pieces together.

'Exactly. Alex, one of your chefs. Tomasz tells me that Alex really likes working for you, and he loves the restaurant. But by all accounts, he's worried about both you and The Balancing Act; he thinks there's something wrong. Tomasz says that Alex is convinced Mike Nation is to blame, and he seems desperate to help out somehow.'

'I see,' said Rosie thoughtfully. She was surprised that Aleksandr had figured out so much. 'Well, he may believe that something is wrong, but he can't know for sure. And while his fondness for the business is nice to hear, it's not really any concern of his, at the end of the day. And nor, for that matter, is it any concern of yours.'

'No, you don't understand. If it *is* true, then I know exactly what you are going through.'

'You do? Why would that be?'

'You see, I also own a business, much like you. I run an architect's firm in the city. It's small but ambitious, and up until recently, it was a very well-managed, profitable little company. But we got into some financial difficulty during the COVID crisis. Overnight, everything stopped being built, and the whole industry just ground to a halt. And if there is no need for new buildings, there is no need for architects.'

'This is beginning to sound very familiar,' said Rosie.

'I thought it would. I'm sure you remember how it was impossible to find any meaningful capital to get through that whole dreadful period. The company was draining its savings at a rate of knots, and there was a chance it would go under. That is, until Mike Nation turned up. We'd done some business with Nation Construction in the past, and he had heard that we were struggling financially. He injected some much-needed cash into the business and basically saved us from administration.'

'Let me guess. It was all good news at first, but things turned very sour, very quickly.'

'Precisely. He started pressurising us to lowball our tenders. He was getting us to "buy in" new business on terms that made no sense. When the business was on our books, we had to contrive ways of guaranteeing that his firm, Nation Construction, would get the order to build all the new projects we were designing. It's been an absolute nightmare.'

Rosie shook her head despondently. It was all sounding so recognisable. 'Stephanie, I can empathise more than you can possibly understand. The man is a tyrant. But, without wanting to sound dismissive, how would any of this help me out? It simply sounds as if we are two sides of the same coin. Surely yours is just another story of Nation ruining a decent local company?'

'I'm getting to that. But first I need to tell you something else. You see, my story isn't just about Nation forcing his way into winning all these new projects for his own business.

That was bad enough, but one day we realised the situation had got even worse. He had started using cheap materials in the building projects. Poor-quality materials, compromised stock. He gets them on the black market, from an overseas contact who fakes their quality certifications. None of it is up to standard, nowhere near the quality that it ought to be. And this all means that, in much of his current construction work, there are structural deficiencies throughout the buildings. Serious safety concerns. Some of the sites could just collapse, with people in them! One small failure and the whole thing could come down.'

'Jesus Christ.'

'Exactly. But the trouble is, I can't tell anyone. I can't blow the whistle because of all the influence he has on my business. He's basically blackmailing me. If I do file official complaints, he'll withdraw all his funding and I'll lose my business. And if that happens, he might even make it look like it was my firm that requested the dodgy materials in the first place. He'll blame me for it all. I'd never work in the industry again…'

Stephanie went red with rage and her eyes welled with emotion. Rosie gently touched her shoulder. Twenty metres away, Brian saw the gesture and wondered what on earth was going on up ahead.

'Stephanie, that's awful. I'm so sorry,' said Rosie. 'But I still don't understand what this all has to do with me…'

Stephanie composed herself, took a couple of breaths, then got to the core of the matter. 'Tomasz reckons that there may be people you know, people you can rely on, who might be willing to help. And these people may have access to equipment, and they may have certain rather specific skills.'

She had to be referring to Brian and Sammy. 'Go on…' said Rosie cautiously.

'Well, the projects that Nation is working on that are at the greatest risk of failing, the buildings that I reckon are the most vulnerable, also happen to pose the most risk to the public. You see, he's constructing the new railway stations.'

'Bloody hell, of course he is!'

'However, this might be where our opportunity lies. You see, I know all about those sites because my firm designed them. And I also know that there's a grand opening planned for the train line in a few days' time. So, I've been thinking. If the opening of the line was cancelled for some reason, maybe because one of the station buildings collapsed beforehand, then the implications for Nation both financially and politically would be huge. The embarrassment would be massive. He would be utterly humiliated if the big celebration was postponed due to his own firm's failings.

'But more importantly than that, the subsequent investigation into the cause of the collapse would be certain to uncover the substandard materials that Nation Construction has been using. He might lose his business; it could even ruin him. But even if that didn't happen, there would have to be implications for him. At the very least, all his firms would be probed for irregularities and it would force him to go straight.

'This would be game-changing for us, Rosie, and for our businesses. No more blackmail, no more dirty money, no more undue influence. We would get our livelihoods back! At least, that's the idea, anyway.'

Rosie couldn't fault the logic of the argument. Stephanie was right; Nation would probably lose everything. But even if he didn't, he would be so tied up in red tape and under such scrutiny that it would be impossible for him to continue his illegal activities.

'So, what would you need from my theoretical associates?' Rosie asked.

'The way I figure it, the station collapse just needs a little helping hand to make sure it comes down before the ceremony. It has to happen before the line opens to make sure none of the public gets hurt. But obviously, that means there needs to be a degree of, let's just say, specialist intervention. And I don't know anyone who could arrange that sort of thing, someone who could guarantee the timing of a building failure like that. Tomasz, however, seems to think that you might know some people who could assist...'

'What do you mean, exactly, when you say *specialist intervention*?'

'Based on my blueprints, I know that the site most vulnerable to collapse is Moseley Station, and I know exactly where the main structural weaknesses will be because I designed the damned place. It will be the two main steel girders that form the outside frame of the station. There's one on either side of the railway line at Moseley, and they run all the way up from the platforms right up to the ceiling of the station building above.'

'Ok, go on...'

Stephanie looked very nervous at what she was about to propose. 'The *specialist intervention* would be, well, I'm thinking...' she paused again and cleared her throat, '... positioning some sort of small explosive charges on these vulnerable points. They'd be designed to not cause too much damage in their own right but create just enough disturbance to ensure the immediate structural failure of the station…'

Rosie stared at her wide-eyed. 'Hang on! Are you telling me you want to blow up your own station? Surely you aren't being serious? It sounds utterly ludicrous!'

'It wouldn't be blowing it up, Rosie. Make no mistake. That building, it's coming down under its own steam anyway, and at some point very soon, I would imagine. All we are doing is ensuring it collapses before the railway passengers start using the station. Look at it this way: we'd actually be saving people from serious injury by guaranteeing the failure happens *before* the line is open. Meanwhile, we would have the significant added benefit of maximising the embarrassment to Nation.'

It was an astonishing plan, almost unbelievable. But the more Rosie thought about it, the more it started to make sense. And they would potentially be saving lives in the process. Maybe, in reality, they had a duty to do something?

Stephanie continued. 'Hopefully, you'll now understand why I wanted to have our conversation face to face and in this rather clandestine manner. It's not the sort of thing I would want to write down or discuss over the phone.'

'Yes, I understand.'

'Look, you don't have to answer me now, and I'm guessing you may want to speak with those friends of yours. But we do have a tight timescale. As I said, the grand opening is soon, in just three days' time. So if the plan is going to be activated, it needs to be sooner rather than later, if only for the sake of the public. Let me leave you with my phone number. If you decide you want to proceed, and if your associates want to know precisely where those weak points are, give me a call and I can arrange delivery of all the plans and drawings.'

Rosie scribbled the number down on the back of her hand, and when she'd finished, the two women looked at each other, uncertainly.

'Thanks for listening, Rosie,' said Stephanie. She gave the stunned chef a little hug and then hurried off towards the nearest park exit. Rosie watched her disappear into the distance, then looked around to get her bearings, feeling a little dizzy as she did so. She found herself next to the Boer War memorial at the northern end of the park, and luckily there were a few vacant benches nearby, so she picked one and collapsed into it, staring blindly beyond the monument and off into space. Her mind was racing wildly.

Within seconds, Brian had joined her and sat beside her on the bench.

'Well, what happened?' he probed eagerly.

'Umm... She wants to blow up Moseley Station,' Rosie said vaguely.

'I'm sorry, what? What are you on about? Who the hell is she?'

'She's an architect, and she's one of Nation's victims, just like me. She reckons the best way for us to get out of our predicament is to humiliate Nation. To ruin him. And she thinks she knows how.'

Brian didn't follow her. He was struggling to understand, and Rosie could tell as much. So she composed herself, refocussed and, turning to Brian, started again.

'OK, let me tell you exactly what that lady said, starting from the very beginning.'

It took Rosie a full fifteen minutes to repeat Stephanie's story and explain her incredible plan. Brian listened intently. He absorbed all the information and wrestled with the whole concept. On the face of it, the idea sounded totally implausible and ultimately very dangerous, but the more he thought about it, the more he had to admit there was a degree of credibility to the argument. Could Stephanie's plan actually work? It could. Theoretically. And anyway, he found the very thought of those stations being opened to the public in such a reckless condition contemptible.

At the end of the story, Brian knew one thing: he needed to do some research. Luckily, he already had some limited knowledge of the opening ceremony, since Nation had regularly bored him to tears about his supposed 'greatest project'. But he needed to know more, much more. Train line openings, collapsing stations, steam engines, politicians and celebrities like Sir Johnny Weaver. There were a lot of moving parts, which meant a lot of unpredictability. Brian had to get as much information as he could about the opening day, and he had to take the opportunity to reflect on it all.

'I need to have a think,' he said, finally. 'I need to read up on this opening ceremony business. I need to get hold of everything I can on the subject. Would we be able to meet up later today?'

'Yes, of course,' replied Rosie. 'The restaurant's closed today, so why don't we meet at The Balancing Act this evening?'

'That sounds like a plan, and I'll bring Sammy along with me. Oh, and Rosie, maybe you could ask those brothers, Aleksandr and Tomasz, to come along too. They seem pretty keen to get involved, and I have a feeling we might need all the help we can get.'

'Sure thing.'

At that moment, Brian's phone pinged. It was a text message from Sammy.

Have located Dixon's car.

Brian heaved a sigh of relief. This was great news, and he hoped to God that they would find the cash in the boot. The contradiction of his now working both for and against Mike Nation at the same time was not lost on him. Nonetheless, the money could still be the answer to everything. If Nation had the cash to clinch the retirement home deal, it might just get him off everyone's backs. He texted Sammy straight back.

Great work. Need you to gain access and search vehicle ASAP. Then meet me at Rosie's restaurant this evening for a debrief.

He got an immediate response.

OK, will do.

CHAPTER TWENTY-NINE

It was 8 p.m., and given that The Balancing Act was closed that day, it would normally have been deserted. Instead, a team of five people had gathered together around the large chef's table in the main dining area to discuss strategy and share information.

Brian had spent the day online, researching and analysing every piece of information available regarding the train line opening ceremony. He knew only too well that the secret to pulling off a successful tactical operation was all in the planning, and so planning was precisely what he had been doing.

Through various searches, he had managed to uncover a stack of documentation relating to the event, including the full itinerary, a list of invitees, security and maintenance arrangements for the day, the steam train itself, the speed limit of the track and the train timetable. Almost everything was online somewhere; you just needed to know where to look.

It turned out that the route wasn't opening to the public for a further week, the upcoming ceremony being a one-off event by special invitation only. This meant the only station that would actually be open on the day was the starting location, Stirchley. The train would then set off with its VIP party and travel slowly along the route, passing through the remaining stops, until it arrived in the city with great pomp and ceremony. This was excellent news. It meant there would be no members of the public at Moseley Station, the site that needed to collapse. The only people there would be the small maintenance team from Nation Construction.

Brian had worked his way through various imaginary scenarios, played around with different permutations of events and concluded that Stephanie's idea was just about workable. So he'd begun devising a formal plan.

He had wanted to come up with a strategy that would maximise the humiliation caused to Mike Nation. The spotlight that would fall on Nation and his businesses after the collapse needed to burn as brightly as possible. After several hours of work, he finally thought he had come up with just such a proposal.

Sammy, meanwhile, had been busy hunting down and then carefully breaking into Paul Dixon's car. She had successfully hacked the penalty charge notice database, having used her back door into the council's main system. Once in, she had found two outstanding parking tickets that had been assigned to Dixon's vehicle during the previous forty-eight hours. The tickets tracked back to the Navigation Street car park in the centre of town.

Having packed wire cutters, a hammer and a tea towel into her rucksack, she had headed into the city. The cycle ride had taken her no more than half an hour, and once there, Sammy had quickly found the accountant's car on the second floor of the structure. The car park had been deserted, so she'd retrieved the hammer and wrapped the tea towel round it to muffle the noise. With one swift motion, she had smashed one of the vehicle's side windows. As expected, the alarm had sounded, so she'd speedily entered the vehicle, popped the bonnet and skipped round to the front of the car. Sammy had checked on the make and model of the vehicle beforehand, which meant she was quickly able to locate the secondary fuse box, the alarm sounder and the alarm's backup battery, all of which were disconnected within a matter of seconds with the help of the wire-cutters.

With quiet restored, Sammy had conducted a thorough and methodical search of the vehicle, starting with the main cabin and glove box, then moving to the boot, the spare wheel well and even the spaces between the trim and the bodywork. She checked everywhere but came up blank. There was nothing of interest, certainly no eight hundred thousand pounds.

Rosie had had her tasks to complete as well. She had contacted Aleksandr, and during the difficult phone call, she had finally admitted that he had been right about Mike Nation all along. He was indeed damaging The Balancing Act and putting the business at risk. Swearing him to secrecy, she had explained how his investment in the restaurant had come about and how he was now manipulating the books for his own shady gains.

She had thanked Alexandr for his loyalty and explained that a plan was being developed, something rather radical in nature, which might help resolve the Mike Nation problem. Alexandr had said he was only too happy to assist in any way he could and would definitely make the evening's meeting.

At Brian's suggestion, Rosie had also asked Aleksandr to see whether his brother would attend, and if he was willing to do so, Tomasz was to bring with him the 'vital information his girlfriend held'. Aleksandr had no idea what Rosie was referring to, but by all accounts, it was important to the plan. He had passed on the message to his brother, and Tomasz, who had started the whole chain of events by putting Stephanie and Rosie together, had been only too happy to help out.

And so, at eight o'clock, the team were all gathered together, spread around the imposing table in front of the kitchens, ready to set out their plans. Brian clinked an empty glass with the back of a spoon and brought the meeting to order.

'Thank you for coming, everybody. The first thing to say is that there is one very important rule of the evening. Whatever is said in this room stays in this room. We'll be sharing some facts and saying some things that we don't want going any further. Is everyone ok with that?'

Rosie, Sammy and the brothers all nodded their agreement.

'Ok, then, I'll begin. We're all here because of one man, and one man alone. Mike Nation. Businessman, entrepreneur, tosspot. And as I see it, all of us here have a valid reason for wanting to see Nation and his businesses fail. Let me explain.

'From my perspective, not so long ago, Nation charged me with a very specific task of uncovering the whereabouts of a substantial sum of his money. He stressed to me that failure was not an option; he simply had to have that cash recovered. He made it clear to me that if I did fall short, the consequences for both myself and for others would be significant. And yet, as of right now, I'm afraid to say I have no idea where the money is.

'Meanwhile, Sammy here very recently jeopardised an important business deal of Nation's, a deal he was going to use the lost money to clinch. It was an inadvertent error, but there could well be reprisals for the misjudgement. I don't know exactly what form that payback would likely take, but what I do know is it will be bad.

'As for Rosie and Aleksandr, well, Nation undoubtedly has the power to damage this restaurant very badly, and possibly fatally. With the missing money still not found, his interventions at The Balancing Act will very likely get even worse, and it goes without saying we need to avoid that at all costs.

'And finally, a similar story applies to your friend's business, Tomasz. Nation, unfortunately, has the power to ruin Stephanie's firm, or at the very least blame it for his own failings.

'Right now, Nation is backed into a corner and he needs to find a lot of money quickly, which means his actions are likely to be unpredictable and harmful. Therefore, I believe we all have a collective interest in Nation's downfall. Agreed?'

Everyone nodded enthusiastically once again.

'Let's ruin the jerk!' declared Sammy.

'Thank you, Sammy. Ok, so to that end, a plan has been developed. For those who are unaware, Nation's current pride and joy, his new train stations, have been built using cheap and defective materials, which means one station in particular – Moseley – is already on the verge of collapse.

The plan is to guarantee that collapse and thereby interrupt the grand opening ceremony.

'This would have the short-term benefit of bringing shame and embarrassment to Nation and his business, but the long-term consequences would be even greater. The subsequent investigation into the collapse would be bound to uncover the dodgy supply of material and Nation might well go to prison. Everyone following so far?'

'You said we're going to *guarantee* the collapse. What do you mean by that?' asked Aleksandr. 'Are you on about knocking it down?'

'Effectively, yes, but we will be using a couple of small explosive charges to get the timing spot on.'

'Explosives, what the hell? Isn't that bloody dangerous?'

'Don't worry, handsome,' replied Sammy, patting her boyfriend's thigh. 'It's all under control.' She gave him a wink, but Aleksandr didn't look convinced.

'Even so, surely someone will hear the noise! Won't it be suspicious?'

'We'll be timing the charges together, so there will be only one noise,' replied Brian. 'Hopefully, it will be assumed the sound was just the start of the building failure. Regardless, as long as we get away clean, we won't have anything to worry about.'

Tomasz agreed. 'Even if the explosives are discovered, I'd hazard a guess that people would assume it was an inside job. There are a lot of explosives in the demolition arm of Nation Construction, and a lot of rather dishonourable men as well!'

'Good point,' said Brian. 'Now then, we could theoretically cause the collapse of Moseley Station at any time between now and the grand opening. Any damage at any point from now on would inevitably lead to the postponement of the ceremony. However, I believe we are best served by causing the maximum amount of embarrassment to Nation, so I believe we should cause the station's collapse while the steam train is actually on the move. The carriages will be full of TV reporters and journalists, and if the train is forced to pull up halfway along its route, the photo and film opportunities will be perfect.'

Brian rolled out a large map of South Birmingham on the centre of the chef's table and positioned a wine glass on each corner to keep it in place. The new train line was clearly marked on the map in red. Everyone leaned inwards and studied the drawing.

'Ok, so this is what I propose. The steam train collects its VIP guests and starts its journey here, at Stirchley.'

'Stirchley *Village…*' said Sammy mischievously.

'It then goes on, passing through Kings Heath, here, and up into Moseley.'

'Moseley *Village…*'

'Shut up, Sammy. And finally, the train continues its journey on into town and is due to arrive at Birmingham Snow Hill Station half an hour after its departure, with great fanfare and celebration.

'Now, the only station with any actual access on the day of the ceremony is Stirchley. The other two stops remain closed until real services commence in a week's time. This means there is no danger to the public, even if Moseley were to collapse during the ceremony. If the steam train is forced to stop right at the foot of the Moseley Station rubble, the only people inconvenienced will be all those dignitaries and journalists marooned on the railway line, with all those TV cameras to capture the moment. Nation's downed station would make national news. It could even go global. Utter humiliation.'

'How are we going to manage to get the timing just right?' asked Rosie.

'Well, as long as the steam train passes through Kings Heath Station, there's no way of getting the driver to stop until Moseley, when he'll see the debris lying on the tracks. Which means Moseley has to fall just as the train passes through Kings Heath.'

'Sounds bloody dangerous to me… I mean, will the train definitely stop in time?' asked Tomasz.

'The whole journey is intentionally being made at a low speed. The driver has been instructed to stick to thirty miles per hour for the whole route. Bear in mind Sir Johnny Weaver is going to be on the footplate of the train, and the organisers are expecting a lot of people to come out and try to get a glimpse of him riding into Birmingham. To give them the best chance of seeing him, the train will just be trundling into town. The speed, coupled with the train track being one long, straight line for the run into Moseley, means the driver will see the carnage a long way out and easily stop in time.'

'I don't understand. What you seem to be saying is that you're only going to set off the charges when the train passes through King Heath. How will you *know* when it has passed through?' asked Rosie

'That's where you guys come in. Timing is everything for the plan to work. Tomasz, I've learned that Nation

Construction will keep a small maintenance team at each station to fix any last-minute issues?'

'That's right.'

'Good. Do you think you could get on the team for Stirchley?'

'I think so, yes.'

'Perfect. And Aleksandr, would you be willing to join the crowd at the road bridge next to Kings Heath Station, just here?' Brian pointed to the place on the large map.

'Sure.'

'Excellent. So, here's what I want you to do. The moment the train departs Stirchley, Tomasz, you text the word STIRCHLEY to Sammy and me. That will be our cue to break into Moseley Station. We can't force our entry too early as there will be a maintenance team there too, and if we're spotted, there's a chance the train could be stopped.

'Once we're in, I figure we'll have around five minutes to position the two charges in the right place. Then, Aleksandr, as the steam engine passes through Kings Heath Station, you text us KINGS HEATH. That will be our signal to blow the charges simultaneously, as we'll know the train can no longer be alerted. A few minutes later, the train driver will see the remnants of the station and stop the train.

'And what do I do?' asked Rosie.

Brian looked at her affectionately. 'Rosie, you need to sit this out.'

'Wait, what? Absolutely not. No chance. No way, Brian, I have to do something!'

'You need complete deniability in this whole thing, Rosie. You and Stephanie, your circumstances are different. You guys have entire businesses in jeopardy here, and if any of this got back to either of you, you could lose your life's work. The two of you must be able to deny that you had any involvement in this plan, particularly if something goes wrong. Which of course it won't,' Brian added confidently.

Rosie looked furious, but she didn't say anything. She knew that Brian had come up with the whole proposal, and he was doing it all, in large part, for her sake. She would have to swallow her pride.

'Ok, guys,' said Brian, 'let's make sure everyone knows what's happening. Let's run through it all one more time…'

CHAPTER THIRTY

Three days after the meeting at The Balancing Act, it was the big day, the grand opening ceremony, and the platform at Stirchley Station was crammed. Local dignitaries, VIPs, politicians, celebrities and TV, radio and print news were all in attendance, chatting away excitedly while soaking in the atmosphere and the glorious sunshine. A brass band was positioned at one end of the platform playing pomp and ceremony music, and at the other end, famed local television reporter Trevor Critchley was busy setting up a shot with his cameraman. *BBC Midlands Today* had rolled out their big guns for the teatime news bulletin, and Trevor was there to tape an item for the show.

The *Shakespeare Express*, a heritage steam locomotive normally stabled in the railway museum of Birmingham, was idling adjacent to the platform, periodically letting off hissing noises as the air brakes held the engine in place. Behind the tender, three perfectly preserved traditional passenger carriages completed the train set, their brass door knobs gleaming in the sun.

Sir Johnny, who, as promised, had turned up in the full cowboy outfit he famously wore in *Slow Train to St Louis*, was busy holding court, and he was relishing the attention. A gaggle of photographers jostled and danced around him, trying to get the best snap of the ageing film star. Out of the corner of his eye, Sir Johnny spotted Trevor Critchley coming over to say hello.

'Ah, well, if it isn't "Ten-Takes Trevor"!' Sir Johnny joked. Trevor groaned dramatically but shook the film star's hand nonetheless. The two men had known each other for decades, Trevor having started his TV career in drama rather than television news. Trevor hated the now infamous nickname, but he knew there was an element of truth to the moniker. In those early days, his outtakes and bloopers had made annual Christmas specials with alarming regularity until, one day, the work just dried up and Trevor was forced to take a different path. He had finally found his home specialising in comfy community news pieces and had built a successful career out of it.

'Hello, Sir Johnny. You're looking well,' Trevor said. 'I can't believe you can still fit into that thing.'

'Bloody miracle, old boy!' Sir Johnny replied with a giggle, and he patted his stomach theatrically. His eyes fell on Trevor's colleague. 'And *who* on earth is this?' he asked melodramatically, gazing longingly at the handsome young man holding a TV video camera.

'Well, quite obviously, it's my cameraman, Sir Johnny. I would have thought the big black contraption on his shoulder would have given that away.'

'Well, he can use his big black contraption on me anytime,' Sir Johnny said with a wink.

'Jesus, Johnny,' Trevor groaned, shaking his head in despair.

Sir Johnny sidled up to the cameraman. 'My dear old young thing, you look awfully toned! You must work out, I presume? I can imagine you're exceedingly... dextrous... How wonderful for you! It's a dreadful struggle for me, I'm sad to report. All that exercise and dieting, it's forever been a challenge. But people can get rather carried away over diets, don't you think? It's all Keto this, and Atkins that. Very confusing, wouldn't you say?'

'Erm, I'd not really thought about it, to be honest, pal,' replied the confused cameraman.

'Diets, old boy. There's hundreds of them, and who's to know which one works? Extreme calorie counting, that's another one. People count the calories in literally everything! Even the things you simply can't do without. Like toothpaste!'

'I see.'

'And aspirin!'

'Blimey.'

'And bacon!'

'Madness.'

'Well, quite, old boy.'

This was going rather well, Sir Johnny thought. He hoped that Trevor Critchley and his cameraman would be joining him on the footplate for the journey into Birmingham. All nice and snug in such a confined little space. That really would be marvellous.

'Do you like my gun?'

'I'm sorry?' the cameraman spluttered.

'My gun, old boy! It's the original, you know. From the movie!'

Trevor Critchley decided it was time to interject. 'Billy, stop annoying Sir Johnny, would you? Let's set up over there; I need to do my piece to camera. And get the bloody steam train in the background, ok?'

'Yes, Trev.'

Sir Johnny beamed like a Cheshire cat as he watched Trevor and the cameraman squeeze down the platform to get a better shot of the steam engine. Each time Billy glanced behind him, Sir Johnny was there, happily waving back in his direction.

When the TV crew reached the front of the train, Billy put the camera on his shoulder and gave Trevor the thumbs up. Trevor coughed, cleared his throat, and made a peculiar gargling noise that made Sir Johnny feel slightly nauseous. The reporter straightened his tie and turned to the camera.

'You join me here at Stirchley Station for the ceremonial opening of a new train line which is being launched to serve residents in the south of the city. Passenger services last ran along these tracks in the 1940s, and while services don't start today, and none of the stations along the line are, as yet, officially open, a regular timetable will run from next week.

'In the meantime, a one-off service on the *Shakespeare Express*, this glorious Pullman train hauled by an old Great Western Railway steam engine, will today travel from Stirchley, right up the route and into the City, carrying dignitaries and VIPs alike. And while the stations may not yet be open, residents are nonetheless lining the route in numbers, all trying to catch a glimpse of this beautiful steam train making the inaugural journey to Birmingham.

'Riding on the footplate for the journey into the city is local hero and global film legend Sir Johnny Weaver. Sir Johnny will be officially opening the line, and he will be joining me later for an exclusive interview. He's here in the very same outfit he made famous in the classic 1970s film *Slow Train to St Louis*, and I can tell you, it's quite a sight! So make sure you tune in to this evening's full report. This is Trevor Critchley, for BBC Midlands Today, in Stechford.'

'We're in Stirchley, Trev,' said Billy.

'Oh, for God's sake… Ok, one more time…'

They repeated the piece, and fortunately old Ten Takes nailed the second go around. 'Did you get all that, Billy?' he asked his cameraman.

'Yes, Trev'

'Great. Ok, let's go and do the interview with the mad old fart, then…'

From the relative seclusion of the station master's office, Tomasz watched the man from the television news interviewing the strange old bloke in the cowboy outfit. He didn't recognise the cowboy chap at all, but whoever he was, he was having a bloody good time.

Tomasz, however, was not having a bloody good time. In fact, he was very much on edge. His anxiety wasn't being caused by any fear of being discovered; after all, he was at the station in an official capacity, having secured a spot on the maintenance team. Instead, his nerves were entirely driven by a very real and conscious concern that the station roof might fall on his head at any moment.

Ever since he had learned about the shoddy materials that he'd unknowingly been using to help build the stations, being inside one of them was the last place he had wanted to be. Tomasz longed to be out in the relative safety of the open air, alongside all the oddballs he had been watching through the office window. If they only knew the truth about their surroundings, they wouldn't be quite so bloody cheerful, Tomasz thought.

Tomasz had two sets of orders to follow. His instructions as part of the maintenance team were simple, in that he was to stay in the station master's office and out of sight unless called upon. So far, his services had not been required.

His instructions from Brian as part of the "screw-over-Nation" team were equally simple. The moment the train departed Stirchley, he was to text Brian accordingly. Fortunately, the station master's office had a clear view out onto the platform area, and so his posting had afforded him an excellent position from where he could watch the action. All he had to do now was wait. And hope the roof held.

Trevor Critchley wrapped up his interview with Sir Johnny just as Mike Nation arrived, accompanied by his special guest from America. Colonel Kicklighter had once again chosen to wear his full military uniform for the ceremony. He had had it pressed by the hotel the previous day, figuring that it was the most suitable attire for civil formalities such as this. Plus, he goddamned loved wearing his military uniform when meeting overseas dignitaries.

Nation made a beeline for Sir Johnny, and The Colonel followed hot on his heels, looking as excited as a kid at Christmas.

'Sir Johnny! Allow me to introduce myself. My name's Nation, Mike Nation.'

'Delighted to meet you, Nation, old boy. And what brings you to this little function of ours?'

'Well, my firm did build the bloody place, so it seemed as good an excuse as any to come down and join in with the festivities.'

'Is that so? Well, jolly good show! And what a lovely job you have made of it, too. My congratulations to you and your team.'

'Well, thank you, Sir Johnny! We do build more than for any other reason!'

'I'm sorry?'

'Oh, nothing. It's just a thing we like to say. Anyway, may I introduce you to a colleague of mine? This is Colonel John P. Kicklighter. He's a huge fan.' Nation gestured towards The Colonel.

'Colonel John P. Kicklighter, you say? Good grief, bit of a mouthful that, old boy! Is that a stage name, by chance?'

'No, sir. It's a one hun'red percent, bona fide, red-blooded, pure Texan name, so help me God!' replied The Colonel. He saluted Sir Johnny stiffly.

'Well, jolly good for you,' said Sir Johnny, and extravagantly saluted back.

'I understand you're actually from Birmingham, Sir Johnny?' The Colonel enquired.

The elderly actor gazed round the platform as if he were surveying the whole of the city. 'Oh yes, this is my home town alright,' he said excitedly. 'The one and only Birmingham!'

'Well, other than the one in Alabama.'

'Ahh… well yes, quite, old boy,' Sir Johnny conceded with a smile.

Phillip Bland, the metro mayor, arrived on the scene. He too was a fan of Sir Johnny's, and he had spotted the film star standing next to Mike Nation, whom Bland knew from the generous "charitable donations" that he had made to his re-election campaign. Bland sauntered over to join the group and introduce himself. As usual for an occasion such as this, he was sporting a high visibility jacket and hard hat, once again looking as if he had built the place himself. In fact, the dazzling gear had been purchased specifically for the occasion.

Bland stood next to Sir Johnny and waited for an opportunity to interrupt. Meanwhile, Nation stared at the men in front of him. Something was ringing bells in the deep recesses of his mind. Sir Johnny in his cowboy outfit, The Colonel in his army uniform and Bland in the construction worker's apparel. He looked at them again, one after another. Army man, cowboy, construction worker. Army man, cowboy, construction worker. Suddenly it clicked: it was the bloody *Village People!* Nation momentarily let out a loud snort of laughter before swiftly recomposing himself. Dear Lord, he was staring at a Village People tribute band!

The three other men looked confused, but Nation said nothing. It was all he could do to avoid launching into a spirited chorus of *Y-M-C-A*. Instead, he closed his eyes and pictured the three dignitaries in front of him bursting into song.

The council leader, Colin Smith, appeared. Following the fiasco of the *Floozie in the Jacuzzi* reopening when Bland had upstaged him once again, Smith had been waiting patiently to take his revenge. His time had arrived, and he had turned up wearing not only his very own hard hat and high visibility jacket but matching high visibility trousers and gloves as well. He was sweating his bollocks off in all that shiny paraphernalia, and he was becoming concerned that he might pass out at any moment. But sod it, he had figured it was well worth it. He saw Bland and waved, a smug touché smile planted across his face. Bland was furious.

Nation, meanwhile, who was still quietly enjoying his vivid daydream of the disco band, spotted the council leader in his own bright yellow outfit. Once again he let out a quiet, involuntarily snigger before whispering under his breath, 'We've already got one of them, pal. You should have come as an American Indian…'

Closing his eyes once more, he imagined the council leader joining the band. '*Y-M-C-A*' the four of them sang out in his head, and he imagined the brass band dropping the pomp and ceremony music to join in with the tune.

Back in the real world, Sir Johnny, The Colonel and the two politicians, who had all been politely chatting away, paused momentarily and stared at Nation. His eyes were shut and his head was bobbing up and down, and they feared the poor fellow had gone completely mad.

Nation's musical fantasy was interrupted by an announcement over the tannoy system that the official ribbon-cutting was about to commence. A long pink silk ribbon appeared from nowhere and was extended across the line in front of the steam engine.

The VIPs pushed and shoved to gain a better view as Sir Johnny was invited up to conduct the formalities. He was handed an absurdly oversized pair of scissors, much to his delight. He cleared his throat and the crowd hushed. All that could be heard was the occasional click of camera shutters.

'Howdy, pardners!' he began. The crowd chuckled in appreciation.

'I know I'm not the tallest man in the world, which is why I'm wearing my *platform* shoes…!'

Quiet coughs echoed across the station.

Sir Johnny persisted. 'I'll keep my speech short, in the hope that I don't get *de-railed*…!'

Silence. Someone at the back whispered, 'Jesus Christ….'

'Right, well, anyway, my passion for the railways is well known to all. Ever since *Slow Train to St Louis*, my enthusiasm for all things trains and railroads has remained undiminished. The rich history and romance of train travel, particularly steam travel, must surely be unrivalled. I doubt any of us could envisage choosing to read or watch *Murder on the Orient Bus!*'

The gathering offered a sympathetic murmur this time, while collectively hoping the old man would get on with it.

'And now the honour bestowed upon me by the city of my birth is to open this brand new railway line, which will serve the great citizens of Birmingham for years to come. This privilege brings together my two life passions: my city and my trains. And so, without further ado, I declare this new railway line open!'

'In about a week...' Nation added, under his breath.

Loud applause rang out through the crowd as Sir Johnny cut the ribbon with the ridiculous pair of scissors. Bottles of champagne were popped, and the fizzy liquid shot up into the air.

At the back of the platform stood Phillip Bland, who had surreptitiously fastened a small brass plaque to the wall. It was covered by a tiny curtain.

'Thank you very much, Sir Johnny,' he called out. 'And now, ladies and gentlemen, please allow me to announce this *particular station*, Stirchley Station, also officially open.' He grinned with delight as he pulled the little string that drew the curtains.

The second official opening in as many seconds took the crowd by surprise, but they quickly recognised the unscheduled act was just part of the two politicians' ribbon wars. Unconvincingly, they clapped briefly once again. Inside his sweaty heap of high viz kit, Colin Smith, the council leader, was livid. Bland smirked.

Up and down the platform, well-dressed attendants appeared from nowhere. They opened the carriage doors with one hand while holding silver trays laden with champagne glasses in the other. The tannoy hummed into action once more, and the tinny voice made another announcement.

'The eleven hundred hours *Shakespeare Express* special service will be departing from platform one in ten minutes. Would all passengers please now board the train at your convenience.'

CHAPTER THIRTY-ONE

Dynamite was famously invented by Alfred Nobel, the man who inadvertently read his own obituary in a French newspaper, having not in fact died after all. He was appalled to learn from his own notice of passing that he was to be dubbed 'the merchant of death', thanks to his infamous creation. This stark realisation prompted Nobel to leave his entire fortune, upon his actual death some years later, to the benefit of mankind with the creation of the five Nobel prizes.

It was Nobel's initial invention, however, that Sammy was collecting from the safe inside the lock-up on the small south Birmingham industrial estate. Brian had asked her to collect two sticks and some fuse wire and meet him at Moseley Station. Dynamite had always been Brian's explosive of choice, and luckily Terry could source it relatively easily. It was extremely reliable and not particularly expensive in the grand scheme of all things explosive, so he always made sure he had a couple of sticks in stock.

Brian checked his watch. He thought Sammy would have reached the station by now. Timing was everything today, so he dropped her a text to make sure nothing was wrong.

Where are you?

Ten seconds later the reply beeped through.

Poundland

Brian typed quickly.

WHAT?

As soon as he hit send, he received another text from Sammy.

Joking... Three minutes out.

That girl is going to be the death of me, he thought.

He had been in position for around a quarter of an hour, hidden deep in the trees to the side of the station car park. Earlier that morning, Tomasz had told him that the maintenance 'team' for the Moseley site was rostered to be just one man: Derek Penrice, the foreman. Given that the station remained closed and the train was not stopping at Moseley, Nation had cut the team to a single employee to keep his overtime costs down. Brian had spotted Penrice through the portacabin window. He seemed to have fallen asleep in the chair behind the desk, and Brian knew that it would be extremely handy if he remained asleep throughout the entire event.

The plan was simple enough. On receipt of the text STIRCHLEY, Brian and Sammy were to scale the security fencing, cross the car park, gain entry to the station and secure the dynamite at the specific locations Stephanie had pinpointed in the blueprints. The target positions were the vertical girders at the top of each stairwell on either side of the railway. Once fastened securely in place, Sammy and Brian were to wait for the KINGS HEATH text, at which point they would light the fuse on each stick and then get the hell out of there. It was a good plan, Brian thought. He believed he had reduced the list of unknowns dramatically, what with the timing of the text notifications and their own delayed ingress into Moseley. The only factor outside of their control, Brian figured, was Derek Penrice.

While he waited for Sammy, Brian's mind wandered back to the phone call he had taken from Mike Nation earlier in the day. Nation had wanted one final update regarding the missing money before he linked up with The Colonel to head off for the ceremony. He had sounded increasingly manic as the days passed without any positive news, and it seemed that he was resigning himself to the fact that he would have to raise the money from elsewhere. Brian had felt sick to his stomach when, with a final passing comment at the end of the most recent call, Nation announced there was nothing else for it, he would have to bleed The Balancing Act dry.

So much was riding on the success of the morning's operation, far more than he was comfortable with. He considered his own views of Nation and the journey those opinions had taken over the course of just the last week or so. Brian's position had shifted full circle, from an attitude of complete apathy towards Nation and his dodgy dealings to one where his eyes had been forced wide open to the damage he was causing. Where once he had seen Nation as a useful and profitable contact, a slightly clownish orange man with a reliable stream of business, he now saw him as something else. His blackmailing activities did awful harm, and Brian knew he could not let it go on. For Rosie's sake, if nothing else.

The noise of a revving engine broke Brian's train of thought, and he glanced over his shoulder to see Sammy parking the clapped-out van in the layby nearby. She had understandably decided that cycling to the meeting point with a couple of sticks of dynamite would be ill-advised, so she had reluctantly used the van, despite the lingering scent of *Eau de Dixon* hanging in the cabin air. She grabbed the dynamite sticks and the fuse wire and headed over to Brian's location, then handed him the explosives.

'Any issues?' she asked.

'None so far. Just the one man on site, as Tomasz suggested. The foreman, Penrice. And I think he's fallen asleep in the portacabin.'

'Handy,' she said. She checked her watch. 'The train should be leaving Stirchley in a few minutes.'

Brian nodded. From his jacket pocket he took out his penknife and a small measuring tape. Carefully he measured out a fifteen-centimetre length of fuse wire and made the cut. Fifteen centimetres equated to thirty seconds of time, based on the type of wire he was using. That would be more than enough time to get clear. He repeated the process a second time and attached the fuses to the dynamite sticks. He looked at Sammy. 'When it's time, I'll do the farside girder, you do the nearside, ok?'

'How very noble of you,' Sammy replied with a smile. She would be clear of the station a few seconds before Brian as she would be nearer to the entrance.

'OK, it'll be any minute now. Get ready.'

Four miles back down the line at Stirchley Station, time was marching on. The driver of the *Shakespeare Express* was preparing for its departure, but there was a problem. It seemed that pretty much all the VIPs thought they were invited onto the open-sided footplate of the cab for the ride into town, and there was a danger of a fight breaking out among the guests. The entire group of *The Village People* was certainly expecting to be invited onto the locomotive. Sir Johnny was, of course, bound to be on the footplate, being the guest of honour. Mike Nation absolutely needed to be on the footplate; he argued he'd built the damned train line in the first place. His personal guest, Colonel John P Kicklighter, also had to get a place. The metro mayor had previously been promised a position, and if the metro mayor was on the footplate, the council leader was damned well going to be on it as well. But the actual driver and the fireman were also required, so that made seven people stuffed into the tiny cab for the journey into Birmingham. And they just didn't all fit in.

At first, Sir Johnny had tried to get Trevor Critchley and the handsome cameraman onto the footplate as well, but that idea had been kyboshed at a very early stage. Sir Johnny had apologised to Trevor. 'Awfully sorry about this, old boy. Tell you what, why don't you bugger off back to first class and get a nice glass of champers, and we'll have a proper catch-up at the end of the ride?'

Critchley reluctantly complied and wandered back down the platform with his cameraman, then took a seat in the first carriage. But that hadn't solved the problem; there was still too much congestion on the footplate. The seven dignitaries had finally got on board the footplate, but none of them could move. The driver was simply unable to drive with all of them in the cab, so he announced that he would not pull out of the station unless at least one more person left the engine.

Arguments erupted, with each suggesting that someone, indeed *anyone* other than themselves should be ejected from the locomotive. They insisted that under the hierarchy of VIP-ness, their own importance was most certainly higher than any of the others', so they had every right to stand their ground. It appeared that they had reached a rather ugly impasse until Sir Johnny had an idea. He pointed to the fireman.

'What about him?' he asked.

'Don't be ridiculous – I'm the fireman!' exclaimed the fireman.

'So what?'

'You need a driver and fireman to drive the train!'

'Nonsense, old boy!' declared Sir Johnny, and there were murmurs of agreement from the remaining guests.
'The crazy old fruit bat might be onto something,' whispered Nation to The Colonel.

'This isn't the bloody movies now,' argued the fireman, getting agitated. 'It's against health and safety to drive a steam train without the two professionals on the footplate. I'm not going anywhere, and that's final.'

'But you see, you're missing the point, dear boy! I was fully trained as a locomotive engineer while filming *Slow*

Train to St Louis! I am very well capable of shovelling a bit of coal and checking the pressure on a couple of little dials! Old Johnny boy here shall fulfil the role of fireman and *you* may enjoy the ride into town from the passenger carriages.'

The fireman looked as if he was going to explode, but Sir Johnny was getting more and more vocal support from the rest of the group. Phillip Bland, the metro mayor, a man normally so health and safety conscious he would wear a hard hat in the bath, decided he was fully supportive of the proposal. He knew that it would be politically disastrous if he missed the photo op of the engine arriving in town, particularly if the council leader was on the footplate, so he went along with the plan, which meant the council leader had to follow suit.

It was clear that neither The Colonel nor Mike Nation was going anywhere, and the driver looked exasperated. The train was now running late. The driver figured it was only eight miles to the terminus and they were capped at thirty miles per hour maximum speed. What could go wrong? Reluctantly he turned to his fireman.

'Look, why don't you head back to the carriages for this run?'

'But the bloody regulations!' complained the fireman.

'Screw the regulations!' Nation barked. He was getting annoyed that he couldn't get YMCA out of his head, and the delay was putting him in a bad mood.

Fuming, the fireman stood his ground for a few seconds, but the driver cast a desperate, pleading look in his direction. Reluctantly he threw his gloves to the floor, climbed down from the driver's cab and skulked across the platform to sit with Trevor Critchley in the back. He grabbed two flutes of champagne as he clambered inside the first-class compartment, muttering swear words under his breath as he went.

The VIPs cheered loudly at their victory. Meanwhile, the driver saw that he had a green light from the signal ahead.

'Just try and keep out of my way, all right?' he said to them all. They nodded their agreement, and the driver blasted the train whistle twice before releasing the locomotive's air brake. The engine slowly lurched forwards.

Back inside the station building, Tomasz, who was still located in the station master's office at the side of the platform, speedily typed

STIRCHLEY

into his phone and hit send.

CHAPTER THIRTY-TWO

'Go! Go!' said Brian urgently as he received the message from Tomasz.

The pair dashed over to the security fencing. Sammy scaled the mesh wiring, flipped over and landed silently on the other side of the fence in one smooth movement. Through the latticework of metal, Brian passed her the two dynamite sticks and then followed her over the top, with slightly less grace but with no less speed. Once on the station side, Brian took one of the dynamite sticks back from Sammy and the pair deftly crossed the station car park while keeping a watching brief on the portacabin. No sign of Derek the foreman.

They reached the station entrance, which, as they had guessed, was once again padlocked. Brian fished out his lock-picking kit from his jacket pocket and set to work once again. Grabbing the lock in his hand, he realised that the padlock had been upgraded since their earlier visit. The new mechanism was far sturdier than previously, with a much bigger shackle securing the door and a considerably longer cylinder, as well.

'Bugger,' he whispered under his breath. They didn't have time for this.

Two miles further down the line, Aleksandr was in position on the road bridge near Kings Heath Station, looking southwards and staring intently in the direction of Stirchley. His brother had sent him the same text message as the one he had sent to Brian, so Aleksandr knew the steam engine was on its way. He had his mobile phone in his hand with the messaging app open in readiness.

A further two miles to the south of Aleksandr, the steam train was speeding up. It was approaching its designated limit of thirty miles per hour and was rattling across the railway tracks. The familiar clackety-clack noise rang out as the train made its journey north towards the city centre, and the engine's cab began rocking and shaking as the train picked up speed. The movement had an unbalancing effect on the five VIP guests on the footplate, and they bumped and jostled each other as they tried to stabilise themselves in the tiny cab.

Despite the commotion, Sir Johnny was in dreamland; he was living his best life. He called out an excited 'Yeeha!' reached down into his holster and drew his gun. From the edge of the speeding footplate, he pretended to fire shots at various imaginary rail-side baddies, just as he had done in his movie all those years ago. Colonel Kicklighter watched the actor with delight as his hero re-enacted his greatest film. He couldn't help but join in with the carnival atmosphere, so he took off his Texan hat and waved it in the air, launching into an impassioned verse of 'She'll be coming round the mountain when she comes'.

The pushing and shoving were getting out of hand. 'Stop doing that!' yelled the driver at the two of them, but Sir

Johnny and The Colonel were having too much fun. They ignored the driver completely and did a little jig together in the middle of the footplate.

Sir Johnny decided that his view out of the opposite side of the train was not what it could be, as the driver was frustratingly in the way. There were bound to be imaginary baddies over on that side of the track that needed shooting, so mid-dance he decided to give the driver a little nudge out of the way to give him better aim. As he did so, the train lurched over a set of points, which meant the little push unexpectedly became a rather heavy-handed thrust. It caught the unsuspecting driver completely off-guard and he lost his balance, staggering back a couple of steps towards the edge of the footplate. The VIPs were frozen to the spot as the driver frantically reached out for a non-existent arm to help him regain his footing. Grabbing at thin air, the driver toppled backwards out of the cab, sailing through the breeze and landing with a thud on the grass verge at the side of the tracks. He tumbled down the embankment, gambolling over himself as he went, before coming to an abrupt stop in a small pond. A disturbed frog leapt onto his head as the driver, dazed, confused and soggy, watched his runaway train continue its now completely uncontrolled journey towards Birmingham.

Back on the footplate, the dancing, singing and shooting had stopped. Sir Johnny Weaver, Colonel John P. Kicklighter, Mike Nation, Phillip Bland the metro mayor, and council leader Colin Smith all stood motionless and in total silence. The only noises that could be heard were the mechanical hissing of the steam engine and the clackety-clack, clackety-clack of the rails below.

Finally, Mike Nation spoke up. 'So, did we need him, then?'

Utterly panicked, Phillip Bland screamed, 'Of course we bloody needed him! He was the bloody driver!'

They were all acutely aware that the only other engineer on the train, the fireman, would be completely oblivious to the situation and was no doubt sipping champagne and chatting to Trevor Critchley back in the first-class compartment.

Everyone looked at everyone else. Bland pointed at Sir Johnny. 'You need to drive this thing. You said you could drive it, right? You were the one that sent the fireman away in the first place. Tell us you can drive the bloody train!'

'Good grief, of course I can't, old boy! Wouldn't have a clue!'

'But you said you had training! For your stupid movie!'

'Well, you see, that was all just a touch of old bollocks, I'm afraid to say. I only said it to get rid of that fireman chappy and keep us all in the cab. The steam train in *Slow Train* didn't even work! We had a smoke machine for the chimney, and most of the time we were being shoved along by a lorry. Alas, I'm sorry to report I've as much chance of driving this contraption as I do landing a jumbo jet.'

The locomotive was speeding up. It was now doing over the thirty miles per hour limit and no one was in control.

Bland buried his head in his hands and murmured weakly, 'We're all going to die...'

Meanwhile, at Moseley Station, Brian wiped a bead of sweat from his brow. The lock was taking much longer to pick than was planned; there must have been at least seven spring-loaded pins that needed coaxing into position on the new device.

Sammy watched on nervously but said nothing while Brian carefully teased the tension wrench and pick into place. Finally, the last pin slid into position and the shackle popped open. Sighing with relief, Brian shoved open the station door and let himself in. Sammy joined him in the main ticket hall and quietly pulled the door closed behind her.

The pair looked around the lobby and were confronted with a building that looked anything but finished and ready for service. There was cracking and damage everywhere. Halfway down the hallway, there was a huge fissure on one side of the wall, running all the way from the floor to the ceiling. Some areas of the concrete landing looked uneven, and the whole hallway seemed to have sunk below the level of the metal staircases at either end of the lobby.

'What a shithole,' Sammy commented. 'Not sure we need the dynamite, Bri. We could probably just push it down.'

Brian nodded in agreement. 'I'd say we have about two minutes until the train passes Kings Heath. Your girder is just here, and I'm over there by platform two.' He pointed to his intended location at the other end of the ticket hall.

Sammy darted over to the stairwell that led to platform one. The concourse had sunk to such an extent that she realised she now needed to shimmy up the girder to secure her dynamite at the point where the vertical and horizontal frames met. She looked over to Brian and saw him doing exactly the same at his end of the lobby. Sammy straddled the steel column and hauled herself up, but she had only shimmied a couple of feet when she heard a yelling voice echo around the empty waiting room.

'Oi! What the hell do you think you are doing?'

She turned to the main entranceway and saw Derek Penrice glaring at her. Derek spotted the dynamite in her hand. 'What the *bloody hell* are you up to?' he repeated.

Brian glanced back towards the noise from the other side of the hallway and saw Penrice bearing down on Sammy. He dropped back down to the lobby, delicately placed his dynamite on the floor and hurried over towards Sammy's side of the station, but she called back over to him.

'No, Brian, I've got this. Just fix the explosives.' With that, she tossed him her dynamite stick, which he caught cleanly. Brian nodded. He knew Sammy could handle the situation, so he dashed back to the far end of the lobby and clambered back up the far column.

Penrice came at Sammy with all his weight, but Sammy was light on her feet and she deftly avoided his attack by weaving smartly to one side. As Penrice passed by, she aimed a kick to the back of his leg. He winced with agony and sank to one knee. She turned to him and adopted the classic southpaw stance of a leftie, hands up protecting her face. Penrice got to his feet and drew a knife from his belt.

'Bugger,' Sammy whispered under her breath; she wasn't expecting the man to be armed. Not to worry; mentally and physically she knew she was much more agile than the foreman, and she had far superior training. Penrice lunged at her for a second time, but once again she easily avoided the attack. She pivoted round perfectly on her right leg and landed a second, hard kick to the back of the aggressor's knee with her left. Penrice's leg buckled and he collapsed to the floor, letting out a shriek of pain.

Meanwhile, Brian had secured the first dynamite stick to the girder at the far end of the hallway. He grabbed the second stick from the floor and hurried over to Sammy's side of the station. He chose a route that arced around the pair who were fighting in the middle of the lobby. Brian could tell that Sammy was more than holding her own, despite the presence of Penrice's knife; nonetheless, he decided to even up the fight a bit, so he took out his own penknife, which he'd earlier used to cut the fuse wire, and called out Sammy's name. She glanced over to see Brain tossing the weapon towards her. She caught it single-handed and immediately turned back to the foreman.

The train hauled itself through Kings Heath Station and the five VIPs waved frantically at the crowd gathered on the road bridge above them, crying out desperately for help. Completely ignorant of the situation below, everyone on the bridge simply waved back happily, cheering enthusiastically as the train steamed under the bridge and onwards towards the city. Everyone, that is, except for one member of the group. The odd man out was Aleksandr, who was busy typing

KINGS HEATH

into his mobile phone and hitting the send button.

Brian had scaled up the edge of the nearside column and was securing the second dynamite stick to the girder joint when Aleksandr's message flashed up on his phone screen.

'We've got to get a move on,' he called out to Sammy.

'Gotcha,' she shouted back. With the penknife in hand, Sammy had been able to make some pretty effective counterattacks and had drawn blood on a couple of occasions, each time across Penrice's right arm as he had lunged forwards with his blade. Together they had danced over to the top of the stairwell that led down to platform one, very near to where Brian was busy working away attaching the final stick.

Sammy had her back to the stairwell. She felt the uneven crumbling concourse under her feet and knew that the sunken level of concrete was about to give way to the metal staircase that was now at a higher level. She egged Penrice on, calling him forward with a wave of her hand, daring him to attack one more time. He was unable to resist the petulance of the girl and launched himself at her. For the umpteenth time, Sammy expertly avoided his attack and pushed him towards the stairwell as he passed her.

Penrice hadn't spotted the raised metal first step and tripped painfully on the hard iron corner. He yelped in fear as he tumbled head-first down the staircase. He tried to break his fall with outstretched arms, but his knife was still clenched tightly in one hand. The weight of his body landed full and heavy on the top of the blade, and it plunged deep into his chest. He screamed with pain as he rolled uncontrollably down the entire flight of stairs. Halfway to the bottom, his head bounced off a metal balustrade, and his neck snapped immediately on impact with the cold metal steel. Penrice's body continued down the remaining steps until it finally landed in a disfigured heap, face up on the concrete platform below. The handle of Penrice's knife stood proudly out of his chest, the blade wedged tightly inside his rib cage.

'Oops,' said Sammy.

'I think he got the point,' added Brian, parodying the classic James Bond line.

'Bit soon, I think, Bri,' said Sammy, rolling her eyes.

On and on the steam engine travelled, ferociously covering the distance between the stations. Sir Johnny was yanking at every handle and lever he could get his hands on, trying to make sense of the myriad of steam valves and gauges, but it was hopeless. Nothing any of them did would slow the train down, and if anything, the train had sped up somewhat, what with the downward gradient of the railway line.

Panic had well and truly set in. The Colonel grabbed Mike Nation by his blazer lapels and screamed at the pumpkin-like face in front of him. 'You fuck! Jesus, Mike, you absolute son of a bitch! Is this how you repay me for all my goodwill and kindness? *This?*' He let go of one lapel to wave a hand across the carnage on the footplate.

'I introduced you to paradise, Mikey!' he continued. 'Goddammed paradise at goddammed Golden Valley, Arizona! With the sun, with the restaurants, with the poolside bars. And what have you got me? A one-way ticket on the Shitsville Express, driven by Duke Dickbrain, the hundred-year-old cowboy! I shit you not, Mike: if we get out of this alive, I am going to kill you.'

'Easy, old boy,' Sir Johnny complained, having overheard the slur. Kicklighter ignored him.

'Come on, Colonel,' argued Nation, 'how the hell was I to know the senile old coot would shove the driver out the window? Christ! Look, calm down, think for a moment.

The engine's bound to run out of coal at some point, surely? Or it'll run out of water, or something like that. Maybe we'll hit an incline and it'll slow down, and we can just hop off. Something will happen. Now is not the time to panic, Colonel.'

'We're on a runaway train! If this is not the time to panic, then when, precisely, is panic time? My God, I wish I had my gun with me...'

'Look...'

'Actually, just shut up. Do not talk to me anymore, Mike. I don't want to hear any more of your shit.'

Nation complied and shut up. Sir Johnny turned back to the controls and started fiddling with the levers once more. The two politicians, meanwhile, were cowering in the corner and praying, one to his red god, and one to his blue god. Each of them was wondering which of their gods, if either, would turn up and come to their rescue.

Back at Moseley Station, Brian dropped down from the steel column onto the concrete floor below and then ran down to the platform. 'Nothing we can do for him now,' he said, staring at Derek Penrice's dead body. He removed the knife from the foreman's chest.

'Yeh, well, no great loss. The guy was clearly an absolute face flannel,' replied Sammy.

'Without the knife in him, the authorities will just think he was killed by the collapsing station,' Brian added before sprinting back up the metal staircase. 'Come on, get ready to light this one. I'll go and light the other one.'

Sammy clambered up the steel column and glanced over to the far side of the lobby. Brian had made it to the same position at the opposite end of the station.

'Ready?'

'Ready.'

'Three, two, one, light!'

They simultaneously lit their fuses, dropped down to the concourse and sprinted for the main entrance. Sammy hightailed it through the door a couple of seconds ahead of Brian who was hot on her heels. They scampered across to the far side of the car park and then crouched down in the corner behind a tree. Peering around the trunk, they focussed back on the station building.

Precisely thirty seconds after lighting the fuse, the charges detonated, and both sticks of dynamite exploded with a loud crack. Almost immediately, one side of the station started subsiding and collapsing in on itself, quickly followed by the other side. The creaking and straining of bending metal reverberated across the car park, and the ceiling crashed down onto the concourse floor below. Finally, the whole structure failed, and the shattered station building tumbled down onto the railway line with a deafening roar.

Moments later, when the dust started to settle, Sammy and Brian reappeared from their position behind the tree and headed over to where the station building once stood. They peered down into the railway cutting below, which was now strewn with concrete rubble, broken brickwork and contorted metal debris.

'Well, it's definitely fucked,' said Sammy.

Peace eventually returned to that little corner of Moseley. The only noise emanating from the base of the railway cutting was the sound of small bits of falling remains, bouncing down onto the rubble below. But after a few moments, a completely new sound cut through the silence. It was the quiet but distinct puff-puffing of an approaching steam engine. The tracks started vibrating, and a high-pitched whine danced up from the metal rails into the air, announcing the approaching train from the far end of the line.

The pair transferred their attention further along the route. From their orientation, they could see perhaps half a mile down the line in the direction from which the train was approaching. They stared silently, intently, waiting. The chugging noise grew louder and louder, and puffs of steam appeared in the distance. Then suddenly it was there, coming into view and homing in on the remains of Moseley Station and the rubble-covered tracks.

It seemed to be approaching at a bit of a pace, much more quickly than either Brian or Sammy had expected. Sammy turned to Brian. 'That's not thirty miles per hour, Bri.'

'No, it's not.'

They stared down into the railway cutting, shifting uncomfortably on their feet.

'It's not slowing down, Bri…'

'I see that, Sammy…'

The *Shakespeare Express* speeded relentlessly into Moseley Station far above its thirty miles per hour limit. The brakes offered no assistance, since no one on board the footplate knew how to apply them, and so the collision was inevitable. The train careered into the debris at the other end of the station with a shattering and almighty blast of noise, sending shards of concrete and rubble into the sky. The screeching sound of scraping metal resonated across the site.

Very quickly, the steam train came to a halt in the middle of the rubble, and the whiplash effect caused Sir Johnny to lurch violently forward, smashing heavily into the back of Colonel Kicklighter near the edge of the footplate. The chain reaction caused The Colonel to be thrown from the train, tumbling through the air towards the remnants of the platform. His head smashed into the corner of a broken Moseley Station sign that lay upright and fastened onto a fallen lamppost, killing him instantly. Sir Johnny, however, having been cushioned by the back of The Colonel, slumped onto the floor of the footplate, dazed and sore but otherwise healthy.

The metro mayor, Phillip Bland, was also flung violently forward. He lost his footing and smashed his head fiercely onto the metal control panels in front of him. Fortunately, the hard hat that he had worn completely pointlessly to every opening ceremony he had ever attended finally proved its worth and protected him from serious injury. He too collapsed to the floor in a confused and disoriented state, slumping alongside Colin Smith, the council leader, whose own hard hat had also saved him from serious injury. Smith's life was most likely saved by imitating his political nemesis's choice of clothing.

Mike Nation, however, was the luckiest of them all. The impact of the crash propelled him from the opposite side of the train to that of The Colonel, but rather than smashing into a station sign, he landed slap bang in the middle of a large bed of flowers, the massive decorative trough of plants being perfectly placed for his touchdown at the top end of platform two. The flowers, plants and shrubbery broke his fall, and he came to rest in the soil almost completely unhurt.

The trio of carriages behind the steam engine all derailed, though thankfully remained upright, which meant that the injuries to the passengers in those three first-class compartments, who were all afforded comfy seats and cushions, were limited to mere cuts and bruises.

Looking down on the carnage from the demolition site above, Sammy and Brian were left to survey the shambles with utter disbelief, wondering what the hell they had done.

'Bollocks,' said Brian calmly. All Sammy could do was nod in agreement.

The walking wounded began clambering out of the carriages and down onto the battered platforms alongside the train. There was no way for Sammy or Brian to get down the railway cutting to try and help out since the two stairwells on either side of the railway had disappeared into the bedlam below. In any event, Brian considered that the pair would be wise not to be found at the crash site when the authorities arrived. The last thing they needed was to be quizzed about their presence.

He glanced behind him, back towards the station slip road and the high street beyond. A small gathering of people was already congregating at the still-locked security fencing on the other side of the car park. The rescue services would arrive soon, he thought, so they had better make their escape.

He peered down one last time at the havoc on the railway. Shaking his head, he was about to suggest they get going when his eyes happened upon a shiny silver piece of metal that, despite the chaos, seemed strangely out of place. It was halfway up the ramshackle platform and had the appearance of a shard of steel, like the corner of a metal object. And then it dawned on him. It was the corner of Paul Dixon's box, sticking out of the platform tomb in which it once lay.

'Bollocks,' repeated Brian, as the pair beat a hasty retreat.

CHAPTER THIRTY-THREE

It was five days after the spectacular crash at Moseley Station, and with Mike Nation officially 'helping the police with various enquiries', the whole gang had met up at The Balancing Act for drinks. Rosie had shut the restaurant for the day, and she had laid on celebratory cocktails for her new friends, who had all gathered around a large walnut coffee table in the bar area.

Tomasz was there with Stephanie. The two had officially announced themselves as a couple, so they sat together, chatting away on a snug grey sofa. Opposite them, swilling merrily from their cocktail glasses, were Sammy and Alexandr. Brian and Rosie made the rest of the line-up, taking the final two sides of the coffee table and occasionally stealing a glance at each other while the group merrily chatted away.

The six of them were engaged in a very intense and enthusiastic discussion regarding what constituted the best bacon sandwich. Aleksandr and Tomasz insisted that you couldn't have a bacon sandwich without an egg on it. Rosie disagreed. She was convinced that all you needed was good quality bread and good quality butter. Stephanie, who was vegetarian, went for bacon-flavoured tofu. Everyone groaned. Sammy said the best bacon sandwich had a sausage in it. But Brian was adamant that all you needed was a big old dollop of HP sauce.

'Of course, we used to make HP sauce here in Brum, you know,' Brian added.

'Did we?' asked Tomasz.

'Yep, right here in the city. In a lovely old factory on the Aston Expressway. Whenever you were out of town and you had the long drive back to Birmingham, you always knew you were home when you saw the big old HP sign winking at you in the distance from the top of the factory building. And guess what happened to it…'

'Here we go,' said Sammy.

'Did we knock the sodding thing down?' enquired Rosie, beating Brian to the punch.

'Damned right we did. We knocked the sodding thing down,' said Brian with a sigh, but he smiled back at her warmly.

'Has he always been this cheerful?' Rosie asked Sammy.

'Oh yes, I don't think he's ever changed. Except he probably used to wear less beige.'

Throughout the previous five days, the runaway train and collapsing station story had run on loops across local and national news. It had even been reported on CNN on the other side of the Atlantic, such was the interest in the story. With an ageing film star on the footplate and a retired US marine among those flung from the steam engine, it was quite the unique news piece.

Local TV reporter Trevor Critchley, who had been on the train at the time of the incident, led the coverage and had been thrust back into the national spotlight once again. He and Sir Johnny had lapped up the media attention.

Just the previous day, Critchley had reported that the crash investigation team had analysed the building materials used in the fabric of the station. Initial results had indicated that the quality of the materials had been compromised and there had been a deliberate misuse of cheap and inappropriate steel and concrete. As a precaution, the remaining stations on the line had been secured as off-limits and the opening of the line postponed indefinitely.

Critchley had said that the owner of the construction firm that built the structures, Mike Nation, had been arrested on charges of intent to endanger life. The financial crime unit of the police had also been called in following the discovery of suspicious accountancy practices within Nation Construction. All of Nation's assets had been frozen and his passport confiscated, the authorities having decided that there was a possible flight risk. Police had uncovered plans for an imminent one-way trip to Arizona.

The news had been met with delight by the whole group, but in particular by Stephanie and Rosie. Those iron chains with which they were shackled to Nation had been broken, at least temporarily. As soon as the story had broken, Rosie had arranged the celebratory cocktail afternoon.

There was still plenty for the police to investigate, however. For a start, there were three dead bodies at the crash site, two of whom, it was ascertained, were not even on the runaway train at the time of the crash. In fact, one of the bodies was discovered decapitated and buried in a box. For that reason, the rolling news continued, and the story was hardly ever off the TV screens. Rosie had moved a television set into The Balancing Act bar area so the gang could keep tabs on events while they drank the afternoon away.

The discovery of the decapitated body hadn't come as a surprise to Rosie. Ever since he had seen the metal box protruding from the platform, Brian had known the accountant's corpse would be found and that he had to forewarn his friend. At first the news had panicked her, but Brian assured Rosie that there was no way for the body to be traced back to them. The only person who had any knowledge of the connection was Nation, and he would never blab. He had enough problems to contend with, without having the authorities learn that the beheaded corpse was once his secret accountant. Other than that, the trail was by now completely cold, and Brian had guaranteed there was nothing to be concerned about. His arguments had been convincing, and Rosie's concerns were once again assuaged. And anyway, she had since decided that nothing was going to spoil her mood, what with Nation being in handcuffs.

Aleksandr offered to get another round of drinks and headed behind the bar counter to fix everyone a top-up. When he had finished preparing the refreshments, he balanced them carefully on a tray and wandered back to the low coffee table. As he strolled across the room, he spotted Critchley's face appearing on the TV screen.

'He's on again,' he announced to the rest of the room.

They looked up and saw the reporter, microphone in hand, talking at the camera lens from the car park of Moseley Station. Rosie turned up the volume on the television, and the six of them stopped chatting to listen to the latest update.

'…and the cause of the runaway train now seems certain to be recorded by the investigation team as a catastrophic failure to follow regulations. It has become apparent that only one locomotive professional, the driver, was in the cab when the train departed Stirchley Station. The fireman had been sent to sit in one of the carriages to the rear of the train to make room for members of the public. Furthermore, it seems that overcrowding on the footplate, with six people present in the cab at the time of departure, almost certainly led to the unfortunate jettisoning of the driver shortly before the train ran through Kings Heath. These failures directly led to the train being uncontrolled and ultimately caused the death of one of the men in the steam engine's cab, a Colonel Kicklighter, from Texas, USA.

'Meanwhile, fingerprint analysis has now confirmed the identity of one of the two hitherto unidentified dead bodies that were discovered under the building rubble and who, it appeared, were not actually on board the train. The man has been confirmed as one Derek Penrice, a fifty-one-year-old man from Solihull, who was a foreman at Nation Construction, the firm that had built the new stations, whose owner is currently under police investigation. Interestingly, Penrice had knowledge of explosives, having previously worked in the demolition arm of the business, and as previously reported, the use of explosives in the building failure has not as yet been ruled out. Forensic analysis is ongoing in that area, and this follows reports of a loud bang immediately prior to the station collapse.

'The second body, meanwhile, a decapitated adult male discovered in a steel box submerged in the station fabric, remains unidentified. The working theory regarding the unidentified male is that once again, Penrice, the foreman, was involved. Police believe he killed the man and dumped the body in a hole in the newly concreted platform. Penrice's fingerprints were discovered on the inside of the steel box where the decapitated body was found, and no other fingerprints were present on the container. Furthermore, a van that was registered to Penrice was spotted at Moseley Station by local police, late at night, three nights before the crash. A man who answered to the name of Penrice when quizzed by the authorities at the time claimed he was checking on a reported break-in. Police now believe this was when the body was dumped...'

Sammy shot a surprised but delighted look at Brian. Good God, that had all worked out remarkably well for them! It seemed their unfortunate run-in with the police that fateful night had actually done them a huge favour in the end. Penrice was going to cop it for Dixon's death! And possibly the dynamite as well! Brian nodded imperceptibly in acknowledgement.

Critchley was wrapping up his latest report.

'...Now, law enforcement officers are appealing for help from the public in order to identify the unknown man in the steel container. They have released this photo-fit of his likeness. For obvious reasons, it would be inappropriate to televise his actual face, but police artists have put together this picture and they are urging anyone who believes they recognise the man, likely to be in his forties, to get in touch as soon as possible...'

A coloured drawing of Paul Dixon's head flashed up on the television screen. Rosie shuddered to her bones and looked away, unconsciously flinching as she did so. She, of all people, knew the likeness was unnerving.

Tomasz, who had just taken a big gulp from his bottle of beer, wiped his mouth with the back of his hand. 'Bloody hell, I think I know who it is! That looks like Mr Dixon...' he announced, before taking another mouthful.

Sammy and Brian exchanged looks for the second time in as many minutes. That was highly confusing. How on earth would Tomasz know the accountant? Sammy turned to him. 'What makes you say that, Tommy? Who's this Mr Dixon bloke?'

'Oh, just a guy I did some work for,' Tomasz replied. He turned to Stephanie and added, 'Maybe I'd better phone the police?'

Stephanie was about to reply when Sammy interjected. 'Hang on, what do you mean, you did some work for him?'

'I just did some work for him, that's all. What's the big deal?' he asked, looking confused.

'Well, it's just such an amazing coincidence, don't you think? How did you meet him?'

Sammy was dying to fully interrogate Tomasz on the subject but instead was desperately trying to tease some information out of him surreptitiously. Brian could tell what was going on and kept quiet; he knew Sammy was better equipped to run with the questions.

'Well, I don't know why you'd be interested, but basically, I was doing some cash-in-hand work for his neighbour, you know, to top up the wages. Alex knows I do a bit of domestic work on my days off because Nation's pay is so crap. Anyway, this was all about six months ago, and one evening I was about to head off home when this Dixon chap came up to me. He said he lived next door and he needed some work doing. He asked if I'd be interested. I said sure thing, so I popped round the next day to see what he was after. He wanted a kind of hidey-hole, a little secret compartment, put together. He'd designed it himself, and he just needed a tradesman to build it out for him. It was quite clever, really.' Tomasz took another gulp of beer.

'How amazing,' said Sammy as calmly as she could, barely able to control her excitement.

'Yeh, it was mad, really. He said he'd pay me well, and all in cash, as long as I promised to never mention this little cubbyhole to anyone. And in fairness to the bloke, he did pay well. I don't suppose it matters talking about it now, though, what with him being dead and everything.'

'Yeh, I think you're ok to talk about it. He isn't gonna sue you now, mate!' joked Sammy, her heart racing. 'So this compartment, how did that work?'

'Well, the recess was inside the chimney breast in the main front room. It was a bloody awkward piece of work, to be honest. I had to remove about three dozen bricks to the left-hand side of the hearth and strengthen the hole so it didn't fall in on itself. Then I had to put a fake wall at the front of the compartment. I put it on a hinge with one of those magnetic mechanisms, you know, where you have to push them in at a specific area and the mechanism releases and then the door pops open. Anyway, the mechanism was on an electronic lock, and the only way of unlocking it was to first press a hidden button tucked behind a big mirror hanging over the mantelpiece. It drew power from the house mains, with backup batteries in case of failure. I had to channel a hole for the little wire right the way from the button and down into the mantelpiece, then all the way to the bottom of the chimney breast and into the hearth. Bloody fiddly. But as I said, all very clever, really.'

'Yeh, yeh, fascinating,' grumbled Aleksandr, who was clearly bored with the story. The weather forecast started blurting out from the TV screen and Rosie turned the volume back down. Brian and Sammy didn't move, but their mouths hung ever so slightly ajar.

'I see,' said Sammy finally. 'Well, it sounds like you did a grand job for him, Tommy. And you're right, you probably should phone the police at some point. But I tell you what, there's no rush is there? After all, the guy's already lost his head! Might as well do that tonight, back at the flat.'

'Yeh, good idea. I'll call them this evening,' Tomasz replied. He glanced at Stephanie and grinned. 'Anyway, I'm having too much fun right now...'

CHAPTER THIRTY-FOUR

The relief on Rosie's face was almost tangible, as much as she tried to hide it. Shaking slightly, she put the remote control back down and tried to process the news report she had just heard. She realised that Penrice was going to take the fall for Dixon's murder, and no one would care because Penrice himself was dead. There was nothing to link her to the crime at all. Just as Brian had promised, it seemed that the events in the multi-storey just over a week ago would never come back to her. And on top of that, Nation was deep in the shit, and she felt the weight of his influence lifting from her shoulders for the first time.

These were all really good reasons for a proper celebration, so she was desperately disappointed when Brian unexpectedly jumped to his feet and announced that there was a very important errand he needed to run. She implored him to stay for another drink, but he said that it would take him less than an hour if he was quick, and he would come straight back when he was done. Sammy decided she needed to go with Brian, and while the four others protested, the pair were insistent.

Reluctantly, the remaining group acquiesced, on the promise Brian and Sammy would rejoin the party within the hour. They agreed, and so the two left The Balancing Act, waving cheerfully back through the window while strolling as calmly as they could past the restaurant. But when they rounded the corner and were out of sight, they burst into a full-on sprint towards the Brindleyplace car park nearby.

'It's got to be the money, don't you think? It's got to be the eight hundred grand,' panted Sammy as they approached the car.

'We'll soon find out,' Brian replied as he jumped into the driver's seat. He started the engine and screeched out of the car park, heading for Edgbaston and the now familiar side street one block down from Dixon's house.

'Bet you didn't think we'd *be heading* back to Dixon's house again so soon, did you Bri? Get it? *Beheading?*'

'How long have you been working on that one, Sammy?'

'Couple of days…'

On the drive over, Sammy couldn't help but quiz Brian about the events of that day back at the multi-storey. She had seen the way Rosie had reacted to the news report that implicated Penrice in the murder of the accountant.

'You know what I've been thinking, Bri? I've been thinking that Rosie killed Dixon, not you. That's why she was in such shock, back in the car park. The way I figure it, he probably had his gun trained on you, and she killed him. And because of that, you owed her. That's why you've been so keen to help her with her Mike Nation problem. And now that the foreman is going to take the fall for Dixon's death, it's a weight off her mind. What do you think of my little theory?' She glanced over at Brian, a quizzical glint in her eye.

Brian had to admire her. She was becoming quite the skilled operative. But he shook his head and told her that her hypothesis was utter nonsense.

Sammy ignored him and carried on regardless. 'And you do realise that if I'm right, in the past ten days, three people have died, and you, the contract killer, didn't actually kill any of them. Which is a shame for you, really, because they all died in such exciting ways! I mean think about it. Dixon was beheaded with a meat cleaver by Rosie, Penrice stabbed himself to death with his own knife while rolling down a staircase, and that Colonel Kicklighter tosser bought it having been thrown from a moving steam train and headbutting a lamppost. Bloody unusual, wouldn't you say?'

'It's certainly all very bizarre, Sammy. But I killed Dixon, ok?'

'Whatever you say, Bri.' She studied his face. He was giving nothing away. But she was sure she was right.

They made the four-mile journey to Edgbaston in double-quick time and parked up in Brian's usual spot. They leapt out of the car and covered the distance to Dixon's house as quickly as possible without bringing attention to themselves. With no one lingering on the pavement to see them, they nipped into the driveway and hurried up to the front door.

Brian dug his mobile out of his pocket and flicked to where he had previously saved the passcode. 'Put this number into the keypad, Sammy. Six, four, two, one, nine, one.'

Sammy obliged and the pair heard the electronic clicking of the deadlocks. The door swung open.

'This way,' said Brian as he led Sammy into the lounge at the front of the house. He raced straight over to the large mirror hanging above the mantelpiece on the chimney breast. Carefully, he lifted the whole thing off its fastening. It was a lot heavier than Brian expected, so he struggled over to the sofa as hastily as he could and rested it on the seat cushions. Then he turned back to the chimney breast and searched for the little button. Now that he knew what he was looking for, he spotted its location fairly quickly, despite it being flush with the wall.

'Can't believe I bloody missed it last time,' he grumbled.

'Well, nobody's perfect,' Sammy offered in support.

Brian pressed the button. Once again, the pair heard a hushed electronic click. Their hearts were racing. Brian dropped to his knees and poked his head into the hearth.

'Have you got a torch?' he asked.

Sammy selected the torch function on her phone and passed it to Brian. He studied the false wall on the left-hand side of the hearth carefully and examined the dust on the fireplace floor below. He saw a faint arc of soot on the floor, circling from the left to the right. The hinge must be on the right, he thought. He pushed gently on the left side of the wall and heard the magnetic mechanism detach. The door swung open.

Brian shone the torch into the chamber and made out the shape of a bag. He passed the phone back to Sammy, stretched his arm deep into the compartment and grabbed at the bag. Finally, he caught one of the handles and tugged the bag out of its home. He swung it round and deposited it onto the lounge carpet next to the fireplace.

Sammy got to her knees next to Brian and stared at the leather duffel bag in front of her. 'Moment of truth,' she said, nervously. They held their breath as she unzipped the top and threw the flaps apart.

Sitting proudly in the belly of the bag, filling it almost to the brim, were hundreds and hundreds of bundles of notes. Fifty-pound notes. Thousands of them. Hundreds of thousands of pounds in total, sitting neatly in stacks and staring back up at Brian and Sammy from their soft leather shelter.

'Christ almighty, Bri...' Sammy cackled with joy and yelled, 'Jackpot, baby! It's payday!'

Brian and Sammy leapt into the car with the money, dashed straight back to their Hall Green flat and counted it all. It totalled a little over seven hundred and ninety-five thousand pounds. It was all the missing money, bar Dixon's expenses purchasing grey jackets and revolvers.

Brian put twenty thousand to one side. 'For a new van,' he said with a wry grin. Sammy nodded.

He then counted out another fifty thousand for his own wages and expenses and handed Sammy a further fifty thousand. 'Couldn't have done it without you,' he said.

Sammy gave him a hug and grabbed the money greedily. 'What about the rest?' she asked.

'The rest is going to two small business owners. Two women who really deserve the money. And it will mean they can pay off every penny of debt they have. So, even if Mike Nation somehow manages to get out of the legal shithole he's got himself into, they will never have to cross paths with him ever again.'

Sammy nodded her agreement, and the pair rushed back to The Balancing Act with the duffel bag. Once there, they tipped its contents onto the walnut coffee table in front of the rest of the gang. They all stared in disbelief at the cash, before launching into cheers of delight, hurling the cash into the air and watching it fall back to earth like confetti.

***

A week later, Brian and Rosie had just finished their first one-hundred-percent bona fide official date. They had spent the afternoon in a little Italian restaurant in Moseley that Rosie was keen on and were strolling up the High Street, heading for cocktails in The Phoney Negroni. As they ambled up the road, walking off their lunch, they passed Nation House, and Rosie glanced over at the building. She noticed that there was some yellow police tape across the main entranceway.

'What are you going to say to Nation if he asks about the money?' asked Rosie.

'I'll just say it never turned up,' Brian replied. 'After all, it almost didn't.'

'Do you think he'll get off? Or will the charges stick?'

'Don't know, and I don't much care, bab. And neither should you,' he added, shooting Rosie a smile.

'I suppose his difficulties will be bad news for you business-wise?' she suggested.

'I guess it might be a little quiet for a while. But I've been thinking lately about the types of jobs I take on. It might be time to be a little more discerning, regarding potential clientele. And anyway, there will always be people who need things "cleaning up" as it were. For a start, Terry got a weird call from a Dora Kumquat the other day, which I'm looking into.'

'*Dora Kumquat?* You're kidding!'

'That's what Sammy said. Odd name. Not sure it's one for us, though. She lives a long way away.'

'Overseas?'

'Effectively. Lichfield.'

Rosie chuckled as they walked arm in arm, taking in the last of the summer heat.

'You know, the sun hasn't stopped shining for over a fortnight now,' she said in passing.

'Sun always shines in Birmingham,' replied Brian.

'Well, that's bollocks for a start…!'

They reached the entrance to the bar and Brian got the door.

'Oh,' said Rosie as she walked through the entrance, 'have you heard about *The Floozie in the Jacuzzi*?'

Brian followed her in, and they took a seat in a bay window. 'No, what about it?' he replied.

'It's broken again. Turns out the original repair job was a Nation Construction contract. They used botched tooling and equipment from start to finish. All cheap and tatty materials. Nine months of work down the drain. Quite literally down the drain: the leaks are bloody everywhere. The whole square is cordoned off.'

'You don't say,' said Brian, and he ordered some drinks from Sandra, the waitress.

'Yep. They've had to siphon off all the water from the fountain once again. They've put the work out to tender, you know, the repair job to the repair job. It's going to take six months to choose a contractor, then another nine months to complete the repairs. Meanwhile, Alex reckons the council are finding a few plants to stick in there for the time being to keep her company....'

Brian rolled his eyes at the thought of the poor Floozie being trapped in the middle of another crappy flowerbed for more than a year. Their drinks arrived and he picked up his glass with one hand, while he took Rosie's hand in the other.

'At least we'll have another opening ceremony to go to,' said Rosie, optimistically.

They clinked glasses and Brian replied, 'Well, that's Birmingham for you, bab. You never really know whether to laugh or cry. I guess it's all a bit of a balancing act...'

THE END

AUTHOR'S NOTES

This is a work of fiction. There are *no* dogging problems in Moseley Village! (As far as I'm aware, anyway…) The suburb is, however, quite the eclectic mix of characters and places, and it's well worth a visit. There isn't a *Phoney Negroni* bar in 'the Village', but its predecessor in the book – *The Jug of Ale* – did once exist. The venue is now a curry house.

There really is a new train line being built along the route described, albeit the terminal station won't be called Stirchley since its location isn't anywhere near Stirchley Village. Instead, the stop will rather delightfully be called Pineapple Road. I just used the nearest suburb's name in the book for ease of reference.

The Floozie in the Jacuzzi did break down. It was eventually fixed and almost immediately broke down again. It was finally re-repaired in July 2022. Nation Construction was not on the job.

There are anecdotal suggestions that underworld bosses used Spaghetti Junction to hide dead bodies during its construction, but nothing has been proven as far as I can find. Certainly, there is no evidence that members of the Kray Twins gang were buried there, although the Battle of Snow Hill does seem to have occurred, when a Brummie gangster family, the Fewtrells, sent the Londoners back home with their tails between their legs.

Birmingham is home to the largest city council in Europe, and as part of the West Midlands conurbation, it also has an elected metro mayor. At the time of writing, the council and the mayor really do hail from opposing political parties, and that has been the case for more than five years. However, as far as I can ascertain, there are no 'ribbon wars', and the two offices do seem to work reasonably well together, for the good of the city. Normally.

The *Shakespeare Express* is a real vintage train service, hauled by a beautifully preserved Castle Class locomotive. It runs weekend summer excursions between Birmingham and Stratford-upon-Avon and frankly is infinitely more reliable than West Midlands Railway's commuter service on the same line...

If you haven't visited Birmingham you really should, *for more than any other reason...*

(Nation's catchphrase borrows heavily from a real slogan used by an estate agent in Mansfield, Lincolnshire. According to their own signage, "More people use Sankey than for any other reason!")

ACKNOWLEDGEMENTS

Thank you to everyone who made it this far! I've wanted to write a book for years, and finally it's been ticked off the old bucket-list.

Huge thanks to my family for their support and help over the last year, in particular my dad Mike, step-mum Alison, my uncle David, and most of all my mum Rosie, for struggling through those early drafts and providing invaluable feedback.

Thanks also go to all my mates who volunteered to read the manuscript, despite no doubt having much better things to do with their time. I'm particularly indebted to Ruth Reaney, Jo Hunt, Mandie McGarry, Dave Canning and Mick Tomes for their opinions and advice.

Finally, I'm indebted to Scott and the whole team at Publishing Push, without whom, this book would not exist and the bucket-list frustratingly unaltered.

Printed in Great Britain
by Amazon

19249915R00185